Swords, Sandals and Sirens

MARILYN TODD

Swords, Sandals and Sirens

by MARILYN TODD

Crippen & Landru Publishers
Norfolk, Virginia
2015

Cover Design by Gail Cross

ISBN (limited clothbound edition): 978-1-936363-10-0
ISBN (trade softcover edition): 978-1-936363-11-7

FIRST EDITION

Printed in the United States of America
on recycled acid-free paper

Crippen & Landru Publishers
P. O. Box 9315
Norfolk, VA 23505
USA

Email: crippenlandru@earthlink.net
Web: www.crippenlandru.com

For Julie-Ann Palma
who understands perfectly that too much of a good thing is absolutely wonderful

TABLE OF CONTENTS

INTRODUCTION

When I was little, maybe nine or ten, I asked my Dad what he was reading. He looked at me over the top of his book. "It's about the Lion Gate," he said, and in the blink of an eye, my world changed. While other kids were disappearing through wardrobes to find lions, witches and Narnia, I'd stepped through my own Lion Gate to Mycenae. To a world where heroes rubbed shoulders with cyclops and centaurs, sirens lured sailors to the rocks and their death, and gods came to earth in a shower of gold.

As it happened, my Mum was also a reader. The difference was, she devoured whodunnits and locked room mysteries, so that by the time I was fifteen, I'd read *I, Claudius, the Iliad,* the Greek myths end to end, and every Agatha Christie going. No yellow-jacketed Gollancz in the library was safe.

Crime and ancient history are the twin passions underpinning this collection. Some of the stories feature series characters like Claudia I-may-have-my-faults-but-being-wrong-isn't-one-of-them Seferius, set in Ancient Rome. Along with Iliona, High Priestess of the Temple of Eurotas, blackmailed into working for Ancient Sparta's feared and hated secret police, the Krypteia. Which, incidentally, is where the word cryptic comes from.

But there are other stories in here, too. The Delphic Oracle becomes drawn into murder. Cleopatra herself is forced to solve crime. Plus it's tough to prevent a coup among the gods on Mount Olympus, when you're just a little Echo.

Echo…

Echo………

Comic fantasy's brilliant! You're given free rein to let your imagination run wild, so puns come thick and fast. Like poor old Orpheus, charged with lute behaviour. The gods playing eeny-meeny-maenad-mo. And dear me, Pan will keep piping up at the most inopportune moment.

BAD DAY ON MOUNT OLYMPUS

The meeting was going well. Boring, but hey. They only come round once a year. Who's going to quibble about the odd satyr too fond of his own voice to relinquish the floor? Or some nerd of a faun who's all presentation-this / flip-chart-that? Let it ride, that's what I say. If these guys get off on pie-charts and graphs, who am I to begrudge them their fun? Not everyone's idea of a good time is freeflowing wine and the chance to get to know one another afterwards.

By which, of course, I mean sex.

And lots of it.

Also, you get to catch up with the gossip. After all, Cupid's still a kid. Not every shot is on target. Some really interesting alliances can result. *Plus* — a real bonus, this — we get to see who's been turned into what animal, tree, bug or whatever. Naturally, this year's big story was Io. *Apparently* (and this you didn't get from me), but *apparently* Juno walked in on Jupiter relieving Io of the rather cumbersome burden of her virginity and...

Look. Let's just say the wife wasn't any too pleased at the picture, OK?

Well, we all know what a bitch Juno can be when she's mad. Look what she did to me. I'm her friend. Anyhow, Jupiter's thinking he'd best get in first, if he's looking to protect the girlfriend, so. . . Spotting a herd of cows on the hill, quick as a flash, he turns Io into a heifer. Find her among *that* lot, he smarms to the wife. But this was the thing, see. Juno didn't *want* to go looking for Io. 'Who needs it?' she says. 'Didn't I always say she was a scheming little cow?' (Incidentally, Io's apologies for absence at this AGM have been duly noted.)

Anyways, like I said, the meeting's going well. After a few millennia you get to know the pattern and this was the point on the schedule when whichever river god was spouting off this time would begin to run out of steam. Happens every year. Someone, somewhere, gets fed up with what he's doing and wastes hours of precious drinking time by making out a lengthy case for changing course. The response from the rest of us is the same each year, too. We let the old windbag make his speech and then say yes. The reason we don't say yes straight off is that then some other windbag would get up and start making demands. So we let it run and then pretend to vote according to our conscience. Of course, the reason we *all* say yes *every* time is that if we didn't, we'd lose even *more* drinking time during the debate. This is democracy, see. It's the only way to do business.

So we vote. The motion's carried. Some little stream in Arcadia (or was it Thrace?) will change course and the river god, bless his sediment, duly gets his change of scenery. Tedious or wot? But any minute now Sagittarius, half-man, half-horse who's chaired the last three hundred meetings, will start to wind things up. We'll get the usual jeers of Sagittarius always wanting to be the "centaur of attention". Some wag will ask Pan, doesn't *he* want to, ho ho, "pipe up" with a question. And someone else will accuse Orpheus of "lute behaviour" in a public place. The usual stuff. Old as Olympus. And call us sad, but we still find it funny.

By the time our equine chairman was rolling up his scrolls and murmuring 'Any other business?' Bacchus is already on his cloven feet, heading for the wine. We almost missed the voice boom out 'Yes' from the back…

Yes? You could have blown me down with a feather. (Well, you could have, if I'd had a body to blow down).

'Er.' Sagittarius stamped a hoof, whinnied a bit, and you can see what was going through his head. Nothing like this had ever happened before on Mount Olympus. 'Did someone say yes?'

See, after him asking 'Any other business', there's always the same short silence, when everyone *pretends* they're trying to think up a question (most of us being more polite than Bacchus). Then we shake our heads, like how we'd all have *loved* to raise a point or three but since the meeting covered everything on *our* agenda, boy, were we stumped. At this point, when Sagittarius pronounces the AGM closed, a cheer goes up loud enough to cause a landslip in Crete followed by a stampede to the wine. Hey! It's not called the "Amorous Gluttonous Massing" for nothing, you know.

Except now someone was spoiling the fun.

'Me,' the voice said. 'I have a point I'd like to raise.'

Necks craned for a better view. Who was this party pooper, we all demanded. And couldn't someone tear his damned head off or something?

The reason we couldn't see him was that, until now, he'd been sitting down. Wise move. Had we noticed him beforehand, we'd all have guessed he'd be trouble and taken the necessary counter measures to keep him quiet. Like sit on him or something. Because no-one wears the full lion's pelt on a sweltering hot day like this without courting *some* kind of disaster.

'Ah. Hercules.'

I don't *believe* it! Sagittarius, the knucklehead, was inviting him up to the front. At the same time, I noticed a lot of eyes turn longingly at the wine jugs. Not least Bacchus's. Although, in fairness, I have to say most of Hundred-Eyed Argus's gaze was directed straight down the bosom of that little wood sprite from Corinth.

Swinging his olivewood club as though it weighed no more than a sunbeam, our doughty hero stepped onto the stage. 'Mister Chairman,' he drawled, flexing his pecs. 'Fauns, satyrs, nymphs, dryads, maenads—'

'Gonads!' yelled a heckler from the crowd, and you can see where *his* thoughts were headed. OK, so we all know that sex isn't everything. But come on. There's more than enough hanging around in between as it is.

'— and all my fellow Immortals.' It was satisfying to watch the sweat pour down Hercules' face under the heavy lion's head. Not so good that he produced a thick wad of notes from somewhere deep in its pelt. 'For some considerable time,' he read, 'there has been an awareness among each and every one of us that all is not well on Mount Olympus. Morale has never been lower —'

How swiftly the mood of the crowd changed! With each bass syllable which carried across the clearing in the woods, they forgot about the wine, the partying, the reason they came here in the first place. Ears pricked up. Backs straightened. Lips pursed in concentration. At last they were not forced to endure some nebulous whinge, a trivial piece of planning which needed approval, an excuse for self-congratulation and praise. This speech embraced them all. *Their* needs. *Their* hopes. *Their* ambitions, *their* prospects. A breathless silence descended as Hercules proceeded to outline the riches he felt the Immortals deserved. What rewards they should reap.

Page after page turned in the big man's hand until, having raised them right up, having lifted the crowd to the very summit of spiritual aspiration, cleverly he began to trawl through their grievances. He listed the niggles which had eroded their confidence over the years. The petty bureaucracies imposed by the gods which stood in their way. I felt, rather than heard, the rumble which surged through the clearing. An emotion pitched somewhere between approval, fear and excitement...

Couldn't they see what he was planning? *Didn't they care?* With each fervoured agreement, each enthusiastic nod of the head, each vociferous 'hear, hear!' which fell louder and louder from their lips I myself grew that much colder.

'So I put it to you, brothers, that the gods — those men and women who laughingly refer to themselves as our masters — have not only grown lack-lustre and idle, they have become spiteful and careless, abusing their powers. Moreover, brothers.' Hercules paused. 'These presumed masters, these so-called invincible beings, have not only lost interest in the running of mortal affairs on earth, I say they have proved themselves *incompetent* here on Olympus.'

Oh, shit. There it was, out in the open. An overthrow. A coup. A take-over. Revolution.

'Incompetent,' he repeated forcefully.

You can say it six times over, *brother,* but this is not for me. I am out of here...

'By way of example, take little Echo here.'

'Here!' I protested. Oh, I do *so* not want any part of this—

'Look at the spiteful way Juno punished that poor little nymph.'

Well, that bit was true. Juno's revenge *had* been harsh. But hell, I knew the risks when I took them, keeping her talking time and again while Jupiter made his getaway from whichever pretty young thing he'd been seducing. I knew full well what would happen if she ever found out. She'd deprive me the power of speech — and for ever. Only Jupiter's intervention left me with some kind of voice. The gift, if that's what it is, of repetition.

'Not once did Juno punish the poor creature,' Hercules said, 'but little Echo was made to suffer twice over. What a bitch! What a spiteful, malicious bitch. And this, brothers, is supposed to be justice under the rule of the Queen of Olympus, the one and only Mighty Juno!'

'No!' I cried out.

Not true. Juno played no part in my doomed love for Narcissus. But, alas, no one could hear me...

'Not content with robbing Echo of her voice,' our muscled hero was saying, 'she takes the poor kid's body away, too.'

'Ooh,' I protested.

Unfair. Hercules knows damned well I pined away out of love. That was my choice, my decision. You can't pin that one on Juno. If I could not belong to Narcissus, I would not belong to anyone else. And I tell you something else, *brother*. I've never regretted that. Not for an instant. But Hercules had his audience right where he wanted them. Which meant he wouldn't let a little thing like the truth get in the way...

'When Juno saw Narcissus waiting for Echo at the pool, she couldn't resisting adding insult to injury. She made him fall in love with himself.'

'Sylph,' I corrected firmly.

No one but me and Narcissus knows what happened down there by that pool. Being dormant right now, Narcissus can't tell and I sure as hell won't. Some things are personal. But I won't have it bandied around that Narcissus fell in love with his own reflection. That just wasn't true. And frankly it bothers me that if Hercules goes on repeating that rumour, that's how it will end up being believed.

Look how he was playing them now! Not a dry eye in the clearing, and that included Hundred-Eyed Argus. Hell, I know everyone's a sucker for that somebody-done-somebody-wrong shit. I just didn't approve of Hercules using *me* to win his audience over. To show them that the deities on Olympus weren't as intelligent or as resourceful as they'd have us believe.

And now he was about to muscle in and oust them, with the backing of this gullible band! I looked round at my comrades. Woodnymphs and fauns, gorgons and sirens, cyclops, titans and sibyls. Over there, Arachne, turned by Pallas into a spider for no better reason than having woven a better tapestry than the goddess. Lycaon, changed into a snarling, howling wolf for doubting Jupiter. Midas, given the ears of an ass for siding with Pan against Apollo. Atalanta turned into a lioness by Venus just (would you believe!) for consummating her marriage, poor cow.

Up they surfaced, though. Grudges which had festered over the centuries. Rancour which had grown bitter with each passing millennium. Centaurs, bacchants, fountain nymphs, muses, harpies, furies, those unfortunate men and women turned into stone all began to dredge up their resentment. For most, though, the prospect of power was simply too tantalising to resist...

'No more tyrants!' Hercules cried, thumping his fist into the palm of his hand.

'No more tyrants!' came the rallying chorus.

'Democracy for Olympus!' he roared.

'Democracy for Olympus!' they cried, and I thought, yeah. Io isn't the only one stuck in a herd.

'In place of Jupiter and Juno,' Hercules said, 'I propose a triumvirate.'

Took him long enough to get round to it, eh? The tyrant is dead, long live the tyrant. But the baying mob cheered him on.

'Are you with me?' he urged. *'Are you with me?'*

Back came the predictable roar, the applause, the tumultuous stamp of approval.

'Then I propose three men at its head — myself, and the heroic twins. What do you say, Immortals? What do you say to democracy led by Hercules, Castor and Pollux?'

I knew what I had to say.

'Pollux!' I said. And I sighed. Dammit, *someone* had to put paid to this midsummer madness.

I just wished that someone didn't have to be me...

Don't get me wrong. I'm no fan of the gods, I don't fawn and flatter them like some I could mention. Well, all right. Who I *will* mention. Ganymede, for one, the oily little oik. OK, so he was a shepherd boy plucked from obscurity to become cup-bearer to the gods, but does he really have to suck up to them in the repulsive way that he does? Then there's Janus. He's not two-faced for nothing, you know—

But you're right. This is not the time to start bitching. We'll go into that later, once we've got this revolt bedded down. The problem was, of course, *how* to stop Hercules from toppling Jupiter from his throne.

Now it's not as though I personally believe the gods are infallible. Hercules made many valid points and I'd be the first to admit there's ample room for improvement. The Olympians *have* grown indolent. Mistakes *have* been made. They've become careless, underhanded, ethics have gone out the window and if ever there was a time to wheel out the clichés this was it. Power corrupts, blah, blah, blah. But! And this is the thing. *The same would be true if Hercules and the twins took control.*

Within no time they, too, would become self-serving tyrants, who would notice the difference? Find me an altruistic politician and I'll show you glaciers on the equator. Oh, and cut the crap about doing it for the Good Of The People. Hercules performed twelve Labours all right, and magnificently so I might add. But they were not for the Good Of The People. He mucked out stables and slew lions and hydras and wot-have-you for his own ends, remember. That this son of a mortal might himself become a god.

And you can forget Castor and Pollux. One's a wrestler, the other's a boxer — sporting heroes without doubt. But have you spotted a single brain cell between them? Keep looking! No, in Hercules' book these brawnballs were nothing more than walking, talking advertising hoardings. "You are safe in our hands" was the message. The Immortals flocked to their feet.

So what was *my* problem, you ask? If one order is the same as another, why not go with the flow? We-ell. Ask yourself this. Would you want *your* destiny in the hands of a group of drunken revellers who yawn their way through their own AGM and who change sides at the first bit of oratory? I rest my case.

The problem was, where to start. Jupiter was off on one of his wenching sprees, and who knows what disguise he'd adopted this time. Swans, showers of gold, husband impersonations, there was no telling — and certainly not enough time to find out. Hercules wasn't stupid. He knew full well he was carrying the Immortals along on the tide. He intended to strike before they changed their minds. So who did that leave? Neptune? Uh-uh. Too busy whipping up storms and sinking the ships of some little Greek island he felt had neglected him. Apollo? Still driving his fiery chariot across the skies over our heads. As for Mars, well damn me, hadn't he turned himself into a ruddy bull again? (After Io, I'll bet!)

This, then, looked like being a job for the girls.

After a hard day's chase through the forests or a bit of post-prandial nookie, there's really nothing quite like unwinding over a good gossip with friends. OK, so I use the term loosely. Maybe the girls meet up more for the mutual massaging of egos than friendship, but who cares? On this particular occasion I hit lucky. It was the A-Team splashing about under the waterfall.

Diana, needing the usual reassurance that she was the swiftest. Venus, bragging about Adonis, so everyone knew she was the fairest. Minerva, head in a book. (Like we didn't know she was the brainy one!) Plus, of course, Juno, angling for sympathy now that everyone knew Jupiter was out playing eeny-meeny-maenad-mo again.

Diana was practising her javelin stance in the water's

reflection. 'Where's Cupid today?' she was asking his mother.

'That little pest!' You could never accuse Venus of suffocating Cupid with maternal instincts. 'I sent him off to practise in the butts.'

An order, believe me, which Cupid takes literally. And it's bloody painful, I tell you, when that arrow hits home. I heard Adonis couldn't sit down for a week and Vulcan says his scar *still* won't heal.

'I don't know what he sees in these mortal women,' Juno was saying. 'Strumpets, the lot of them.'

'Ahem,' I said. It invariably takes an age to catch someone's attention. You have to wait for just the right moment.

Bugger. This wasn't it.

'Well, you know what they say about husbands, darling,' laughed Venus. 'They're like fires. They go out if you neglect them.'

'Ahem!'

'Are you suggesting I'm not stoking Jupiter's passions, you bitch?'

Oh-oh. This wasn't going the way I had hoped. They were too busy starting a catfight to listen to echoes round the edge of the pool. Briefly, listening to the squabble break out, I was tempted to call it a day. Let Hercules *lead* his raggletaggle band to glory.

I slipped away at the point where Venus was offering to give Juno lessons in techniques of the bedchamber. I was willing to bet that, at this rate, the next time I saw Venus, she'd have her fringe combed over one eye to hide the shiner.

What do do, what to do...

Back in the clearing the Immortals were drunk with both power and wine. Not so much ambrosia and nectar for them,

I thought. More like lotus eaters. One taste and everything else is forgotten. I looked at them. Sons and daughters of mortal women rising up against their own parents. Even Hercules, son of Jupiter and fostered by Juno at one stage, was prepared to overthrow his own father and that, I thought, told the story. That was what separated men from the gods.

Olympians might throw tantrums.

Mortal men yearn only for violence.

That's why Hercules would never be King of the Gods. OK, Jupiter has his faults. Serial adultery by no means the least. But was Hercules — indeed were any one of the rabble massed in the clearing — genuinely interested in the welfare of ordinary people? Did they see them as anything other than pawns in their own selfish power game?

Back at the pool, Juno and Venus had joined forces to turn on Diana.

'You can shut your trap,' Juno was saying. 'The day I take advice from virgins about sex is the day my husband turns celibate.'

'How dare you!' Diana snarled. 'I value my virginity—'

'Rubbish,' Venus sneered back. 'No man will have you, you prissy little cow. That's why, after all these millennia, you're still a virgin. You're frigid.'

'Frigid?'

Diana's spluttering drowned the splash of the waterfall and, since it was turning into a right old scrum over there, I left the three of them to it. It was Minerva I focussed on. You notice she hadn't uttered a squeak about Jupiter's philanderings or Diana's chastity bent? (Told you she was the brainy one). I waited until she came to the end of the scroll she was reading — or at least pretending to read, take your pick. Because I know which I'd have sooner been watching, kiddo.

Three top goddesses at it hammer and tongs or a dull old page of poetry? No contest. Anyway, as Minerva reached down, I gave the signal.

With a groan that cut through to the marrow, my old friend Boreas, the north wind, spread out his feathers, beat his grey wings and scattered Minerva's scrolls to all points of the compass.

Everyone shivered at the unexpected drop in temperature. Even me. It had been ages since I'd dallied with Boreas, I'd forgotten how icy his embrace could be. But Boreas whipping up Minerva's papers was the signal for Daphne to start. The distinctive rustle of her leathery leaves echoed round the wooded glade, a cue for Myrrh to begin weeping thick, sticky ooze from her bark. Suddenly, all my other friends descended. Ceyx and Alcyone, whose wish to become seabirds had been granted, swooped out of nowhere. Snakes rustled among the long grasses. All those gentle creatures who had asked — yes, *asked!* - to be changed from human shape descended now round the pool, calling at the tops of their voices as Boreas kicked up a din of his own.

'What the hell's up?' Juno was forced to shout over the racket of birdsong and animal sounds and the wild woodland echoes.

'Up!' I yelled back.

'It's that bloody AGM,' Diana snapped, rubbing the goosepimples on her arm. 'Happens every time we leave them alone. Something always goes awry.'

'Wry,' I said, fixing hard on Minerva.

'What the blazes does Apollo think he's playing at up there?' Venus said, glancing up at the sun, still blazing brightly in its innocence. 'I'm bloody freezing.'

'Zing!'

'Did you hear that?' Juno sniffed. 'Even scatty little Echo has got in on the act.'

Ooh, you don't know how much I wished she'd said something that I could have replied to at that!

'Sssh,' said Minerva, and the other three goddesses swung round on her, ready to lay into Jupiter's favourite daughter. (You notice how quickly they change sides, these girls. Loyalty changes hands faster than coins in a pickpocket gang).

'Don't tell *me* to shut up, you bossy cow —'

'No, listen,' Minerva said, and there was a tone to her voice that made everyone shut up, not just the three squabbling beauties. The glade plunged into silence. Even the tears of the cataract seemed to fall softly. The laurel stopped shivering. The bird calls ceased. The serpents stopped writhing. Only Myrrh's resin continued to weep.

'All of you, listen to Echo,' Minerva ordered.

Oh, bless you, Minerva. You're not the Goddess of Wisdom for nothing! I let my repetitions echo into the still summer air.

'Up,' I repeated. 'Wry. Zing.'

'Do you hear that?' Minerva reached for her armour.

'Up. Wry. Zing,' I said, softly now. Hurry up, ladies. I was running out of zing here myself.

'By the heavens!' Diana thundered, strapping her quiver on to her back. 'We hear you, Echo. By all the gods, we hear what you're telling us. Trust me, you'll find the Olympians grateful!'

No-one ever accused Juno of being quick on the uptake, but finally the bronze penny dropped.

'UPRISING?'

Oh-oh. I recognised *that* tone from the Queen of Olympus. Someone, somewhere was going to pay.

For once, I was thankful that that someone wouldn't be me!

I won't bore you with the details. No coup is bloodless, and suffice to say there are a lot of wild bears and boars and snakes running about who'd far rather have remained river gods, satyrs and fauns. Especially now the hunting season's nearly upon us.

But there you go.

For my part, I'm pleased with the outcome. One day, perhaps, men *will* take over from the gods and that will be a sad day for mortals. It is the nature of men to always want to war with one another — and who will be there to quench the fires of hatred, if not Jupiter, Juno, Minerva, et al?

My only regret was that Hercules was taken out of circulation before he could retract his scurrilous lies about me and Narcissus, but what the hell? My lover and I might be condemned to false history, but the truth of our love shows itself every spring. And don't tell *me* some bloke called Wordsworth or Jobsworth or whatever won't want to write a poem in the future about the fruits of our ardour!

As for Hercules, he and the twins didn't disappear entirely. Being a son of Jupiter, his Twelve Labours were given a positive spin in the history books, while at the same time any mention of this little episode was duly deleted. Ditto Castor and Pollux. The gods, being gods, wouldn't kill them, of course. That's not in their nature. So, if you care to tilt your head upwards on a clear night you can see them. Up there in the heavens.

Only you and I know the real reason the three of them have been placed in the Constellation.

And I, of course, am not telling.

At least. Not unless you top up my glass…

If there's one thing the Romans excelled at, it was organizing a good knees-up. They'd hire everything from musicians to poets to performing apes, with no expense spared on gourmet food such as stuffed honeyed dormice, flamingo tongues, peacock brains, and sows' udders. Think I'll pass.

BAD TASTE

When a senator throws a banquet, you know it's going to be good. When that senator happens to be a second cousin to the Emperor, even if it is three times removed and through a second marriage, you know it's going to be memorable. And when he's Horatius Clemens Stolus, Clem to his friends, you know it's going to be something really special.

Forget the river running with red wine, and the rose petals that fell like fragrant snowflakes from a contraption rigged to the ceiling. Clem had brought in Sicilian jugglers, Corsican conjurers, acrobats all the way from Dalmatia. He'd arranged for dancers to be dressed up like the gods—blue-skinned Neptune wielding his trident, Apollo in gold, Hades in black, Jupiter flashing his dark, goatskin thundercloak. And that was only the start. To the gentle strains of lyres and harps, he had satyrs chasing wood nymphs with balletic precision. Clowns and buffoons telling jokes, making riddles. He had slaves reciting poetry. Boxers and wrestlers. An Egyptian who could mimic anything from voices to birdsong.

'Claudia! My dear Claudia, there you are! Sorry I didn't get chance to welcome you personally. Got nabbed by some bore of a general just back from the Rhine, who insisted on giving me every detail of how he quashed the latest uprising.'

There's something about powerful men, isn't there? Clem was beyond the first flush of youth, he was losing his hair, cultivating a paunch, and an overlong nose prevented him from being handsome. So why this magnetic pull?

'And here's me, thinking you'd run me to ground in a dark corner for an ulterior motive,' she purred.

'Don't think I'm not tempted,' he laughed. 'But mind telling me what you're doing behind a bust of my great-grandfather? Don't say you're not enjoying yourself?'

On the contrary. For a girl who'd screwed and schemed her way out of the gutter, hobnobbing with the Empire's elite was as good as it gets. But when she'd also spotted the marble merchant she'd swindled out of eight thousand sesterces, a quiet corner seemed the perfect retreat.

'It's hot.' Claudia wafted her fan. 'I was taking a breather.'

'Exactly why I opted for an informal gathering. Can you imagine if we'd had everyone squashed together on couches in this heat? We'd have poached to death in our own perspiration.'

'Only the men, Clem. Ladies don't perspire, it's beneath us. We'd have elegantly glowed to death.'

'Talking of death.' The smile dropped from his face. 'I can't thank you enough for—'

'I didn't do anything.'

'You saved my life, Claudia. Those men would have beaten me to a pulp, if you hadn't come along.'

'Nonsense.' She dismissed any heroism with a wave of her hand. 'Thieves are rarely that industrious. How *are* the ribs, by the way?'

'Sore. But not half as sore as my pride. It's we men who are supposed to rescue maidens in peril, not the other way round. As for getting beaten and robbed, I'm ashamed to say, I followed through with my threat and told everyone I was knocked down by a wagon. Seems more ... manly, somehow.'

'Run over, rolled over, it doesn't matter to me. I'd still have put you in my litter, patched you up, and brought you home.'

'Which is why I am indebted to you, Claudia Seferius. And as a reflection of my gratitude, there are several wealthy merchants here today that I'd like you to meet.'

'In which case, senator, you are looking at a hero. Lead the way.'

'Seriously, my dear, it's the very least I can do, but a word of advice? Give it an hour.' He lowered his voice to a conspiratorial whisper. 'Once they've been caught canoodling with someone else's wife behind the laurels, or the wine's made them disclose confidences that should have stayed secret, you'll find they're infinitely more amenable to signing contracts.' He chinked his goblet against hers. 'Trust me.'

No one trusts a politician. Although it went a long way to explaining how certain votes got passed.

'So while I butter up the foreign dignitaries and get my ear chewed by some wearisome judge, you go enjoy the rope walkers, the fire-eaters and the quick-change artists,' he murmured. 'Then I'll come back, make some introductions, and we'll see just how much my miserable life is worth! Oh, and Claudia? Don't forget this is supposed to be a banquet. Can't have you going home half-starved, can we?'

Fat chance of that, because if the entertainment was spectacular, the food—dear me, the food was to die for!

Gazelle marinated in honey. Fig-peckers in pastry.

Peppered dormice that had been fattened for weeks. In fact, every imaginable delicacy was laid out on display. Lobsters, sucking pig, hazel hens and quail. Truffles, smoked duck, veal. Just looking at it made Claudia's mouth water. It made her mouth water, her tongue tingle, her mouth burn. Now her face was on fire. She was shaking and sweating. Her breath was coming shallow and fast.

But the funny thing was, as hard as she tried, as hard as she gulped, she couldn't—she just couldn't breathe...

'Drink this,' said the doctor.

'Suck this,' said the herbalist.

'Don't put anything in your mouth,' a rich baritone ordered. 'Not one damn thing, do you hear?'

Through the convulsions, the pain, the numbness and blurred vision, she made out a mop of dark, wavy hair. It seemed to be attached to a horribly familiar face. 'Orbilio?'

'Marcus Cornelius Orbilio at your service, ma'am!' He pressed his fist to his breast in mock salute. 'Although after you threw up over my toga, my tunic and a brand new pair of boots, the least you can do is call me Marcus.'

'For heaven's sake, Orbilio, what do you expect, when you ram your fingers down somebody's throat?'

'Seriously?' A jerk of his thumb cleared the room of doctors, herbalists and slaves. 'You're busting my balls because you're not dead?'

'No one dies from one bad oyster.'

'Nausea plus numbness plus dizziness plus burning equals classic aconite poisoning.'

'Roast goose plus pheasant plus pomegranate plus wine equals classic overindulgence. You're making mountains out of molehills, I'm fine.'

He shot her a wink, which was his way of saying *you look it,* then made her swallow a pile of black, crispy crumbs.

'Fine. I threw up over your boots. That doesn't give you the right to choke me with volcanic dust.'

'I'm choking you with charcoal, actually. Old family recipe, simple, but effective. Absorbs the poison like a sponge.' He sat down on the bed, folding his arms to make himself comfy. 'And while it works its gentle magic, perhaps you'd care to tell me who, at this splendiferous banquet, wants Claudia Seferius dead.'

She tried to roll her eyes, but the painted cherubs on the ceiling were spinning like tops.

'Honestly! Who'd want to kill a poor, defenceless, grieving, young widow—and while we're at it, what are the Security Police doing at said splendiferous banquet, anyway? Other than waiting to stick their fingers down some unsuspecting female's throat?'

'You're not poor, you're not grieving, and the last I heard, rabid tigers backed off fighting you.' He shovelled another handful of dust in her mouth. 'Now then, why am I here? Let me think. Was it to shadow the prime suspect in a nasty case of fraud? The same person, incidentally, who's not paying her taxes? Is also selling her blended wines as vintage? Has run up astronomical gambling debts, even though betting's against the law? Has helped slaves escape, by forging their master's signature? Is up to her big, brown eyes in—'

'I'm sure, if you put more than a token effort into your investigations, you'd find those slaves were owned by some smarmy marble merchant, who treated them so cruelly, it's impossible to believe anyone could be that sadistic. Just as I'm sure you'll find that the eight thousand sesterces your suspect swindled him out of is chicken feed to him, whereas it goes a long way between ex-slaves.'

Less thirty percent commission, but who's counting?

'Thank you, Claudia. Hardly a deathbed confession, but close enough. Mind you.' He cracked his knuckles. 'Had you let me finish, you'd have heard me tell you I was invited for the simple reason that Clem's my mother's cousin.'

Bugger. Thanks to stomach cramps and this terrifying numbness in her limbs, she'd forgotten Orbilio was the only patrician member of the Security Police. Now she'd given him enough ammunition to trace the victim (victim, there's a joke!) and quite possibly the runaways, as well.

'If this *is* aconite poisoning—and that's a very big "if", Orbilio—there are a hundred people milling around downstairs. It has to be random.'

'I tend to think of it as a hundred suspects,' he said cheerfully. 'Random only works when other people are affected, whereas this. This is designed to look like food poisoning.'

Didn't it just. And if Marcus Cornelius Orbilio hadn't been snooping around, she'd have called a litter to take her home, where, by the time anyone realized the situation was serious, it would have been too late. Not so much on the scene, she thought, as on the ball. Goddammit, the lengths some people go to, to have their suspects fit and healthy enough to stand trial!

'Check, and I'm sure you'll find loads of other guests that have mistaken the symptoms and taken themselves home.'

'The Phoenician ambassador passed out from the heat, two magistrates and a consul threw up from drinking too much, the tribune's wife broke a tooth biting into an almond, and my Uncle Petronius's ulcer is giving him hell. Other than that, Claudia, everyone's fine.'

As prisons went, she couldn't complain about this one. Swansdown mattress, gilded mirrors, scented damascened sheets, and if nothing else, Clem showed excellent taste in the fresco department. But for all the marble, bronze and porphyry, that's exactly what it was. A prison, where her next move would be to a dank, dark, communal cell underneath the Capitol. If she had any chance of avoiding ten years exiled on some godforsaken island, with just her cat and the clothes she stood up in, Claudia needed something to trade.

But for once, there were no loaded dice up her sleeve.

'I wouldn't say you were lucky, but you certainly got off lightly.' Orbilio pulled her eyelid down, checked the temperature of her forehead, and generally inspected her as if she was a horse. 'You ingested a very mild dose and, all things being equal, should make a quick recovery. But since no self-respecting poisoner slips their victim a mild dose of aconite, can you think of anything you spat out, because you didn't like it?'

'Nope.'

'Something that tasted odd, that you pushed to one side of your plate?'

'No, and before you ask, I selected every one of those delicacies myself.' No question of any tainted food being passed by a third party. 'Nor did I sneak titbits off anyone else's plate.'

'And you have absolutely no idea why you were targeted?'

'For once in your life, Marcus, you'll have to accept that I'm telling the truth.'

She must have slipped into unconsciousness at that point, because the next thing she knew, the sun was sinking over the Palatine, an oil lamp flickered in the corner, and someone was lying on the counterpane next to her, his head propped up on a mountain of pillows. That someone appeared to be reading a book of poetry, Catallus unless she missed her guess, just as that someone smelled of basil, instead of his customary sandalwood unguent. Without the usual hint of the rosemary, in which his posh clothes were rinsed. Claudia wondered what kind of household kept an entire wardrobe of clothes on hand, for their guests to change into. The sort of household, obviously, where female guests regularly throw up over male guests.

'Why aren't you downstairs, clapping poisoners in irons?'

'You're awake, then.' Orbilio tossed the poems aside. 'Feeling better?'

Much. The room had stopped spinning, the cramps had turned to dull aches, and Claudia could feel both her legs, her left arm and two, possibly three, of her toes. But if a girl's going to be in prison, it might as well be a comfy one. 'Terrible. In fact… if anything, Marcus, it's getting worse.'

'Hm.' His grunt had the word *Capitol* written all over it, you could practically hear jail keys clunking. 'In that case.' He stood up and stretched. 'Before you have another relapse and take that final ferry ride over the Styx, why don't you walk me through the sequence of events? Every last detail, every conversation you took, from why Clem extended the invitation until the moment you wrote off my boots.'

'He owed me a favour.' No good deed goes unpunished. 'At least, he thought he did.'

Pure chance made her peer between the curtains of her litter the other day, and instead of the usual yellow-wigged street walkers or dirty children begging for scraps, she saw a man being set upon in an alley between two tenement blocks. Both attackers were armed with cudgels, and while one beat the shit out their victim, the other was cutting his purse.

Orbilio had reached for a quill and was dipping it in the inkwell. 'Where was this?' he asked without looking up.

'Just off the Forum.'

'Can you be a little more precise?'

'The Subura.'

'Precise means specific, Claudia. I need to know *exactly* where this took place.'

What hadn't improved was the crushing fatigue. She was just too bone weary to lie. 'The Street of the Wig-Makers.'

Orbilio leaned back in his chair and let his breath out in a slow whistle. 'Now what would a senator devoted to moral reform be doing in an area renowned for prostitutes, gamblers and hemp-dens?'

'He said he was lost.'

'Not impossible for the average merchant, perhaps. The slums being worse than a warren.' Marcus was grinning from ear to ear. 'But my mother's fine, upstanding cousin ... ?'

'Mock all you want, but I believe him. Nobody chooses to wander down alleyways running with sewage, cabbage water and despair.'

'You did.' If possible, the grin had become even wider.

'I had an appointment,' she sniffed. With her bookie, but that was none of his business. 'Besides. I had four sturdy litter bearers along for protection.'

'My point exactly. Men at Clem's level don't set foot outside without a small army of minders, much less into the tenements. Yet not only were there no bodyguards to protect him, he was attacked in broad daylight, where even the most dim-witted felon knows that assaulting senators is a serious offence.'

The tingling in her neck was fading rapidly, and the feeling had returned to nine of her toes. 'Why should they think he was a senator?'

'You don't think the purple stripe on his tunic and high, black boots with a silver C on the ankle might have been a clue?'

'If you weren't such a stuffed shirt, you'd know that men who have shameful vices tend not to advertise their status.'

Senator, orator, father of four? Small wonder he told everyone he'd been knocked down, and dear god, how her stomach lurched when she saw him curled up on the cobbles, trying to make himself small. And if the crunch of wood against ribs wasn't sickening enough, it was the hatred on the thieves' faces. The loathing of rich men, who had it made—

Not just the mansion, the money, the slaves and the comfort. We're talking men who have everything from fresh water to their own teeth, and doctors who ensured they stayed in good health. Men who wouldn't be dead before their fortieth birthday. Whose diet was more than just porridge and beans. Who had grave markers set up when they died, so they would not be forgotten...

Seeing him—seeing *them*—the years fell away, pitching Claudia back to the yelling, the touting, the shouting, the sobs. To sores that refused to heal. To babies crying from hunger, and dying of it, too. To the stench of urine, house fires, oppression and eggs. That was why she'd ordered her litter bearers to stop. The reason she'd rushed to Clem's aid. To rescue him, not so much from the attack, but from the grip of the slums.

To re-wind the past, and make everything right—

'Orbilio?' She looked round. 'Marcus?'

Surely she hadn't passed out again, but suddenly the room was empty. Just a swish of a drape to show the speed of his leaving.

And there you go! One minute you're in prison, facing a horrible, lonely, penniless exile. Next thing, those loaded dice are back up your sleeve. Who says the gods don't smile on the righteous?

Claudia massaged her legs, rubbed at her arms, flexed as much life as she could back into her fingers and toes. She felt like shit, no question of that. But Clem's slaves had replaced her soiled gown with a magnificent creation of soft peach shot with gold, and her tiara would hide any sweat-streaked strands of hair. Step by step, no matter how long it took, she would inch her way round to the back of the house, call for her litter and take off to the country until the dust had died down—

'Sorry, ma'am.' An oak of a guard was blocking her exit, and by blocking, she meant he filled the whole bloody doorway. He also had the sort of face that looked like it had fallen out of a tree and hit every branch on the way down. 'The boss said not to let anyone in before he's apprehended his suspect. Or, for that matter, miss, let anyone out.'

Sod the sweaty ringlets. 'Orders are orders, I appreciate that,' she said sweetly. 'But it's urgent I go home.' While she rattled off her address, she stabbed herself with a hairpin hard enough to make her eyes water. 'I've just received news that my daughter is dying ...'

'Very sorry to hear that, ma'am.'

Not sorry enough to move out of the way, though. 'I need to be with her at the end, I'm sure you—no doubt a father yourself—understand?'

'Well—'

'Oh, thank you. Thank you so much, you're a good man. Maybe your wife would like this? I'd intended to pass it on to my daughter, only—'

'That's right kind of you, ma'am.' The tiara disappeared inside his tunic with the speed of greased lightning. 'Only Master Orbilio said you'd try these sorts of tricks. You don't got no kids, miss. And trying to bribe an officer is against the law.'

'Really? Well, unless you hand that tiara back, I'll report you for accepting backhanders.'

Ideally, she'd have glared him to death, then slammed the door in his face. In her current state, it was more a gentle waft.

'And in future, you mind your manners,' she called over her shoulder. 'When you address me, it's "you don't got no kids, *my lady*".'

How long Marcus Cornelius had been gone, Claudia had no way of telling. When you're aching from head to foot, feel like you've been kicked by a mule, and your mouth tastes—and probably smells—like rancid goats' cheese, time loses all meaning. Darkness fell. Through the thick, stone walls of Clem's magnificent mansion, she could hear muffled laughter and clapping, cheering and gasps, as the entertainment played through the evening and into the night. Occasionally, she heard the crash of dropped china, the clang of a gong, even, once, the slap of a face, when a kiss went too far. Music ebbed and flowed in time with the revels, varying from strings to pan-pipes, and at one point the harsh blare of trumpets, suggesting speeches or some kind of announcement.

Why it was taking so long to arrest the marble merchant, though, was beyond her. Perhaps he'd got wind of Orbilio's intent and made his escape? Perhaps he'd resisted arrest and needed further restraining? Or maybe he'd simply come clean and was making a detailed and lengthy confession? No matter, the sadistic little prick was in irons, that was the main thing, though with hindsight, it was obvious who'd slipped Claudia the poison. Who else had she defrauded out of eight thousand sesterces?

Apart from that Syrian merchant, but then he was just passing through.

Oh, and that one-eyed Macedonian, though that was purely to recoup the money he'd taken from her by cheating at dice.

If you can call it cheating, when he'd swapped her own loaded dice for a new set, but that was beside the point.

The point was, she hadn't just defrauded the marble merchant out of eight thousand sesterces, she'd robbed him of seven house slaves, each worth around the same sum. Making sixty-four thousand reasons for wanting revenge. Because, for a man for whom money means nothing, humiliation is beyond price—

And how naïve to imagine he hadn't seen her at the banquet. Worse, the bastard had come prepared. Which was some consolation, she supposed. When it came to trial and she was called to give witness, she'd have the satisfaction of knowing he'd be paying twenty times over. Of course, since she hadn't actually died, he'd probably argue that he simply intended to teach her a lesson, meaning he'd escape with exile rather than be forced to take his own life.

What irony, if they ended up on the same bloody island.

Because if Orbilio was here on a family invite, Claudia was the Queen of bloody Sheba. He'd been trailing her like a bloodhound from day one.

And talk of the devil—

'That went well.' He looked like the cat that had got the cream, the duck and the family parrot, as he breezed back into the room. 'Even his wife hasn't twigged that he's missing.'

The old medical emergency ruse to draw him outside, he explained, where two burly guards had been waiting to bundle him into a litter, with two more inside to restrain him with shackles.

'Not because I didn't want to put a dampener on the party. I just don't want his accomplices getting wise to what went down.'

Accomplices? Plural? She knew she'd pissed him off, but just how many marble merchants does it take to slip poison into— 'How *did* he manage to dose me with aconite?'

'When you chinked goblets, he dropped it in your wine, no doubt expecting you to drink it quickly in this heat. Silly man still had the phial on him when we arrested him, and that alone's a capital offence. Did you know it's illegal to even grow the plant in your own garden?'

Stuff landscape gardening. 'You're not talking about the marble merchant, are you?'

'Hardly, although now you mention it, he had a nasty accident earlier. As I passed him at the top of the stairs, poor chap took a terrible tumble over the rail. Broke his shoulderblade on the marble, apparently. As well as a sprained ankle, broken jaw and three crushed fingers.'

Orbilio did all that? Well, well, well.

'Accidents will happen,' Claudia said solemnly. Try taking a whip to your slaves now, you sadistic bastard. 'So given that Clem was the only person with whom I chinked goblets, I assume it's our illustrious senator you took into custody?'

The Security Police perched itself on the edge of a table. 'First, I take a job my father feels taints our fine aristocratic heritage. Then my wife divorces me for a common sea captain and I refuse to enter into another political marriage. Now I arrest my mother's favourite cousin.' Orbilio rubbed his hands with glee. 'The old man will be climbing the walls for months, when he hears about this.'

'It's called job satisfaction, Marcus. But back to Clem a minute, I'm guessing he didn't try to kill me, just to hush up some tawdry commerce in a house of ill-repute?'

Any moral crusader worth his salt would maintain he was conducting research incognito. Murder took it to a different plane. Especially premeditated.

'Rumours have been circulating for some time about plans to assassinate the Emperor—'

'Why would anyone do that?'

Augustus had stabilized an unstable Empire after years of civil war, he'd made Rome a force to be reckoned with, and brought prosperity to every single one of its citizens.

'Power.' Orbilio picked up a silver elephant paperweight and tossed it from hand to hand. 'Power was the one thing Clem didn't have, and the one thing he wanted more than all the rubies in the desert and all the gold in Egypt.'

For months, he'd been gathering a band of co-conspirators, plotting how, and indeed when, to take over from the current administration. What the authorities lacked was hard evidence. What the traitors lacked was a professional assassin, since, like Caesar's wife, they needed to appear above suspicion when this monstrous crime went down.

'As soon as you mentioned the Street of the Wig-Makers, I knew we had him,' Marcus said. 'It's the haunt of a well-known hit-man, where, again, we've never had enough proof to pin him to any of his fine achievements. Witnesses either disappearing, too scared to testify, or floating in the Tiber.'

So far, so good, Claudia thought. Dressed in ordinary clothes, and without his bodyguard to verify his whereabouts, Clem obviously paid a visit to the assassin. No doubt cut a deal. Then had the misfortune to be set upon by thieves.

'Why me? All I did was save him from a bigger kicking than he'd already had.'

'You're the only person who could tie him to the assassin, and how better to eliminate you, than by staging a simple bout of food poisoning in full sight of a hundred of our city's finest?'

Crafty bugger made sure no one saw them together. Didn't even come forward to welcome her when she arrived, biding his time until she took refuge behind his great-grandfather's bust. 'You really weren't shadowing me, then?'

'I work for the Security Police, Claudia. Our role is to keep the Empire safe, not worry about who's fiddling her taxes or fleecing Syrian merchants and one-eyed Macedonians.'

Janus, Croesus, he knew about *them?* Was nothing in her life secret any more?

'So why the Cyclops outside the door?'

'To stop Clem—or one of his associates—coming in and finishing the job. And, of course, to stop you sneaking out and preventing Clem—or one of his associates—from waylaying you and finishing the job.' He replaced the silver elephant on the writing desk. 'Can't have our star witness giving evidence from Hades, oh and congratulations on that miraculous recovery, by the way.'

The only thing to do with sarcasm is ignore it. 'In other words, I'm free to go.'

'As a bird.'

No charges, no probes, no stains on her character. Free as a bird—to fleece another poor sucker.

'And I really did ruin your tunic, your toga—and did you say *brand new* boots?'

'The softest kid leather, with the most elegant tooling.' Orbilio clucked his tongue in regret. 'Best boots I ever had, those. '

'Beyond fixing?'

'Way past.'

Claudia tucked her hair behind her tiara, slipped into her sandals and pocketed the silver elephant for a souvenir. 'Quite honestly, Marcus.' She shot him a smile as she swept past. 'Today just gets better and better.'

When three generations of women are found hanged, High Priestess Iliona wonders whether it was a suicide pact — or something more sinister?

COVER THEM WITH FLOWERS

Below the majestic peaks of Mount Parnon, Night sloughed off her dark veil and handed the baton of responsibility to her close friend, the Dawn. Daughter of Chaos, mother of Pain, Strife, Death and Deception, Night continued her journey. Gliding on silent, star-studded feet towards her mansion beyond the Ocean that encircled the world. Here she would sleep, until Twilight nudged her awake and her labours would begin all over again.

At the foot of the temple steps, Iliona rinsed her fingers in the lustral basin, carved from the finest Parian marble, and lifted her face to the sun. In the branches of the plane trees, the bronze wind chimes tinkled in the breeze. White doves pecked at the crumbs of caraway bread that was baked daily, especially for them. Whether the seeds were addictive, or the pigeons were simply content with their lot, the High Priestess had no idea. But the doves rarely strayed from the precinct, and it wasn't because their wings had been clipped.

Another few minutes and the first of the workers would

start to arrive. Scribes, libation-pourers, musicians and heralds. Basket bearers, janitors and the choirs. Every day was the same. They would barely have time to change into their robes before the sacred grounds were swamped with merchants, wanting to know if today was the day they'd grow rich. Wives, desperate to know if last night's efforts had left them with child. The poor, fearful of what lay ahead. Cripples would flock to the shrine, seeking miracles. The sick would come seeking cures. Wisely or not, Iliona had taken it upon herself to interpret their dreams, sometimes the behaviour of birds, even the shapes of the clouds, to give them the peace that they needed.

But for now — for these precious few minutes — that peace was hers, and she basked in its solitude. The soft bleating of goats floated down from the hills. Close at hand came the repetitive call of a hoopoe. Letting the sun warm her face, she breathed in the scent of a thousand wildflowers carried down from the mountains and over the wide, fertile meadows. Narcissus, crown daisies, crocus and muscari ... along with, unless she missed her guess, a faint hint of leather and woodsmoke.

'I'm beginning to think the rumours are true,' she said without turning round. 'That the *Krypteia* never sleeps.'

'You should know better than to listen to gossip,' chided the leather and woodsmoke through a mouth full of gravel. 'I sleep.' He paused. 'Upside down in a cave, admittedly. Cocooned in my soft velvet wings.'

The hair at the back of her scalp prickled. If the Chief of Sparta's Secret Police was making jokes, it must be serious.

'What can I do for you, Lysander?'

Had he discovered that she was still aiding deserters? A crime punishable by being blinded by pitch and thrown, bound and gagged, in the Torrent of Torment. Or that she was rescuing deformed babies that were thrown over the cliff ... ? Slipping food to prisoners in the dungeons...?

'Me? My lady, I wouldn't dare to presume.' His voice was slow and measured, but the teasing note was unconcealed 'Your country, on the other hand would be immensely grateful for your input and wisdom.' He cleared his throat, instantly changing the mood. 'Three women have been found hanged.'

Now she turned.

'Three?' But for all the shock, what was uppermost in Iliona's mind was that he looked older than the last time they'd met. The lines round his eyes were as deep as plough furrows, and there were more silver strands framing his temples. On the other hand, his short, warrior kilt showed no weakness of thigh muscle, and his chest still put a strain on the seams of his tunic. 'On the same night?'

'Same night, same house,' he said, explaining how they were three generations of the same family. 'Girl of fourteen, her mother and grandmother. And as much as I would like to dismiss this as some eccentric death pact, or even double murder followed by suicide, there were no stools that could have been kicked away. No chairs, no tables, no blocks of wood. Nothing.'

Small wonder he looked weary. However feared and hated the Secret Police, when it comes to women being strung up like hams, even the toughest among them are affected.

'It's no mean feat to creep into a household, overpower three women and hang them,' she pointed out. There would be servants. Dogs. Any number of obstacles.

'The alarm horn wasn't blown,' he said. 'In fact, there were no signs of a struggle in or outside the house.'

Which might, she mused, be because the killer was cunning

enough to cover his tracks. Or maybe obsessively tidy—

Now that acolytes had begun milling round the precinct, lighting the incense in the burners and sweeping the steps with purifying hyssop, Iliona suggested a stroll down to the river. Here, shaded by willows and poplars, they would able to speak without being overheard. Gathering up her white pleated robes, she found a perch on a rock and watched a heron stalk the lush grasses on the far bank for frogs, while moorhens dabbled in and out of the rushes and butterflies fed off the thistles. The river was at its fullest, thanks to the snowmelts, but the Eurotas was one of the few rivers in Greece that didn't dry up in high summer. That's why the river god was so revered by the people, and why so many flocked to his temple.

Why peace was so hard to come by.

'This is a monstrous crime, truly it is. But I don't understand why the *Krypteia* is involved.'

Unless the victim was royalty or a member of the Council, murder was hardly the preserve of the Secret Police. Much less its ruthless commander.

'Two reasons.' Lysander picked up a pebble, dropped to one kilted knee, and skimmed the stone over the water. Flip-flip-flip, eight times it jumped. But then everyone jumped for the *Krypteia*. 'Primarily, this triple murder will send shock waves round Sparta, and I need to neutralize the situation before it undermines morale.'

To remain the strongest land power in Greece, Sparta had turned itself into a nation of warriors, with boys joining the army at the age of seven. In the barracks, they would learn the values of endurance through discipline, hardship, deprivation and pain, pushing their bodies to limits that most men couldn't stand. Not for nothing was the mighty Spartan army feared wherever it went. But with the men away, protecting smaller and weaker city states from being gobbled up by their neighbours, they had every right to expect their womenfolk to be safe. Murder had suddenly become a political issue.

'Also.' Flip-flip-flip, another eight times. 'This was the family of one of my generals.'

'And naturally you owe it to him, to bring the culprit to justice?'

'Not exactly.' His smile was as cold as a prostitute's heart. 'This man is after my job, and I don't intend to give him a reason to get it.'

Iliona watched the swallows dip over the river for flies. Smelled the wild mountain thyme on the breeze. 'What has this to do with me?'

Something twitched in his cheek. 'Who else sees through the eyes of the blind, and hears the voice of the voiceless? You count the grains of sand in the desert, and measure the drops in the ocean.'

She jumped to her feet.

'How dare you mock my work! You know damn well that the poor, the weak, the dispossessed and the lonely come to this temple because they need something to lean on. Well, the support I give them is solid and sound, and it matters this—' she snapped her fingers '—that my oracular powers are fake. I set riddles, Lysander, in order that these people can find the solutions to their problems themselves, and don't get me wrong. These murders are tragic.' Desperately so. 'But since I don't know the women, I have nothing useful to contribute. On this occasion, I am unable to help you.'

Without pausing for breath, she rattled off a long list of tasks that could not be abandoned. Oracles aside, who would preside over the endless rituals and sacrifices? Dispense oaths in the name of the river god? Log donations and offerings in the various treasuries?

'The altars would not be properly purified, there are mountains of letters to dictate, and let's not forget the accounts that need overseeing, the various marriages and funerals that needed officiating, and not least, the preparations for the forthcoming spring carnival.'

'Hm.'

For a long time he said nothing. Just kept flipping pebbles over the water. She waited. Baiting him might be argued as the height of stupidity, but if he had come to arrest her, he would have done it by now. A girl had her pride, after all! At the same time, High Priestesses aren't exactly naïve. She knew it was only a matter of time before he resorted to blackmailing or bullying her into co-operating, as he had so many times in the past. Even so, she had no intention of making it easy for him, and job security wasn't her problem. In fact, many more deserters would be helped, babies rescued, prisoners comforted, with a new man at the helm of the *Krypteia*. One who did not know her past.

So it came as a surprise when Lysander rose to his feet and said quietly, 'That is your answer?'

She squared her shoulders. Wondered what pitch smelled like, when it was close to the eyes. 'It is.'

'Then I bid you a very good day, Iliona.' He placed his fist on his breast in salute. 'May Zeus bring you all that you wish for.'

A chill ran from her tiara to her white sandalled toes. He was a fighter, a warrior, a leader of men, who used every weapon in the book to win and get what he wanted. The Head of the Secret Police did not back down. He was up to something, the bastard.

'Wait,' she called, but he'd already gone.

Fear crawled in the pit of her stomach.

Night rose, slinking through the Gate of Dreams, to work again her dark powers over the earth. The days passed, the nail on the wall calendar marking their journey, highlighting those days which were propitious for planting, those which were auspicious for building, as well as those which cursed folk for telling lies. Not once did Iliona stop looking over her shoulder, but, as time passed, she began to relax.

Sacrifices were presided over with ritualist precision, oaths were dispensed in the name of the river god, donations and offerings were logged in the various treasuries. The altars were purified. Properly, of course. Those mountains of letters were duly dictated, the accounts managed with customary efficiency, and, thanks to the High Priestess's efforts, the spring festival went off without a hitch. Even the procession of children, carrying cakes stuck with burning torches, managed to reach the sacred pine tree without anyone tripping up. Usually at least one child would set fire to the carpet of needles, and last year the bee-keeper's daughter exceeded all records, setting the harp player's tunic alight as she stumbled, then singeing his hair when the poor man tried to stamp out the flames.

'You're working too hard,' said the Keeper of the Sacred Flame, one of the few true friends Iliona had.

'It's the season,' she lied. 'Everything comes at once in the spring.'

And to prove it, she went off to burn incense.

'You're not sleeping,' observed the temple physician.

'It's the season,' she shot back. 'The nights are too hot.'

And to prove it, she walked round wafting a fan.

As for the triple murders, the entire State was indeed sickened by the slaughter of three defenceless women. What kind of monster would do this? And yet, thought Iliona, in a country of full-time professional soldiers who virtually lived at the barracks, Spartan women were strong. How was it possible to overpower three at the same time?

As well as horrific, she found the crime deeply unsettling. Being a second cousin to the king, she had many contacts at the palace and, through them, kept abreast of events. She learned, for instance, that, with typical *Krypteia* thoroughness, Lysander's agents had explored every avenue in their attempt to bring the killer to justice. Could this have been a grudge killing, to punish the husband? Goodness knows, an uncompromising general collects enemies like a small boy collects caterpillars. Except there was nothing in his military history to point to a need for such dire retribution, nor in his personal life. Was the wife having an affair which had soured, inspiring the lover to take revenge? Apparently, running the farm in the general's absence left no time for romance. Had the mother-in-law upset someone? Again, this was ruled out—but the daughter? Wasn't she engaged to be married next year? What about the family of the future in-laws? Was there someone who didn't approve of the political union? At the time of the killing, the general was heading an assault in the Thessalian hinterland, making his alibi more solid than iron. Which was not to say he couldn't have paid an assassin to wipe out his womenfolk. But why would he???

Through those same contacts, Iliona read the reports of every interview and interrogation that had been conducted, and monitored the leads on the literally dozens of suspects. Consequently, she grew as frustrated as the investigators, since everyone and yet no one was in the frame for these murders.

Was one woman the target, she asked herself? Forcing the killer to silence the others after his crime was discovered? But why hanging? Why in a line ... ?

Meanwhile, life at the Temple of Eurotas continued on its daily course of setting riddles, interpreting dreams and committing enough treasonable offences to tempt Iliona to blind herself with pitch and save the authorities the trouble. Out across the valley, the buds on the vines uncoiled into leaf. Willows were cut to be woven into baskets, the olive trees were pruned back, oxen were gelded, and thousands of baby birds hatched. But as the spring progressed and the nestlings left home, the killings continued to dance at the back of her mind. As did the shadow of the *Krypteia*.

A month to the day after Lysander's visit, Iliona was at the house of her cousin, Lydia. Now in most city states, the decision to expose weak or deformed babies was the preserve of the father, thus leaving a certain amount of room for manoeuvre. In Sparta, however, where virtually every male citizen was a warrior of one kind or another, this decision was down to the State. And the State liked to decide very early on whether his little limbs looked like they would grow straight enough to grow up and march thousands of miles in full battle dress. Or whether he had a good, loud bawl, indicating that he would eventually be strong enough to throw spears and go hand-to-hand with the enemy. Those who failed the test were taken to the Valley of Rejection up in the mountains and thrown into the abyss.

Little room for manoeuvre in that.

Unless, of course, someone happened to have a fishing net rigged up and ready to catch them. Someone who, when the little mite was hurled into space, was also on hand to heave a blanket-covered stone into the gorge. One that made the right kind of thud when it landed.

The State called it treason. Iliona called it giving childless artisans the family they craved.

Aware that, one of these days, her luck would run out.

But for now, the sun shone on the jagged peaks of Taygetus, still capped in snow, and the Hoeing Song drifted on the breeze from the men working the fields. Lydia's husband, like the rest of the army, was off fighting someone else's battles, an annual exodus which, with spectacular regularity, sparked a glut of babies nine months after their return. Another reason why the fathers did not make that all-important decision. They weren't here.

'Who's a bonny boy, then?'

Iliona cradled the infant in her arms, while Lydia sat in the corner, grey-faced and shaking with fear. Her son was not deformed, but, arriving eighteen days before his due date, he was certainly a weak little baby. Now, five days after the birth and in accordance with the law, the Elders had gathered at the family shrine in the courtyard to pass judgment on the strength of his bawl.

'They're going to take him.' Lydia had no doubts. 'My baby, my only child, and they're going to reject him.' Tears trickled down her face. 'Suppose I'm unable to bear more children? Suppose— '

'Dry your tears,' Iliona said softly. 'I have cast the runes, read the portents and heard the voice of the river god dancing over the pebbles. Eurotas does not lie, Lydia. You will watch your son grow into a man.'

Runes and pebbles be damned. What didn't lie was the phial of willow bark infusion secreted in the folds of her robes.

'Gentlemen.'

Making ritualistic gestures to disguise the bitter liquid that she dripped on his tongue, Iliona handed the baby over for inspection.

'By Hera,' gasped the astonished Elders. 'They will hear this little man in Athens!'

Consequently, the celebrations were especially fierce, with flutes and trumpets, singing and laughter, and wine flowing freer than midwinter rain.

Which made the herald's announcement all the more shocking.

'On the road to Messenia, just beyond the fork,' he said, 'the bodies of three women have been found, hanging from the beams of their farmhouse.'

Daughter, mother, grandmother. Exactly as before.

Surrounded by olive groves on one side and paddocks on the other, the farm's main output was barley, where field after field of feathered stalks rippled in the warm, sticky breeze. Another week, two at the most, thought Iliona, spurring her stallion up the dusty track, and the crop would be ready for harvesting. Making it all the more poignant that the women would not see it.

Reining her horse as she approached the buildings, she glanced along this green and fertile valley. Enjoying a better climate than most of Greece, and with a constant flow of water, Sparta was not only self-sufficient, but in a position to export large quantities of grain and livestock. Add on a lively trade in iron, porphry, racehorses and timber, and it was easy to see why the State had grown so rich. Of course, like everyone else, land ownership was only available to citizens, just as tax was deemed too degrading for men who put their lives on the line every day. Instead the State taxed the artisans who made their armour and weaponry. And did so without ever seeing the irony of that decision.

'I'm surprised the temple can spare you,' Lysander drawled, coming out of the house to meet her.

Iliona tethered her stallion beside the water trough, shook the red dust off her robes and thought, if he expected her to apologize, he was in for a long wait. 'May I see the murder scene?'

She expected him to make another sarcastic comment, possibly along the lines of surely she, who could see through the eyes of the blind, had seen it in the sacred bowl? Instead, he ushered her past the porter's lodge and through the atrium in silence. Country villas were pretty much the same in design, being built around a central courtyard with a colonnade running round the sides. What differentiated them was the lavishness of the frescoes, the quality of the stone, the lushness of the couches and the richness of the tapestries on the walls. There was little of that here. A hoplite's family, not a lofty general's. A family who were scraping to get by.

'Are you sure you want to go in?' Lysander paused at the entrance to the store room to light an oil lamp. 'We haven't cut them down yet.'

We? As far as Iliona could tell, there was no one else here. In the hush, she could smell vinegar, honey and olive oil, and, when he lifted the lamp to light the way through the archway, she noticed that the air was hazy with flour.

'Yes.' She nodded. 'I'm sure.'

She wasn't. Far from it. But if she'd gone with Lysander one month before, maybe these women would still be alive. Facing them was the least she could do.

'Your frown tells me something strikes you,' he said, setting the lamp on the shelf.

'The distance between them.' It was the first thing she'd noticed. After the obvious. 'The spacing between each noose is almost identical.'

'Not almost.' He held up both hands so that his thumb-tips met, then splayed his fingers. 'Exactly three spans between each rope, just like last time.'

'You didn't tell me that at the temple.'

'I believe you were busy.'

Chip, chip, chip. He wasn't going to let her forget her refusal to help, and frankly, she didn't blame him. 'Still no witnesses?'

'The farm doesn't employ many labourers, and those they do live in huts in the hills.'

'But three women,' Iliona said. 'I mean, look at them. They're hardly pale, puny creatures.'

The grandmother had arms like a blacksmith's, the mother's legs were like tree trunks, and even the girl, not yet fourteen, was a strapping young thing.

'They wouldn't be mistaken for Athenians, that's for sure.' He almost smiled. 'However, one thing is certain.' The smile hardened into a grimace. 'I won't bore you with detail, but if there's one thing I know, Iliona, it's death. These poor bitches were alive when they were hanged.'

Yet there were no scratched fingers, from where they'd clawed at the rope. No dishevelled clothing. Just dolls hanging, three in a row. All evenly spaced. 'He drugged them,' she said.

'That would be my guess.' Lysander rubbed at his jaw. 'After which he either dragged or carried them here to the store room, but if you look around, the herbs on the floor to deter vermin are intact.'

'More likely they've been brushed back into place.'

The killer was as she'd suspected. Tidy to the point of obsession. Worse, he was cunning, careful and intelligent with it. She cast her eyes over the various sacks and amphorae lined up round the storeroom. That was what Lysander had been doing when she arrived. Untying, unstoppering, sniffing and testing. Hence the fusion of smells in the air. He obviously hadn't found anything pertinent, though. More a question of thoroughness than anything else.

'Aah.' Her mouth pursed in compassion as she picked up a small wooden daisy among the dried stalks of rosemary, tansy and lemon balm beneath the daughter's feet. 'This was probably her lucky charm, which fell out of her clothing when—'

'Let me see that!' Lysander snatched at the lantern for a closer look, and then swore. A short, sharp, vicious expletive.

'What is it?' she asked, because suddenly he was scrabbling around beneath the other two bodies, swearing harder than ever.

'I found a carved rose on the floor of the first house,' he said. 'Right below the mother, but—' More expletives. '—didn't give it a thought.' He held out three carved flowers, one under each of the bodies in the storeroom. A daisy, a rose and a lily. 'How could I have been so stupid?'

His anger pulsed through the windowless room as if it had substance and form.

'How could you have imagined it was anything other than trivial?' she replied. 'I also dismissed it.'

But Iliona was not the *Krypteia*. The *Krypteia* don't make mistakes ...

'I need to re-visit the first scene,' he spat.

As it happened, the house had hardly been touched in the month since its occupants were ferried across the Styx to the land of the shades. In no time, he'd recovered three wooden flowers among the strewing herbs on the floor.

A daisy, a rose and a lily.

The moon was full, dulling the starlight, as Iliona stood in the clearing in the hills. Twinkling silver far below was the river whose god she served, and whose annual floods brought wealth and plenty. It took an hour to cross the valley by foot, but three days to travel its length on a horse. Through olive groves, barley fields, paddocks and vineyards. A tranquillity that was now broken, thanks to one man. A monster.

In the two weeks since the second murders, the general had been pushing hard for Lysander to step down. His incompetence had led to a reign of terror, he'd stormed to the Council, and Iliona could only imagine the grief and despair that was churning inside him. With his family wiped out, anger was all he had left.

Which was better, though? For the Secret Police to be led by a man whose impulses were driven by blinding emotion? Or an honourable man, who would not baulk at blinding her with pitch before throwing her into the Torrent of Torment? She stared at the rugged tracks criss-crossing this red, stony land like white scars in the moonlight. Smelled the pungent moss under her feet. Listened to a stream frothing its way downhill, over the rocks. With their dark cliffs and secret caverns, these mountains were at once dangerous, beautiful, treacherous and magnetic. No different from Lysander himself.

But how do you define beauty? The scent of dog rose had suddenly become cloying. The sight of daisies made her feel sick.

She listened to the music made by the squeaking of bats and the soft hiss of the wind in the oaks. If only she could unravel the significance of those flowers! Of the spacing between the nooses! Of choosing three women of the same family …

A twig snapped. She looked round. Knew that, if he wanted, he could have crept up and not made a sound. The smell of woodsmoke and leather mingled with the aromas of moss and wild mountain sage, and in the moonlight his eyes were as hard as a wolf's. She wondered how Lysander had found her hiding place. And whether he'd seen the deserter she'd just helped to escape …

'Would you believe my orders—' He leaned his back against a tree trunk and folded his arms over his chest '—are to identify and protect every household that fits the pattern for the killings.'

An impossible task. Sparta currently had three thousand warriors scattered all over Greece, every last one of them landowners, and given that they were all aged between eighteen and thirty, probably two thirds had widowed mothers and daughters living at home. Their sons, of course, would be in the barracks, while the older men, retired veterans, were either working their own farms or employed in auxiliary military work. Obviously people were keeping an eye on their neighbours, while remaining vigilant themselves. But spring was a busy time on the land. The *helots* who worked it needed close supervision, or they would rise up and rebel, or take off.

'The general hates you,' she said.

'He holds me responsible.'

'Either way, he's engineered it so that you will either fail in your efforts to protect every woman in Sparta, or be forced to disobey orders.'

His lip twisted. 'Providing I can put a stop to this murdering sonofabitch, the Council will forget that I challenged their authority.'

The deserter ... Fifteen years old ... Was he already lying in a gully with his throat slit?

'The moon,' Iliona said, wondering if Lysander's dagger was still warm from the boy's blood. 'The moon has three phases. Waxing, full and waning.'

'Three women!' He jerked upright. 'Also waxing, full and waning!'

'Exactly. And all killed at the new moon.' Iliona dragged her eyes away from his scabbard. Straightened her shoulders, and swallowed. 'Suggesting the daughters might be the key.'

'To what?'

'I don't know,' she admitted. 'But how in the name of Zeus did he manage to drug them?'

'That second family,' Lysander said slowly. 'He had to have drugged them out in the courtyard, otherwise he would have strung them up from the beams in the kitchen like the first three.'

'You think the killer might have been a guest?'

Whoever he was, he was a coward who craved power. And could only get it when his victims couldn't fight back.

'Our investigations haven't turned up any visitors, and don't forget, the first trio. Not many guests are entertained in the kitchen.' Lysander clucked his tongue. 'Not at the general's level.'

'What about wood carvers?'

'What about them? There are hundreds inside the city alone,and none of them sell flowers like the ones placed under the bodies. As a trade, it fits your theory of precise, intelligent and tidy. Then again, every man and boy who's ever owned a knife — which is everyone — has had a go at carving at some stage.'

Needles and haystacks, needles and haystacks.

Would this monster ever be caught?

Two weeks later, when the new moon scratched her silver crescent in the sky, Iliona found her answer. In a house deep in the artisan quarter, three more women were found dangling, with the same flowers under their feet. The daisy, the rose and the lily. Now the terror was palpable. These were not exalted citizens. Landowners and farmers. They were tradespeople. The family of a humble harness-maker, who was away in Thrace, supporting the cavalry.

But that wasn't the worst of the matter. Three days before the moon was due to rise, the women brought in supplies and barricaded themselves indoors. No one had been allowed in, they wouldn't even open the shutters, and the alarm was only raised when their neighbour, an Egyptian gem-cutter, could elicit no response. He and the wheelwright broke down the door.

This, obviously, was the work of no human hand.

Sparta had angered the gods.

'Bullshit.' Lysander paced the flagstones of Iliona's courtyard, spiking his hands through his long warrior hair. 'Complete and utter bollocks.'

While he prowled, Iliona sat on a white marble bench in the shade of a fig tree, surrounded by scrolls of white parchment.

'I agree.'

The gods controlled the weather, the seasons, human fate and emotions. That was why they needed to be propitiated.

To ensure fruitfulness, justice, victory and truth, and offset famine, tempest and drought. True, Deception wove her celestial charms while men slept, as did Absent-mindedness, Panic and Pain. But so did the Muses, as well as Peace, Hope and Passion, and the goddesses of beauty, mirth and good cheer.

'All the appropriate sacrifices have been made,' she continued.

To Zeus, a ram purified with oak. To Poseidon, a bull, another to Apollo, honey cakes to Artemis and grain to Demeter. The gods had no reason to argue with Sparta.

'Also, the Olympians might take life, but not in this way,' she added. 'They kill, but they do not leave flowers.'

'If we knew what it meant, this daisy, roses and lily business— Are these my files?' He picked up one of the scrolls littering her bench.

'Duplicates,' she lied.

There had been too many for her scribes to copy, forcing Iliona to resort to the one thing that always oils wheels in the palace. Bribery.

'These are reports from the initial investigation,' he said, leafing through. 'Why are going through them again—? Ah.' He bowed. 'You see through the eyes of the blind and hear the voice of the dumb, and no, before you throw another tantrum. I am not mocking you this time. You work your oracles with trickery and mirrors. The quickness of the hand deceives the eye.'

Iliona watched an early two-tailed pasha butterfly fluttering around the arbute. Listened to the fountain splashing in the middle of the courtyard.

'Suppose,' she said, 'that the flowers are a smokescreen?'

'Like the precisely measured distance between the nooses?'

'Both suggested a ritualistic murder, but suppose that was the killer's intention?'

'Hm.' Lysander looked up at the cloudless blue sky, and seconds dragged into minutes. 'We didn't question the family of the second victims to check for alibis, therefore no leads were followed up, as we did for the general's women.'

Like a Parthian's bow, this was a long shot, Iliona thought. But suppose there was a cold-blooded killer out there, covering his tracks with a series of murders? If so, how in Hades would they pinpoint which of the six women was the original target?

Dusk was cloaking the temple precinct, softening the outlines of the treasuries, gymnasia, watercourses and statues. Up in the forests, the wolves and the porcupines would be stirring. Badgers and foxes would slink from their lairs. Down by the river, bats darted round the willows and alders. Frogs croaked from the reed beds. As the darkness deepened, Iliona watched moths dance round the flickering sconces, while the scent of rosemary and mountain thyme mingled with incense from the shrine.

'You were right.'

She jumped. One of these days, she thought, and Lysander would slit the throat of his own bloody shadow.

'His name is Tibios, and he did indeed serve the temple of Selene. Well done.'

The moon was her starting point. In the old days, long before the Olympians were born, Selene used to be worshipped in her three phases of womanhood. Developing, mature, then declining. In these enlightened days of science and mathematics, only those initiated into the priesthood even remembered this ancient wisdom — suggesting the killer was familiar with the old ways. Whether the murders were ritualistic, or whether his elaborate methods were simply a smokescreen, was irrelevant. It was a base on which to start building.

From then on, logic prevailed. The new moon was synonymous with youth, implying the intended victim was one of the daughters. But unions between citizens are contracted when the children are still in the cradle, whereas artisan women are free to wed whom they please. At sixteen, the harness-maker's daughter would have been casting around.

'With nothing else to go on,' Iliona said, 'the theory was worth testing. I'm just relieved it panned out.'

'Which is why,' Lysander said, 'my men are holding him in your office.'

Ah. 'You have insufficient enough evidence to bring him to a trial, so you're hoping I will draw a confession out of him.'

'The torture chamber is notoriously unreliable, and besides.' He shot her a sideways glance. 'I always believe in finishing what I started. Don't you?'

She made a quick calculation of what his thugs might find among her records. Surely the *Krypteia* didn't think she was foolish enough to commit incriminating evidence to paper?

'The harness-maker's daughter was called Phoebe,' he said, explaining on their way across the precinct how questioning friends and family had led to a young acolyte, who had been courting her.

'For a while, it seemed promising. Tibios is handsome enough, and he soon proved himself courteous, attentive and generous.'

The problems arose when he became too attentive. Too generous. Instead of one bottle of perfume, he would send her a dozen. It was the same with wine cakes and honeycombs.

He would present her with several new bath sponges every week. And positively showered her with cheap jewels and trinkets.

'Phoebe found it overpowering, but endearing,' Lysander continued. 'It was only when Tibios began to stipulate which tunics she should wear and who she could meet with, and got angry when she refused to comply, that she realized this was not the man she wanted to marry.'

Iliona was beginning to understand. Intelligent, shrewd and obsessively tidy were the hallmarks of a controlling nature. Men like that don't take kindly to rejection.

In fact, many don't accept it, full stop.

'My lady, meet Tibios. Tibios, meet the lady who outsmarted you and secured justice for nine vulnerable women.'

Handsome, certainly. Cheekbones a tad sharp, eyes a little too narrow, but yes. She could see why Phoebe would be attracted to him. Even in shackles, he was cocky.

'I'm the one who needs justice.' The acolyte leaned so far back in the chair that its front legs were off the tiles. 'Bearing false witness is a serious crime, but that's what comes when you misinterpret entrails and cloud formations. Or was it rustling leaves and the warbling of doves?'

'You presume,' Iliona breezed, 'that you were important enough to warrant consulting the river god, but as it happens, Eurotas doesn't concern himself with parasites. You were just sloppy.'

'Sloppy?' The legs of the chair came crashing down. 'From what I've heard, the killer left nothing to chance! *Nothing!*'

As though he hadn't spoken, Iliona dripped essential oils into the burning lamps, driving out the smells of ink and dusty parchment and infusing the room with sandalwood, camphor and myrrh. Behind the chair, the guards had merged into the shadows. Leaning against the wall in the corner, Lysander could have been carved out of marble.

'That last house was barricaded from the inside,' Tibios spat. 'Tell me how getting past that isn't smart.'

'Well, now, that's exactly what I mean.' Iliona picked up an ostrich feather fan and swept it over the shelves as though it was a duster. 'You didn't need to bypass their security.'

'That's because the killer's a god. Passing through walls, or changing his shape to an insect and able to slip under doors.'

Tibios was too full of himself to question why high priestesses should be doing their own housework. Or notice that she was so unaccustomed to it, that she was using the fan upside down.

'Alas, Tibios, the truth is more mundane.' Swish-swish-swish as though he was secondary to her task. 'You were already inside.'

Another shot in the dark, although enquiries at the temple of Selene confirmed that Tibios had been off sick for the three days prior to the murder.

'You knew this family. You knew their habits and your away around, and so, having hidden yourself in their cellar, how simple to slip a tincture of poppy juice into their wine that night, and then pff! Next you're stringing them up like hams over a fire.'

'There you go again. You keep saying *me*.'

'Only because of that little stash of carvings you thought you'd hidden away. Daisies, roses and what was that other thing, captain? Lilies? Not that it matters,' she continued airily. 'Your attitude was that if you couldn't have Phoebe, nobody would, so you killed the first two families as a smokescreen—'

'Like Hades I did!' Even now, believing the lie that the captain had actually found his cache of wooden flowers, Tibios was no less arrogant. 'I wanted those bitches scared out of their skins. I wanted them to *know* they'd be next. To feel the fear in their veins and sit awake at night, worrying — and they were. Even though they'd barricaded themselves in, they couldn't sleep, couldn't eat. It wasn't just Phoebe. They ganged up against me, the whole bloody tribe, so they needed to know that you can't just toss me aside. That I had power over them, over you, over the whole bloody State.' A smug grin spread over his face. 'The smokescreen was the *fourth* family I intended to kill.'

He may have been motivated by vengeance at the beginning, but this boy enjoyed his work. He would not have stopped at four.

'Exactly how did you get that message across to these women?' Iliona laid down the fan, and now there was a contemptuous edge to her voice. 'They were unconscious when you crept out of the cellar. Unconscious when you slipped the noose round their necks, and unconscious when you hauled on the rope. That doesn't sound very powerful to me. In fact, it seems more like the hand of a coward.'

'No, no, I—'

'The trial will probably be halted for laughter, once the jury hears how this big, strong Champion of Vengeance spent three days hiding behind a sack and peeing in an olive jar.'

'It's no different from a hunter lying in wait,' he protested. 'Ouch!'

'Ooh, did that hurt?' Iliona jabbed the inside of his nostril a second time with the sharpened quill of her pen. 'That doesn't bode well, does it?' she asked the Head of the *Krypteia*. 'Remind me again what the punishment is for killing a citizen?'

'First the guilty party is paraded naked through the streets,' Lysander rumbled. 'It draws a large crowd, so of course if someone should throw something nasty at him, or take a shot with their fists, there's little my men can do to protect him.'

'That's not fair,' Tibios whined. 'I'm entitled to civility at my execution!'

'And you shall have it,' Lysander assured him. 'With great civility, you will be thrown into the Ravine of Redemption, where you can — with even more civility — contemplate your crimes as you lay bleeding.'

'That's for traitors! You can't do that to me! I'm no traitor—'

'There will be no food, no drink, no comfort down there. Just you, your broken bones, and the wolves that circle closer each day.'

'Not forgetting the moon, so white and so bright overhead,' Iliona said. 'Which will wane, and then wax again, before you eventually join the Land of the Shades. '

'Don't think you can aid your own death, either,' Lysander rumbled. 'Your hands will be tied behind your back when you're thrown. With the greatest civility, of course.'

Above the rugged peaks and fertile valleys, Night cast her web of dreams to the music of crickets and the nightingale's haunting song. Tomorrow, the countryside would ring with the drums and trumpets of the annual Corn Festival, as the first ears of wheat were offered to the goddess Demeter. How sad that the women who had worked so tirelessly to bring their crops to maturity were not here to lay their gifts on the altar.

'I suppose you were hoping it was the general behind the killings?'

The guards had long since dragged Tibios off to the

dungeons, but Lysander showed no inclination to accompany them. Instead, he'd taken the chair vacated by the killer, folded his hands behind his neck and closed his eyes. It was too much for Iliona to hope he'd nodded off. Like she said before, the *Krypteia* don't sleep. Even in a cocoon of their own velvet wings.

'I can't tell you the satisfaction that clapping him in irons would have given me, after the things he wrote to the Council.' A rumble sounded in the back of his throat. It was, she realized, the first time she'd heard Lysander laugh. 'Unfortunately, as much as the general wants my job, I wasn't convinced he'd go to those lengths.'

'But you checked anyway.'

One eye opened. 'I checked.'

Iliona poured herself a goblet of dark, fruity wine. Somehow, she thought she would need it. 'What's that?' she asked, pointing to what looked like a squishy cushion wrapped in blue cotton under her desk.

'Oh, didn't I say?' The eye closed. 'It's a present.'

She drank her wine, all of it, before unwrapping the bundle. *'A hunting net?'*

'I find it quite remarkable, don't you, how so many women, who were previously considered barren, have been blessed with a much-wanted child over the last four or five years?'

Sickness rolled in the pit of her stomach.

'Spartan justice is famed throughout the world,' he continued levelly. *'Not only done, it is also seen to be done*, to quote the poet Terpander. But then.' Lysander stood up. Stretched. Rubbed the stiffness out of the back of his neck. 'Terpander was a inexhaustible composer of drinking songs, who died choking on a fig during a musical performance.'

'What are you saying?'

'I'm saying it's not a hunting net. It's a bird snare. If you look closely, you'll see the mesh is finer than the fishing net in which you currently catch your flying babies, yet strong.' He didn't even pause. 'It will dramatically reduce the time you spend on maintenance.'

'You're— not arresting me?'

'Whilst a boy with a twisted leg might not make a good warrior, Iliona, I'm sure he can weave a fine cloak or engrave a good seal.' He leaned over the desk and poured himself a goblet of wine from the bowl. 'The same way that not every man can be a cold-blooded killing machine. Some need to break free.'

Iliona's legs were so weak with relief that she had to sit down. 'Helping deserters is treachery in the eyes of the law.'
'The law can't afford to have men on the front line, who cannot be relied on.' He grinned. 'And on a more personal level, the law prefers devoting its precious time and resources to rooting out real traitors, rather than track down weaklings who will only let their country down in battle.' He refilled his goblet. 'Of course, that's only my opinion, and I would prefer you didn't bandy it around.'

Your secret's safe with me,' she said, and for heaven's sake, was she actually *laughing?*

Iliona opened the door and lifted her face to the constellations. The Lion, the Crab, and the Heavenly Twins. Far above the mulberries and vines, the paddocks and the barley fields, Night watched the High Priestess in the doorway. Guided by the stars and aided by the Fates, who measured, spun and cut the thread of life, Night had long since dried the tears of the bereaved and wrapped them in the softness of her arms. Having called on her children, Pain, Misery, Nemesis and Derision, to plague Tibios the acolyte, she was now ready to pass the baton of responsibility to her good friend, the Dawn.

And when the sun rose over the jagged peaks of Mount Parnon, some still capped with snow, Iliona smelled the scent of daisies, roses and, of course, white lilies. This time, their perfume was sweet.

The Festival of Diana, the day on which this story is set, originally took place deep in the Alban Hills on the night of the first full August moon. Carrying torches, women would form a flickering procession round Lake Nemi. The idea being that the light from their torches would merge with the moonlight on on what was believed to be the Goddess's Mirror.

CUPID'S ARROW

'Let me see if I've got this right.'

Claudia stopped pacing and ticked off the points on her fingers.

'In six days' time, we, as producers and merchants of fine wines, celebrate the *Vinalia*, when no lesser light than the priest of Jupiter himself will pronounce the auspices for the forthcoming vintage?'

'Correct, madam.'

'Except.' She turned to face her steward. 'We have no grapes to lay on his altar on the Capitol as offerings?'

'Correct.'

'Because some clod on my estate came down with a sniffle and the bailiff took it upon himself to quarantine the entire workforce?'

'To be fair, madam, the clod in question was the bailiff himself. He did not feel he could jeopardise the harvest by exposing — '

'Yes or no to the grapes?'

'Yes. No. I mean yes, we have no — '

'So in effect, I'm asking the King of the Immortals, God of Justice, God of Honour, God of Faith, who shakes his black goatskin cloak to marshal up the storm clouds and who controls the weather, good and bad, to very kindly *not* drop a thunderbolt over my Etruscan vineyards, even though I haven't bothered to propitiate him this year?'

The steward's adam's apple jiggled up and down as his long, thin face crumpled like a piece of used papyrus. 'That does appear to pretty much sum up the current situation, madam.'

'Oh, you think so, do you?' Claudia resumed her pacing of the atrium, wafting her fan so hard that a couple of the feathers sprang loose from their clip. Dear Diana, it was hot. Small wonder that half of Rome had taken itself off to the cool of the country or else to the seaside for the month of August. She thought of the refreshing coastal breezes. A dip in the warm, translucent ocean. The sound of cooling waves, crashing against rock s... 'Well, let me tell you something, Leonides. That doesn't sum up even *half* the current situation.'

According to the astrologers and soothsayers in the Forum — at least those diehards who hadn't fled this vile, stinking heat — terrible storms were in the offing, unless almighty Jupiter could be appeased. For everyone else in the Empire, storms would be a relief from this torpid, enervating swelter. Sweat soaked workmen's tunics and plastered their hair to their foreheads. Meat turned within the day and fish was best avoided unless it was flapping. Even Old Man Tiber couldn't escape. His waters ran yellow and sluggish, stinking to high heaven from refuse, sewage and the carcases of rotting sheep. But for farmers with grapes still ripening out on the vine, storms on the scale that were being predicted provoked only fear. A single hailstorm could wipe out their entire vintage.

'Prayers and libations aren't enough,' Claudia said, as two more feathers flew out of the fan, 'and I can hardly buy grapes from the market and palm them off to Jupiter as my own.'

It was enough that that bitch Fortune happened to be unwavering when it came to divine retribution at the moment. Claudia didn't want it spreading round Mount Olympus like a plague.

'And you're forgetting, Leonides, that I can't despatch a slave to Etruria to cut bunches until tomorrow at the earliest, because today, dammit, is the Festival of Diana – which just happens to be a holiday for slaves!'

'Oh, I hadn't forgotten,' Leonides replied mournfully.

Claudia blew a feather off the end of her nose and thought at this rate, the wretched fan would be bald by nightfall, and why the devil can't people make things to last any more, surely that isn't too much to ask. She stopped. Turned. Stared at her steward.

'Very well, Leonides, you may go.'

He was the only one left, anyway, apart from her Gaulish bodyguard, and it would take an earthquake, followed by a tidal wave, followed by every demon charging out of Hades before Junius relinquished his post. She glanced across to where he was standing, feet apart, arms folded across his iron chest in the doorway to the vestibule, and couldn't for the life of her imagine why he wasn't out there lavishing his hard-earned sesterces on garlands, girls and gaming tables like the rest of the men in her household.

The girls, of course, had better things to do. Dating back to some archaic ritual of washing hair, presumably in the days before fresh water had been piped into the city by a network of aqueducts, the Festival of Diana was now just a wonderful excuse for slave women to gather in the precinct of the goddess's temple on the Aventine. There, continuing the theme of this ancient tradition, they would spend the day pinning one other's hair in elaborate curls and experimenting with pins and coloured ribbons. Any other time and Claudia would have been down there, too, watching dextrous fingers knotting, twisting, coiling, plaiting, because at least half a dozen innovative styles came out of this feast day on the Ides of August, and all too fast the shadows on the sun dial on the temple wall would pass.

But not today. Today she had received the news that her bailiff was covered in spots and that, rather than risk the harvest by having the workforce fall sick, he had put them in quarantine to the point where no-one was even available to pick a dozen clusters of grapes. There was a grinding sound coming from somewhere. After a while, she realised it was her teeth.

'Junius?'

Before she'd even finished calling his name, he'd crossed the hall in three long strides. Was any bodyguard more dedicated, she wondered? Sometimes, catching sight of his piercing blue gaze trained upon her, she found his devotion to duty somewhat puzzling. Any other chap and you'd think he carried a torch for her, but hell, he was only twenty-one, while she was twenty-five, a widow at that, and tell me, what young stallion goes lusting after mares, when he can have his pick of fillies?

Widow. Yes.

With all the excitement, she'd almost forgotten poor Gaius. Yet the whole point of marrying someone older, fatter and in the terminal stages of halitosis was for these vineyards, wasn't it? Well, not the vineyards exactly. She had married Gaius for what they'd been worth, although the bargain wasn't one-sided. Gaius Seferius had had what he wanted, as well — a beautiful, witty trophy wife, and one who was less than half his age at that. Both sides had been content with the arrangement, knowing that by the time he finally broke through the ribbon of life's finishing line, Gaius would be leaving his lovely widow in a very comfortable position. In practice, it worked out better than Claudia had hoped.

Maybe not for Gaius, who had been summoned across the River Styx a tad earlier than he'd expected, and certainly before he would have wished.

And maybe not for his family, either, who were written out of his will.

But for Claudia, who'd inherited everything from the spread of Etruscan vineyards to numerous investments in commercial enterprises, from this fabulous house with its wealth of marbles and mosaics, right down to the contents of his bursting treasure chests, life could not have turned out sweeter, if she'd planned it. So why, then, hadn't she simply sold up and walked away? It was how she'd envisaged her future after Gaius. No responsibilities. Draw a line. Start again. Instead, she hadn't just hung on to the wine business, she'd taken an active, some might say principal, role. And as for his grasping, two-faced family, goodness knows why she continued to support them! Something to do with not wanting them to root around in her past, she supposed, but that was not the point.

The point was, she must remember to lay some flowers beside her husband's tomb some time. And maybe she'd have his bust re-painted this year, too. After all, it couldn't exactly be improving down there in the cellar.

'Junius, I want you to run down to the Forum and hire a messenger. The ones by the basilica are usually reliable, but if there's no-one left today, and I'll be very surprised if there are, given that it's a holiday for slaves, try the place behind the Record Office.'

'Me?' The Gaul was shocked. 'B-but I can't possibly leave you here alone, madam.'

'I promise that if a gang of murdering marauders come barging in, I'll ask them to wait until you're back to protect my honour, and that way we can both get killed. How's that?'

'With respect.' His freckled face had darkened to a worried purple. 'I don't consider danger a joking matter. These are the dog days of summer. Men are driven mad by the appalling heat, madam, and by the sickness and disease that grips the city. With rich folk decamped to the country, only criminals and undertakers flourish in Rome at the moment.'

Claudia nodded. 'Very eloquently put, Junius. You are, of course, absolutely correct and if you don't hurry, there won't be any messengers at the place behind the Record Office, either.'

'But madam — '

'It's a straight choice, Junius. Either you hire a courier to gallop like the wind to my estate, pick a dozen bunches of the ripest grapes then ride straight back, where we might — just might — make it in the five days we have left and therefore save the day. Or I turn you into cash at the slave auction in the Forum in the morning.'

The young Gaul drew himself up to his full height, squared his impressive shoulders and clicked his heels together. 'In that case, madam.' This time he didn't look at her, but stared straight ahead. 'In that case, I see I have no alternative.'

Excellent. Using the full services of the post houses and

changing stations, the messenger —

'You will have to sell me in the morning.'

What? The remaining feathers sprayed out of the fan as Claudia crushed it in her fist. 'This is not a debateable issue, Junius. You will — '

'I am not leaving you alone and that's final.'

Jupiter, Juno and Mars, that's all I need. The only slave left on the entire premises turns out to be as stubborn as a stable full of mules! She looked at the rigid line to his mouth, the square set to his chin and resisted the urge to punch him on it. Remind me of the position again?

A storm threatens to wipe out this year's harvest.

The offering to propitiate the god who threatens that storm isn't coming.

There's no one available to go and fetch it.

And the only person who *could* help is throwing tantrums. In short, if she wanted a courier, Claudia would have to trek out in this ghastly, fly-blown, disease-ridden heat and hire one herself, a role her bodyguard would be very happy for her to undertake, because at least he could be on hand when robbers, thieves and rapists set upon them.

Was there, she wondered, anything else which that bitch Fortune could throw in her path today?

The goddess's reply came almost at once.

She delivered it in the form of a bloodcurdling scream.

Which came from Claudia's very own garden.

With its stately marble statues and rearing bronze horses, Claudia's garden was a testament to her late husband's wealth and social status. A red-tiled portico provided shade and offered shelter from the rain, the water from its terracotta gutters collected in oak butts to irrigate the vast array of herbs and flowers, whose scent in turn fragranced the air throughout the year. Paved paths criss-crossed through clipped lavender and rosemary, while topiaried laurels and standard bay trees gave the garden depth and height. In the centre, a pool half-covered by the thick, white, waxy blooms of water lilies reflected sunshine, clouds or stars according to the weather. And all around, fountains splashed and chattered, making prisms as they danced, as well as an attractive proposition for birds in need of something more refreshing than a dust bath.

That such a place of beauty and tranquillity could be shattered by such a scream was nothing short of outrage.

The instant they had heard it, Claudia and her bodyguard went flying down the atrium. From then, it was as though the sequence of events had been frozen. Time slowed. She might have been watching them unfold by following their progress on a carved relief.

The screech came from a young man scrambling down the fig tree which grew against the wall. Unlike her villa in the country — indeed like everybody's villa in the country — this house didn't have the room to follow the traditional pattern of four single-storey wings around a central courtyard. For a start, it had two upper galleries for bedchambers and linen storage, each accessed by separate staircases, and a cellar which was accessed by steps outside the kitchens. The only possible site for a garden was behind the house and adjacent to its neighbour's. With one million people crammed into the city, space was at a premium and houses, even those of the wealthy, invariably butted up against each other. Claudia's was no exception. To the right she adjoined with the house of a Syrian glass merchant, while her garden at the rear adjoined with a general's. Paulus Salvius Volso, to be precise. Admittedly a loud-mouthed, drunken bully of a man, but all the same it was from his premises that the youth was making his rather hurried exit.

What he'd been up to in the general's house was clear from the array of golden goblets and silver platters which bulged out of the sack slung over his left shoulder. The contents nearly blinded her when the sunlight caught them. He was halfway down the fig when he let loose a second shriek.

It took a moment before Claudia realised that they were not screams of alarm, but squeals of wild abandon. The grin on his face as he jumped down was as side as a barn.

'Hey!' Junius called out. 'Hey, you! Stop right there!'

The boy spun round in surprise, but didn't falter as he belted towards the wicker gate on the far side of the garden.

'Stop!' This was a different voice. A soldier's bark. 'Stop, or I'll shoot!'

Junius was already racing down the path to try and cut the thief off, so he didn't bother looking round to see who was shouting from the top of her neighbour's wall. Claudia did. It was Labeo, one of the general's henchmen and a retired captain of archers. The thief had used a ladder to make good his escape. His mistake lay in not kicking it away. Labeo had shinned up it like a monkey.

The boy shot a quick glance at the bodyguard charging down the path towards him. Halfway to the gate, he knew he could out sprint him. Claudia knew it, too, and so did Labeo. On a public holiday, the street outside would be heaving. One more thief lost in a crowd.

'Last chance,' Labeo boomed. 'Or I'll fire.'

Claudia saw the grin drop from the boy's face. Realised that he hadn't actually seen Labeo until now. Thought it was a bluff being called by someone from inside Claudia's house, not from the top of the wall.

He turned. Saw the archer. Dropped the sack.

'All right, all right,' he yelled. 'Have it!'

Gold, bronze, copper and silver spilled over the pinks and the lilies. Ivory figurines knocked the heads off the roses.

What happened next would stay with Claudia for the rest of her life.

Watching the cascade of precious artefacts, she first saw its reflection in the pool. An arc of white, flying left to right.

Heard a soft hiss.

Looked up.

The arrow hit the boy in the centre of his back. She heard the splinter of bone. The soft yelp that sprang from his lips.

For three paces he didn't stop running. Then his arms splayed. His legs buckled. Red froth burst from his mouth. Still he kept going. It was only when he reached the gate and tried to unbar it, that he realised he couldn't make it. Junius had caught up by now. Was cradling the boy in his lap. Claudia could hear him whispering words of comfort as she flew to his side.

'Sssh, lad.' Junius wiped the fringe from the boy's face and patted his cheek. 'It's all right. There's a physician on his way now.'

His expression was haunted as it met Claudia's unvoiced question.

'You d-don't understand.' The boy's head rolled wildly and his breath bubbled red. 'N-not s-supposed to b-be like this.' Terrified eyes bored into Claudia's. She could see that they were brown. Brown as an otter. 'I'm n-not going to d-die, am I?' he asked.

'Of course not,' she said, only there was something wrong with her eyes, because her vision was misty. 'It's just a wound, like Junius says.' Her voice was cracked, too. 'You'll be back on your feet in a week.'

But that wasn't quite true.

The otter was already swimming the Styx.

For his part, Labeo had no sympathy for what he termed a dead piece of scum. Indeed, he would have pulled the arrow out of the boy's back to see how the head had compacted upon impact, had he not been prevented by Mistress Snooty from next door here, slapping his hand away. What a bitch, he thought. Shooting me glares which would pole-axe a lesser man. What did she expect me to do? Let the thieving toe rag go?

'The general's instructions was to shoot all intruders, whether they be on the premises or in the process of escaping,' he informed her. 'And it don't matter to me whether this piece of filth were carrying a dagger or not,' he added coldly, when taken to task about killing an unarmed, defenceless fifteen-year-old boy. 'He were guilty and the proof, if it's necessary, lies all over your flowerbeds. Ma'am.'

He weren't accountable to her anyway. The bitch.

But dammit, the sulky cow just would not let it rest. On and on she went, about how young the boy was, and hadn't anyone considered what had driven the poor lad to resort to stealing, because you could see he wasn't used to it, no one in their right mind would run off up a busy street with a sack stuffed full of golden objects and not have the army after them, and anyway what seasoned professional would go round leaving ladders against walls to make life easy for his pursuers?

Labeo let it ride. If she wanted to feel sorry for that little turd, that was her business, not his. He'd done the job he was being paid to do, and he was behind the general all the way on this. Let criminals think you're a soft touch, and every bloody thief will be climbing up the balcony! So while she ranted, he congratulated himself on being such a damn good shot. That arrow went exactly where he'd planned it.

Quite at what point Her Snootyship intended to shut up, Labeo didn't know. But he was mighty glad when he heard the general call his name from the far side of the wall. The master hadn't been expected back for ages, but wouldn't he be pleased to hear his captain had bagged a sewer rat this morning!

Except there were something different about the general's bellow. Every bit as terse. Nothing usual about that! And no less urgent, neither. (The general weren't a patient man!) But … Well, it just sounded different, that was all.

'I'm over here, General.' He called back. 'Caught a burglar stealing your gold. Shot him as he escaped.'

'Is he dead?' Volso wanted to know, scaling the ladder two steps at a time. He was a tall man in maybe his forty-second summer, broad of shoulder and square of jaw, his skin weathered from years of campaigning and thickened from too many nights cradling the wine jar. But he cut a commanding enough figure on and off the field, and regular training in the gymnasium had clearly paid off. It was a lean and nimble figure that swung itself over the adjoining wall.

'Couldn't be deader,' Labeo told him proudly, as his employer dropped to the ground.

'Pity,' Volso snarled, wiping the dirt from his hands down his tunic. He marched over to where Junius and Claudia were conversing quietly over the body and rammed his foot hard into the corpse. 'Bastard didn't deserve an easy death.'

'Volso!' Horrified, Claudia stepped in front before he could land a second kick. 'You are on my property, general, and I'll thank you to have some respect for it, for me, and for the dead.'

'Respect?' Labeo feared the general's bellow would deafen the widow. *'Respect, you say?'* He pushed her roughly aside and slammed his boot into the boy's side as he had originally intended. 'Save your sympathy, Claudia Seferius. If Labeo hadn't killed him, public execution certainly would.'

'Stealing is a civil matter,' she began.

'Stealing is,' the general agreed. 'Murder isn't. That boy you're so protective of didn't just rob me of my gold and silver. He robbed me of my wife.' Volso turned to face his archer. 'Callista's body is still sprawled across the bedroom floor,' he said quietly. 'Where this bastard strangled her.'

Moonlight had turned the garden paths to silver. The feathery leaves of artemisia and the pale purple flowers of sweet rocket released musky perfume into heat that pulsated like a cricket, and mice rustled beneath the fan-trained peach trees, pears and apricots. Bats squeaked on the wing in search of moths. An owl hooted from the cedar three doors down, and a frog plopped gently into the pool from a water lily leaf. The slaves were not back yet. Milking their precious holiday for all it was worth, there was none of the customary clattering of pots and skillets from the kitchens. No bickering coming out of the married quarters. The heather brooms and garden shears were silent. Everything was silent.

Seated on a white marble bench with her back against an apple tree, Claudia watched her blue-eyed, cross-eyed, dark Egyptian cat chase a mouse round the shrine in the corner of the garden and slowly sipped her wine. The wine was dark. Dark as Claudia's mood. And every bit as heavy. Cradling the green glass goblet in both hands, she stared up at the night sky without blinking. The stars would make life easy for navigation out at sea tonight, she thought. Directly overhead, the dragon roared and Hercules strode purposefully across the heavens, wielding his olivewood club. How appropriate, she mused, that it was the constellation of Sagittarius, which was starting to rise over the southern horizon. Sagittarius, the Archer …

The army had come, conducted its investigation in the twinkling of an eye, and departed hours ago. The young man's body had been carted away unceremoniously on a stretcher and Labeo had been lauded for a job well done, both by the army and his bereaved employer. It had been left to Claudia and her bodyguard to stack the stolen objects back inside the sack, where Junius later returned them to their owner.

Still staring at the stars, she sipped her wine.

'So then.' A tall, patrician body eased itself onto the bench, leaned its back against the rough bark of the apple tree and crossed its long patrician legs at its booted ankles. 'Cut and dried.'

Even above the scents of the junipers and cypress, the heliotrope and the lilies, she could smell his spicy sandalwood unguent. Caught a faint whiff of the rosemary in which his trademark long linen tunic had been rinsed.

'I wondered how long it would take before Marcus Cornelius Orbilio arrived on the scene,' she said without turning her head.

Up there on Olympus, Fortune must be wetting her knickers. Claudia topped up her goblet from the jar. Dammit, she couldn't make a move without the Security Police popping up in the form of their only aristocratic investigator, who seemed to view her — let's call them misdemeanours — as his fast track to the Senate. Still. What did she care? She had nothing to hide from him this time. For once, Marcus Make-Room-For-Me-In-The-Assembly Orbilio was whistling in the dark.

She couldn't see him, but knew that he was grinning. 'Why?' he asked. 'Were you running a book on when I'd arrive?'

'Tch, tch, tch. You should know that gambling's against the law, Orbilio.'

'Which happens to be one of the reasons I've called round.' A shower of bronze betting receipts scattered on the path. 'Yours, I believe.'

'Never seen them before in my life,' she replied. Bugger. That was the best boxer in Rome she'd backed with those. Half a brickwork's worth, if she recalled.

'What about these?' he said, showering a dozen more.

And that, unless she missed her guess, was the other half, invested at five to one on a Scythian wrestler from the north coast of the Black Sea. Bugger, bugger, bugger.

'We caught the bookie touting outside the imperial palace,' he said cheerfully. 'You know, you really should be more careful who you have dealings with, Claudia.'

She skewered him with a glare. 'Damn right.'

'How much of Gaius's money do you have left?' he asked.

The old adage was true, she thought ruefully. The best way to make a small fortune is to start with a large one …

'Jupiter alone knows what will happen to the family fortune once I'm married to you,' he continued smoothly. 'We'll probably be celebrating our fifth anniversary in the gutter.'

She supposed it was the moon making twinkles in his eyes, but in its clear, three-quarters light she could see every curl in his thick mop of hair, the solid musculature of his chest, the crisp, dark hairs on the back of his forearm.

'I would go to the lions before I went to the altar with you, Marcus Cornelius, and if you've finished littering my garden path, perhaps you'll be kind enough to sod off. I have a pressing engagement.' She patted the wine jar beside her. 'With my friend Bacchus here.'

'Hmm.' He folded his hands behind his head and closed his eyes. 'You seem to be having a lot of metal littering your garden path all of a sudden. Tell me about this morning.'

'No.'

Why the hell did he think she wanted to get drunk? To forget, that was why. To forget a young man with an ecstatic grin and eyes as brown as an otter. Eyes that she had watched glaze in death …

'Oh, no. There's more to it than that,' he said, clicking his tongue. 'I know you inside out.' He re-crossed his ankles, but did not open his eyes. 'Tell me.'

'If I did, you wouldn't believe me.'

'I don't believe you've never seen these betting receipts. I don't believe you've never defrauded your customers, or that you've never smuggled your wine out of Rome to avoid paying taxes, and that's why I love you, my darling, and that's why I know that when you marry me, life will never be dull —'

'See a physician, you have a fever.'

'— and I know, equally, that I'll never be able to trust you with money or business, but I do trust your judgement, Claudia Seferius. What is it about this morning that bothers you?'

'You really want to know?' Claudia drew a deep breath. Stared up at the celestial Archer. Let her breath out slowly to a count of five. 'What bothers me, Orbilio, is that a woman was murdered today and the wrong man took the blame. A young man who, conveniently, is not around to tell his side of the story.'

'You think Labeo — '

Claudia snorted. 'That arrogant oaf?' In her mind, she heard again the sickening thud as the general's boot thudded into the dead boy's ribs. Heard the youth's exuberant yell as he scrambled down the fig tree on the wall.

'No, Marcus,' she said wearily, 'Labeo did not kill Callista.' She thought of her tiny, fair-haired neighbour laid out on her funeral bier in the atrium next door, cypress at the door, torches burned at her feet. 'The thing is, Volso is a domineering drunk and a bully.' She sighed. 'Who liked to beat his wife and his children.'

Juno in heaven, how often had she heard them. The muffled screams. The pleading. Wracking sobs that lasted well into the night ... Many times she would rush round there, only for the door to be slammed in her face, and the next day Callista's story would be the same. The children had fallen downstairs, she'd say, or she had walked into a pillar. Sweet Janus, how often had Claudia begged her to leave the vicious brute? One day, she'd told Callista, he will end up killing one of the children.

'Think of them, if not yourself,' she'd advised.

Months passed and nothing changed, until, miracle of miracles, last week Callista called round to confide that she was leaving. Enough was enough, she'd said. Claudia was right. One of these days she feared Volso *would* go too far and as soon as she'd found suitable accommodation for herself and the children, she would pack her bags and leave.

'So you think Volso killed his wife?' Marcus said.

'No,' Claudia replied sadly, 'I killed her.'

She could easily have taken Callista and the children in, but she had not. She'd been too busy trotting round placing bets on boxers and wrestlers, ordering new gowns for the *Vinalia* in six days' time, planning parties, organising dinners, garlanding the hall with floral tributes. A battered wife with moping children would have got in the way. Put a dampener on everybody's spirits.

As surely as Paulus Salvius Volso throttled the life out of poor Callista, so Claudia Seferius had provided him with the ammunition.

Orbilio was forced to admit that, when Claudia told him he wouldn't believe what she was going to tell him, he was wrong. He'd said he was convinced that he'd believe her. But. Wrong he was.

That Volso killed his wife he could accept. The minute he'd heard that Callista had been found strangled in the course of a burglary, his suspicions were aroused. Having listened to the report of the centurion sent to investigate the killing of the thief, he'd not been at all satisfied with the army's neat conclusion. Volso's reputation preceded him and Marcus knew him as the type who vehemently believed that his wife and children were his property, that he would say who came and who went, and that nobody, but nobody, left him unless *he* threw them out. That was why he'd called on Claudia this evening. To hear her view on the matter.

But that she was in any way morally responsible was bullshit.

In time, of course, she would come to see this for herself, and surely the best way of helping her to reach this point was for her to help him clap the cold-blooded bastard in irons.

'The killing required a lot of planning,' he said.

And together, as the Archer rose and the level in the wine jug sank, they gradually pieced together the sequence of events.

First, Callista, having made her decision, must have somehow given the game away. Perhaps she had started to put things together in a chest. Maybe she'd confided to one of the older children. Who knows? Hell, she might even have lodged her claim in a divorce court, where Volso was just powerful enough to have the scribe report the matter back. Either way, he knew about her plan but did not let on.

Instead, he went out and hired himself a thief. A military man, he'd know exactly where to look and, as a commander of long standing, he would know what type of character to choose. Someone gullible, for a start. Someone who would believe the story he had spun them about having fallen on hard times and how the debt collectors would be knocking at his door any day now to seize his assets. But if he could beat them at their own game ...? Stage a burglary, whereby the thief was paid handsomely to steal the goods, which he would hand over to the general's henchman outside in the street to be converted into liquid assets, which the debt collectors would not know about.

'How do you know he'd told the boy there would be an accomplice?' Orbilio asked.

'The yells,' she explained. 'The yells were to alert the person he believed would be loitering in the street to move up to my back gate in readiness to relieve him of the sack and pay him whatever price Volso had agreed.' She shrugged. 'As I said, it had to be somebody gullible.'

Older boys would not have swallowed the bait. This boy had to be new at the game. No one else would have been told to leave the ladder up against the wall and actually left it!

'Except his yells alerted Labeo instead,' Marcus said. 'Who had been primed beforehand by his master that, on a slaves' holiday, the house might well be a target for thieves and that he was to shoot on sight.'

Perhaps it wasn't Labeo's fault, after all, Claudia mused. He'd been as much a pawn in the game as the boy, the one lured by greed, the other by pride. The only difference, Labeo was alive.

'So.' Orbilio steepled his fingers. 'The house is empty, because all the slaves are out celebrating. It's just Labeo in there on his own, and Callista, who Volso had undoubtedly drugged. The boy sneaks in, probably through your garden, shins up the fig tree and over the wall. He then places the ladder so he can make his escape. Inside, he fills the sack with the items he's been instructed to pick and then, when he's finished, he screams like a banshee, because it's vital the accomplice is outside for a quick handover.'

'Unfortunately, the yell alerts Labeo, who finds no trouble chasing him, thanks to the ladder Volso thought to set in place.' Claudia could see why he'd made general. In military tactics, timing is crucial. 'Because while we're all nicely diverted by the robbery and the killing, the master of the house is free to walk in through his own front door and throttle his wife at his leisure.'

'Ah.' Orbilio plucked a blade of grass and chewed it. 'That's where it starts to get tricky. You see, Volso refused point blank to give his porter the day off today, and the porter is adamant his master left the house shortly after dawn and did not come back until *after* the boy had been shot. He knows this, because, when Volso came home, the porter told him about the robbery and he was actually with him when he found Callista's body.'

He paused. Cracked his knuckles. Spiked his hands through his hair in frustration.

'Therefore, Volso could not have killed his wife.'

Dawn was painting the sky a dusky heather pink when Claudia finally stood up. The first blackbird had started to sing from the cherry tree, mice made last-minute searches for beetles and frogs began to croak from the margins of the lily pond. She shook the creases from her pale blue linen gown, smoothed pleats which had wilted in the heat and forced half a dozen wayward ringlets back into their ivory comb.

The first of the slaves had begun to trickle home three hours ago. Gradually, the rest had staggered in, singing, belching, giggling under their breath, their footsteps and their voices restoring order to the silent house. Without their presence, it was as though the bricks and mortar had been in hibernation. Now it was a home again, for them as well as Claudia, the rafters resonating with their drunken squabbles and their laughter, the clang of a kicked pan here, the spluttered expletive from a banged shin there, the bawling of too many over-tired children.

For most of the night, she and Orbilio had sat in silence in the moonlight, trying to figure out how Volso could have done it. Twice Marcus got up to fill the wine jar and fetch cheese, dates and small cakes made from candied fruit, spices and honey to help mop it up but now, as dawn poked her head above the covers of the eastern horizon, the Security Policeman admitted defeat.

'He's got away with it, hasn't he?' he said, yawning. There was a shadow of stubble around his chin, she noticed. And lines round his eyes which didn't come from lack of sleep.

'The cold, conniving bastard is going to walk.'

Claudia stretched. Massaged the back of her neck. And smiled.

'You fetch the army and arrest him,' she said. 'I'll give you the proof.'

She glanced across at the garden wall, then back at her own house. Gotcha, you son-of-a-bitch.

It started in the garden, it was fitting that it should end there, she supposed. By the time half a dozen legionaries came clunking in, their greaves and breastplates shining in the sun, Claudia had changed into a gown of the palest turquoise blue and was seated in the shade of the portico beside the fountain, taking breakfast. In her hand was a letter from her bailiff and the news was good. The spots were not contagious, he had written. According to the estate's horse doctor, they were the result of eating tunnyfish. The grapes for Jupiter were on their way.

She should bloody well hope so, too. Caught up in the tragedy of yesterday, she had quite forgotten about sending a courier to fetch them and maybe she might call in at Fortune's temple in the Cattle Market later to drop off a trinket or two. Fickle bitch, but not so bad when you boiled it down.

'You'll pay for this!' Volso thundered, as the soldiers dragged him down the path. 'By Hades, I'll have you in court for slander, Claudia Seferius, and I'll take every penny that you own in damages. This house. The vineyards. I'll have the bloody lot, you'll be so poor, you won't be able to afford the sewage from my gutter.'

'Save it for the lions, Volso.' She bit into a peach, and the juice dribbled down her chin. 'You planned Callista's murder like a military campaign and thought you'd get away with it.' She mopped the juice up with a cloth. 'Only there were three people you underestimated.'

'Come on,' he taunted, his square face dark with rage. 'Let's hear this crackpot theory, you bitch, because believe me, it will make for interesting evidence at your slander trial.'

Behind the group, she watched Marcus Cornelius let the bronze statue of a horse absorb his weight. He hadn't had time to change his tunic, yet she swore that, above the smell of soldiers' sweat, the leathery scent emanating from Volso and the pungent perfumes of the herbs in the flowerbeds — basil, thyme and marjoram — she could detect a hint of sandalwood. An expression had settled on his face as he watched her, which with anyone else, she would have interpreted as pride.

'Firstly, Volso, you underestimated the boy. He was young, keen, gullible, vulnerable, in fact, all the things you'd wanted him to be, and that was the problem. He was *too* young, *too* keen, *too* gullible.'

He ought to have picked someone who was greedy, not needy. The screams gave it away. Yes, he'd yelled as he'd been instructed. But the shrieks he'd let out were wild and exuberant. Whoops of pure joy. *I've done it,* they'd said. *I've got away with the stash, the accomplice is outside, I am going to be RICH!* She remembered the grin as wide as a barn. The dancing light of triumph in his eyes. That was not the expression of a thief who'd just strangled a woman in a burglary that had gone horribly wrong.

'Secondly, you underestimated my steward.'

Volso might run a tight ship next door, checking up for specks of dust and fingerprints on statues, taking the whip to his wife and his slaves if he found so much as one thing out of order. What he'd overlooked is that not everyone gets off on that level of control. It might work on the battlefield, but Claudia's slaves wouldn't know what a whip looked like, for gods' sake, and Leonides wasn't the type of steward to have his crew running around doing unnecessary tasks. The cellar was cleaned thoroughly, but only twice a year, and that was twice as often as any public temple.

She turned to Orbilio. 'Did you find any of the substances I listed?'

'Oh, yes. We found traces of them on his boots and tunic from where he'd bumbled around your cellar in the dark while he counted out the timing. Flour from the grinding wheel, cinnamon where it had spilled out from the sack, a vinegar stain, a smear of pitch, the corporal has the full list.'

'You planted that, you bastard,' Volso snarled.

'We didn't plant your bootprints in the dust,' Marcus retorted. 'The impression from a shoe is almost non-existent unless there's a body inside to make tracks.'

But the general wasn't going down without a fight. 'The fact that I was in the cellar proves nothing. In fact, I remember now. Two or three days ago, I called round to borrow some charcoals, ours had run out.'

Even the legionaries couldn't stop sniggering. Paulus Salvius Volso running next door to borrow some coals? Jupiter would turn celibate first!

Volso turned back to Claudia. 'And the third person I'm supposed to have underestimated? That's you, I imagine?'

'Good heavens, no.' Claudia shot him a radiant smile. 'My dear Volso, that was your wife.'

Apart from the fact that frogs would grow wings before Volso came back early to check on his wife who had not been feeling well, had he not left Callista's body sprawled on the bedroom floor, he might still have talked his way out of it. But what devoted husband wouldn't have lifted the remains of his beloved on to the bed? Only a callous bastard of the highest order could think of leaving her in an ignominious and distorted heap for people to gawp at.

In death, Callista had had the last word after all.

The legionaries were gone, their prisoner with them. The tranquillity of the garden had returned, and there was no indication among the rose arbours and herbiaries of the tragedy that had taken place here. Not just one death, either, but three. Callista's. The boy's. And Volso's to come in the arena.

He had planned the two murders like a military campaign. Coldly and ruthlessly, he chose the day when slaves everywhere, not just his own, would be out. No doubt he'd expected his neighbour to be out, too, as she usually was on the Festival of Diana, but it wouldn't matter unduly.

He would climb into Claudia's garden using the ladder, then kick it away after him. He would hide in the cellar, biding his time until he heard screams and then whoever *might* have been in the house would certainly rush outside. He would give it a count of twenty before he leaving the cellar, but then comes the daring part. He actually walks across the garden while everyone is clustered round the thief's body! If challenged, of course, he can bluff it out by claiming he'd heard a scream as he was returning home and came to help. Then he would just nip over the garden wall to "check on his wife", only to report back that she was dead.

As it happened, no-one saw him. Up and over, throttle the missus, up and back again in no time — before calmly letting himself out of Claudia's house and sauntering up to his own, whistling without a care in the world as the porter had testified.

And now they were gone. All of them. Volso. Callista. The otter.

'Do you think we'll ever know his name?' she asked Marcus.

In reply, he pursed his lips and shrugged. 'I doubt it,' he said. Urchins like him disappeared by the dozen every day. It was the unseen tragedy of the big city and so-called civilisation.

Across the garden, a chink of gold reflected from beneath the mint. A small child's goblet with a double handle. And so the tragedy goes on, she thought …

She looked up into his eyes. Resisted the urge to brush that stupid fringe from where it had fallen down over his face and trace her finger down the worry lines round his eyes.

'I was here,' she said, 'when I saw the reflection of the arrow in the pool.'

There was a pause. *'Here?'* he echoed, frowning.

'Right here.' She pointed to the spot with a determined finger. Sweet Jupiter in heaven, she would never forget it. 'White as snow, I actually watched it arc through the air.'

Orbilio scratched his ear. 'Not from here you didn't,' he replied. 'If Labeo was standing on the ladder and the boy was near the gate, and if he kept on running like you said after he'd been hit, then the arrow travelled like so.'

He indicated the trajectory of the missile with his hand.

'As you can see, the path doesn't curve as you describe it. Also, the arrow wasn't white, it's almost black, and Labeo's is far longer than the one you saw reflected in the water. What's more, if it was travelling at the speed, angle and direction that you say, it would be you who was lying dead, not your little otter. Oh, and by the way, did I ever tell you that you're stunning when you're angry and you're stunning when you're not, and that you're even more stunning when you're breaking generals' balls? I think a spring wedding would be rather fun, don't you?'

'I'd marry an arena-full of Volso's before I married you,' she said, 'but what I don't understand is this. If it wasn't Labeo's arrow that I saw reflected in the pool, what was it?'

Orbilio thought of the suffocating heat that played strange tricks by bending light. He thought of the emotion of the moment, the reflection of a white dove overhead, in fact, he could think of any number of rational explanations. But then ... But then... There was also the matter of a certain mischievous little cherub by the name of Cupid. So he said nothing.

He just pulled Claudia Seferius into his arms and kissed her.

No one really knows what went on there. Did the Oracle inhale noxious gases rising from fissures in the rock that made her ramble? If so, wouldn't she have died young, instead of living to a ripe old age? Was it staged? Was it political? Was it a lust for power? All I know for sure is that the location is breath-taking. And that the Oracle's mystique will run and run…

DEATH AT DELPHI

Smoke, grey and nauseous, swirled round the temple. Laertes recognized bay, hemp and barley grains among the ingredients, but there were others, rich and exotic, that were foreign to him. The heat of the charcoals on which they smouldered fused with the heat of high summer.

Still breathless from the tortuous climb, Laertes bowed before the priest.

'I – '

What should he say? *I have an appointment?* It made him sound as though he was a common civil servant, not head of an army, and besides. The priest already knew why he was here. Laertes had registered his petition, paid his (truly exorbitant) fee and purified himself at the Castalian Spring, all of which was noted in the oracular records. As indeed was the gold statuette, which had propelled him to the front of the queue.

'I have sacrificed a white goat,' he told the priest. 'Its entrails — '

'Suggested favourable omens. I know.' The priest smiled as he bade him lay his armour aside. 'Come,' he said. 'Come with me, and together we will summon the spirit of Apollo, that He may answer the question you lay before Him.'

Ushered deep into the building, Laertes felt the world he knew slipping away. Gone were the crickets that rasped in the scrub. The butterflies that flittered over the cushions of wild thyme on the hillsides. Gone were the jangle of harnesses, the scrape of boots on the march. Even the sunshine was no more, for in the world of the Oracle, oil lamps flickered and strange odours danced. Music came from everywhere and nowhere. Not the music of clashing swords that Laertes was used to, nor the blare of battle trumpets. This was a soft, haunting tune made by lyres and flutes, that spoke of death, and of life, and of dreams ...

From the shadows, two acolytes stepped forward in well-rehearsed unison. Boys of twelve, maybe thirteen, dressed in the same long, flowing robes as the priest.

'Drink,' the priest said, but when Laertes turned, the man was gone. In the distance, he could see small chinks of daylight. They seemed far, so far, away.

The first acolyte handed him a goblet on which the word "Forget" was engraved. The drink was wine, and Laertes drank. Then the second youth passed him a goblet on which the word "Remember" was etched. To Laertes's mind, it tasted the same. With spirals of smoke coiling round his head one second, his feet the next, they steered him towards what looked like a gaping hole in the floor. Squinting cautiously, he could see nothing but darkness below. The acolytes motioned for him to sit, then retreated in silence, taking their torches with them. Even as he'd prepared to face battle, Laertes had never known his heart beat so fast.

How long did he sit there, dangling his feet in the Stygian blackness? A minute? An hour? Time had no meaning in the world of the gods. For was this not the site where Apollo slew the dragon snake that had raped his mother when she was pregnant with him and his twin sister, Artemis? Alone in the timeless void, Laertes set to wondering for the millionth time how best to phrase his question.

Then he was falling.

Tumbling through nothingness, with his arms flailing wildly, since the smooth stone denied him a grip. Down, down he spiralled, funnelling into the blackness. In his struggle, his forehead made contact with rock, then he found flagstones cushioned with reeds. Dusting himself down, his soldier's eyes searched for the hands that had tugged at his ankles. It took only seconds to realise that his only companion was a statue of Apollo –

'Welcome,' a voice echoed. It was thin and crackled with age. 'Welcome to the world of answers and truth.'

Making the sign of the horns, Laertes traced the sound to a narrowed entrance over which "None may enter" was written in gold lettering. From the doorway, he peered into a small inner sanctum lit by the dim flame from a tripod. Its flickering light revealed a solitary female, veiled and seated upon a stool.

'Welcome to the point where heaven and earth and east and west meet. The navel of the world, that is home to the Oracle.'

What had he been expecting? An old woman, to be sure. Wisdom went hand in hand with age and prophesy, and he remembered now that the previous sibyl's trance had turned her into a wild animal, thrashing and groaning as she frothed on the floor, to die only a few hours later. Would that happen now? Listening to drumbeats and doves cooing curiously close by, Laertes was transfixed by the frail figure bent over her tripod, still dressed in the wedding robes of her marriage long ago to long-haired Apollo. To his shame, his strong limbs were trembling.

'Dost thou wish to enquire of the Lord of Light and Prophesy, whose arrows of knowledge shine into the future?' she quavered.

'I do.'

'Art thou pure of body and heart?'

'I am.'

'Then Apollo will speak to thee through the vessel of my body. What is it thou wishes to know?'

'My question ...' He cleared his throat. He was a general, after all. A commander of men. 'My question is this.'

His mouth was dry. Was it the smoke, the vile smell, or the fact that this was the first time he had voiced his intentions so bluntly?

'The king who rules the city-state from which I come is a weak man. He puts the good of himself before the good of his people, and I want to know if ... if ...' The words did not come easily. '... I move to unseat him — '

'Whether thy campaign will succeed?'

He didn't feel better, now it was out in the open. His heart still pounded harder than a blacksmith's hammer on the anvil. 'Yes,' he said eventually.

'Then shall ye know.'

With a twirl of her wrist, an explosion erupted from the tripod, a flurry of sparks flew into the air, then she hugged her arms tight to her chest and began rocking back and forth, keening softly. Swaying himself in the abominable heat of this underground tomb, Laertes watched the flames from her fire reflect in the Pool of Prophesy at her feet and sensed the past and the future fusing together. It wasn't only the crack on his head, he thought, that was making it throb.

Time passed. The Oracle rocked, wailed, muttered and reeled. The flames in her tripod guttered and died. In their place, smoke, white and sweet, welled from the walls, from the floor, from the ceiling. Laertes' tunic clung, sodden, against his skin.

'When a guest of wood doth pass through thy portals.' When she spoke, it was in a voice unrecognisable from the tremulous warble of old age. This voice was low, deep and even. 'Then must thou build a city of metal walls and woollen roofs, and set it beside the dancing pebbles.'

The sweat on his back turned inexplicably cold.

'Sacrifice in this place a creature that makes both music and food, and I, Apollo of the Lyre, will surely march at thy side.'

With a jerk, she slumped forward. The drumbeats fell silent. The cooing of doves ceased at once.

'Leave me,' the old woman quavered, and her voice was so weak he had to strain to hear it. 'Leave me, for I am spent.'

Perhaps he should have thanked her, but she seemed barely conscious, so he turned, and the last sight was of her thin breast rising and falling with unnatural rapidity. He did not understand the riddle, but, as he clambered up the rope ladder that had been lowered through the hole, he knew there was a priest in the temple, a seer called Periander, who would help him unravel the mystery. With the seer's help, and with Apollo's, there was no doubt in his mind that his revolt would succeed.

Tumbling back into the real world, Laertes was positively breathless with relief.

Below, in the underground sanctum, the Oracle threw off the veil that filtered the fumes and stretched her slender arms high.

'How many more?' she asked the wall.

The wall parted, spilling a thin finger of light into the cavern. 'Five,' the young man said, consulting his scroll by the glow of his candle. 'Though none of the other petitioners require such elaborate theatre.'

'Good. I was half-choked with that smoke.'

'You were?' The young man laid his drums aside and squeezed through the gap in the false wall. 'When you tossed those herbs into the tripod and set off that explosion, I had to pinch my nose to stop myself sneezing.'

Cassandra smiled with him. 'Next time, I'll stow a smaller bunch of borage up my sleeve, but at least Laertes should have no trouble interpreting the riddle.' She pulled off her old woman's mask and blotted the sweat off her face with her sleeve. 'I made it simple enough, I thought.'

When a guest of wood doth pass through thy portals — in other words, when a ship enters harbour — that's the time to *build a city of metal walls and woollen roofs* — i.e. set up camp, since soldiers use spears to support their blankets. And if this didn't make it plain that this undertaking should be conducted in the spring, when the seas opened once more for trade, *beside the dancing pebbles,* she had added firmly. It wouldn't take much working out on Laertes' part that this meant when the first snowmelts cascade down the mountains, and as for sacrificing *a creature that makes both music and food* — well, what other animal's flesh is succulent when roasted and whose shell makes the perfect soundbox for a lyre, other than a tortoise?

'Laertes is a soldier, not a politician, my love.' Jason began to knead the muscles in her neck that tightened from hours bent over the tripod. 'Men like him think in straight lines. Not too rough?'

'No, that's lovely,' she purred.

'I'll bet you a chalkoi to an obol that Laertes heads straight for Periander.' He moved down to massage the knots in her shoulders. 'He's the very sort who needs a seer to solve the puzzle for him — and ho, ho, talk of the devil.'

An older man in ankle-length robes, whose craggy face was softened by a beard, shinned down the ladder with the skill of a ship's rat.

'Father!' Cassandra embraced him warmly. 'What a delightful surprise!'

She hadn't seen much of him over the past six months, and he had never, in her recollection, come down here to see her. Was this because she was too engrossed in her new appointment, she wondered? Or because the memories that this sanctum held were too painful for him?

'Did you solve the riddle for our rebellious general? Because all in all, I thought it went rather well,' she decided.

The admission fee, the costs of purification, one gold statuette, plus what? a silver wine cup, perhaps, for the seer's deciphering. Traitor or not, the Delphic Treasury would welcome Laertes back any time.

'I suppose, Cassandra, that depends how one defines the word "well".' Periander's eyes were grave, but then they always were. 'Laertes collapsed at my feet.'

'And?' she cried.

'And he's dead,' her father said quietly.

Ever so softly, Night threw her cloak over the mount of Parnassus. Flexing the stiffness out of her legs, Cassandra paced the portico as, one by one, the priests and attendants made their way home to their wives and their supper and bed. The last of the petitioners was long gone, the temple swept with purifying hyssop in readiness for tomorrow, and the only sound that broke the silence was the grinding of bolts, as the sanctuary was locked up against thieves. She paced and paced until only the creatures of darkness prowled the Sacred Way that zigzagged its way up to the shrine. Fox, jackal, hedgehog and caracal. They moved from shadow to shadow.

Dead? How could Laertes be dead?

In the Pool of Purification, she saw a young woman with hair blacker than a raven's wing and eyes darker than an adulterous liaison. Plunging her hands into the cool, clear water, Cassandra splashed her face with her own reflection.

With the temple physician laid up in splints after a fall, there was no one to confirm or refute the cursory diagnosis that cause of death was a weak heart. Several witnesses testified to the chills and sweats that Laertes experienced beforehand, but then most supplicants suffered similar effects at the prospect of coming face to face with the gods. As for being breathless after his consultation, there was nothing unusual about that, either. The higher a petitioner's status, the harder the temple worked at disorientating him, because farmers, for instance, eager to know the most auspicious time to plant their beans or bring in their harvest, were far less worldly than kings or insurgent generals. Deeply religious, highly superstitious, the peasant folk believed with all their hearts that Apollo's spirit spoke to them straight through the mouth of the Oracle. They didn't need further convincing.

But a crown is not held in place by thin air. Kingship requires plotting and scheming, travel and trade, just as it requires war and diplomacy. Such sophisticates are not easily fooled and are even less likely to trust. Hence, the magic that is brought into play.

Senses manipulated by darkness, by narcotic fumes, by strange haunting music. Rituals take on even greater importance. The petitioners are passed from one priest to another before they are able to take stock of their surroundings. They're given goblets of wine that will supposedly make them forget everything except the focus of their question yet remember clearly the Oracle's prediction. Then they are left alone to commune with the gods, and who would imagine that an old woman's hands could grip their ankles and drag them into the void? Disorientated by their fall every bit as much as the blackness, they do not see the old woman hurry back to her stool. But — ! (And it was always possible). One of these days, this chicanery might just bounce off their defences. In which case, keeping the petitioner outside the inner sanctum, where there was no possibility of him seeing that the face was a mask, was essential.

As indeed was the Oracle's constant monitoring of the supplicant's body language and expression from beneath her veil ...

High overhead, Hercules wielded his olive-wood club and the moon rose full and white through the pines. Cassandra sat on the steps of the temple and buried her head in her hands. Weak heart be damned. While she was teasing Laertes with her riddles, what she had mistaken for nervousness and disorientation were, in fact, the symptoms of a man who was dying. Dying in front of her eyes.

And manifesting all the symptoms of poison.

'Jason.' She had to shake him twice to rouse him. 'Jason, wake up.'

When he saw her, fully dressed and her hair still pinned up, he was on his feet in an instant. 'What's wrong?'

'Laertes was murdered,' she explained, while he pulled on a tunic. In the lamplight, his skin shone like bronze. 'I need you to go down to the temple mortuary.'

She did not need to elaborate. Women, even the most important woman in Delphi, were forbidden to set foot inside.

'Examine his body, check his eyes, his skin colour, look in his mouth, his ears, under his nails, then report back to me on your findings.'

She was pretty certain she knew what had killed him, having ruled out corn cockle, since Laertes had suffered no abdominal cramps, while aconite would have had him throwing up, and with hellebore he'd have been salivating like a rabid dog. Other poisons were either too slow or too fast and so, given the timescale in which he died, Cassandra concluded that only belladonna could have taken his life. But confirmation would not go amiss.

'I love you, I adore you, I would give my life for you,' Jason said, combing his tousled hair with his hands. 'But frankly, my darling, I'd rather face the Minotaur in Hades than ask the Keepers of the Vigil to stand aside while I poke and prod their dead charge at this ungodly hour of the night. What excuse am I supposed to give them?'

'I have absolutely no idea,' she said, smiling in spite of herself. 'But you did so well today, with the drumbeats and doves, that I'm sure you'll come up with something.'

The invisible doves of prophesy were Cassandra's idea, but the drums and the white smoke had been Jason's. All it needed, he'd insisted, was a bowl of hot water and some terracotta pipes to filter the steam. Delphi, after all, was founded on the principle that the quickness of the hand deceives the eye.

'Ah, the birds.' He clucked his tongue. 'I wasn't sure it would work,' he admitted. 'I feared blocking the light from my one tiny flame would make no difference when I threw the sheet over their cage, but bless you, my love, you were right. They stopped talking at once.'

'I wish you would,' she said. 'We have so little time.'

'Why the hurry?'

She pressed her lover's hand in urgency. 'I'll explain later,' she said. There wasn't time now to go into why she needed to unmask Laertes' killer during her first trance of the morning.

'For you, O Prophetic One.' He kissed her lightly on the nose. 'I will borrow Hermes' winged sandals and fly like Pegasus himself.'

Watching him sprint across the courtyard, she thought it wouldn't be the first time that the Oracle had delivered a prophesy, only for it not to come true. Accuracy wasn't essential. Had Laertes died trying to overthrow his sovereign, it would only prove that, although Apollo had been with him, Zeus or Poseidon had sided with his opponent. When it comes to gods battling it out, no one argues.

In addition, many riddles were deliberately open to misinterpretation. Some for political reasons. Some because bribes had been passed (the Treasury was no slouch when it came to filling its storehouses). And some because, quite simply, Cassandra had no idea how to answer. Thanks to the meticulously maintained library of files at Delphi, she knew who the supplicants were, where they came from, the political background. But there was never any advance notice of their question.

And today the Oracle had quite clearly foretold that Laertes would set up camp beside the river next spring.

The Oracle could not afford to be that wrong.

Outside, Selene's silver light spilled over the rooftops, bathing the theatre, the shrines, the fountains in silver as bats squeaked on the wing. With a thousand city states constantly at war with one another, Delphi remained spectacularly neutral. In fact, it thrived on optimism, Cassandra decided, as she waited for Jason to return. And it was her job to keep it that way. Without optimism, one tiny shrine could not have grown into the most prestigious religious centre in the world, bursting with treasuries, overflowing with marble, and where eight hundred statues stared out to sea. Thanks to its oracles, a federation of small (and otherwise insignificant) city states had grown to become the most powerful council in the Greek world. Today, it was not so much a case of consulting the Oracle as obtaining sanction. Kings would not make war without it.

But Cassandra was only one link in the chain and, incredible as it may seem, not even the most important.

If anything happened to her — and the sibyls had a curious habit of dying in agony — there were other girls trained to step into her bridal robes and take that famous seat over the tripod. Girls like her cousin Hermione, for example, who'd been primed to take over, had it not been for Cassandra's outstanding aptitude for deception. She smiled in recollection. The Governing Council, always eager to stock a new treasury, revelled in the fact that each new generation brought fresh ideas to the role. Cassandra's proposal to enclose her lover, Jason, behind a partition to add to the drama cast poor Hermione into oblivion.

'Great Zeus, what are you doing out alone this time of night?'

She spun round. 'Father! You frightened the life out of me!'

Grey eyes stared solemnly at her in the moonlight. She tried to remember the last time he'd smiled, but could not. 'Can't you sleep, child?'

'Can't you?' she retorted. Like her, he was still in his day robes.

'The death of those carried young to the Elysian Fields is tragedy beyond measure,' he said sadly. 'To have them die before one's eyes is a burden greater than Atlas, who holds the whole world on his shoulders.'

Periander wrapped one arm round her shoulder and squeezed. Together father and daughter watched the moon dance on the sea.

'We old folk find consolation in the knowledge and wisdom that comes from maturity, but it is always the young that we envy, Cassandra.' He sighed heavily. 'You have so much to give.' He placed a kiss on the top of her head. 'So much to lose.'

She watched him walk away, stroking his beard in thought, though it was only later, much later, that she realised he wasn't talking about a young general collapsing dead at his feet.

He had been talking about Cassandra's mother.

What befell Periander's wife befell most of the Delphic prophetesses. One day the Oracle was sitting in her sanctum, dispensing riddles as usual. The next, she was a gibbering wreck. Drooling, moaning, writhing, screaming. She saw visions – terrible, marvellous, hideous visions – but these were the visions that killed her. Slowly and painfully, they would torture her to death while she frothed at the mouth, suffered spasms, amnesia, until the final convulsion came as a blessing.

Cassandra was just a baby when her mother had died. She only ever knew her through her father's memories, but, from what he told her, she would have loved her. They shared the same dark hair and eyes, he said, the same sense of joy and laughter.

'Ah, but she was a wonderful actress,' Periander would remind her. 'The minute she donned those robes and mask, she became Apollo's virgin bride, waiting for her adoring bridegroom.'

Then he would explain how it wasn't that the Oracle was a fraud. Just that Mighty Apollo couldn't sit there, day in and day out, with nothing else to do but assure this merchant that his investment was sound or that poet that his next work would be a masterpiece. When the gods spoke, mortals knew it, Periander reminded her solemnly, and when Apollo *did* speak through the mouth of the Oracle, then the poor creature was doomed. But by maintaining the pretence, such was Delphi's standing in the Greek world that men came from all over to receive the god's approbation, undergoing various rituals to win Him over. It was vital their trust in Him was upheld.

Backed by a massive administration ranging from the Governing Council to the countless scribes that toiled to keep the mountain of files up to date, the Oracle hosted Games to rival Olympia and held musical competitions that would turn Orpheus himself green with envy. And thus, for the thousands of pilgrims who flocked to the shrine hoping to have a curse lifted or find love, found a new colony overseas or sue for peace with their neighbours, the Oracle represented stability in a changing and unsettled world.

'You, child, are even better than your mother,' Periander would tell her, and for her part, Cassandra was proud to contribute to the miracle that was Delphi. Rich or poor, every petitioner went home reassured that, if he sacrificed here or did penance there, Apollo would surely be with him. The emancipation of slaves was particularly rewarding for her. You couldn't ask for more than to give a man happiness.

And so, watching her father prostrate himself before the shrine of Zeus, the moonlight turning the lines in his face into chasms, her heart ached for the man whose wife had died after hearing Apollo's voice, and who had never got over the loss. And now, to add to the tragedy, his daughter's prophesies had been brutally sabotaged …

As he rose and poured a libation to the King of the Immortals, God of Vengeance and Justice and Honour, she realised with a start that her mother would have been the same age Cassandra was now. In her twenty-fifth summer.

Despite the throbbing heat of the night, the Oracle shivered. And wished Jason would hurry.

Z*eus is the first, Zeus is the last, Zeus is the god with the divine thunderbolt.*

The hymn kept going round in her mind.

Zeus is the head, Zeus is the middle, of Zeus all things have their end.

As she gazed down over the hillside, across the building works in various stages of construction, at the statues that lined the Sacred Way, Cassandra knew that she would remember this night for the rest of her life.

It was the night she walked into womanhood.

Behind her, the Shining Cliffs lived up to their name, glistening white in the moonlight. Riddled with caves and rich with fountains and springs, they were the playground of Pan, home to the Muses, and the stairway to the pinnacle from which those convicted of sacrilege against the gods were flung to their deaths. From the grove of holm oaks, an owl hooted softly.

Not a seer like her father, or a prophetess as was made out, Cassandra nevertheless saw the picture clear in her mind.

The king who rules the city-state from which I come is a weak man. Laertes' words floated back to her. *He puts the good of himself before the good of his people.*

The files had backed up this assessment, but weak and self-serving doesn't mean stupid. One by one, as Hercules tramped round the heavens, the pieces fell into place.

Laertes' king hadn't trusted his general an inch, and when Laertes set off on that long trek to Delphi, the king knew there could be only one question which needed an answer. Not about to give up his dynasty, he duly despatched his own man, an assassin, to ensure Laertes would not return.

Leaning her back against a pillar, Cassandra realised she'd never know for certain. Had the assassin travelled a different route, which took longer? Had he been caught in a storm out at sea? Taken ill? Who knows, but whatever happened, he must have arrived in Delphi well after Laertes had registered his petition and paid his admission fee. Prowling round on padded feet, enquiring in whispers, the assassin would have noted the power that one gold statuette held, shooting Laertes up the queue of merchants and military men, athletes and musicians, much less the scores of humble smallholders. And the assassin would have quickly realised that, if the Treasury could be bought, so could individuals. It was his nature to probe and investigate. To determine which priest drank from gold goblets at home. Which acolyte kept an expensive mistress. Whether the Guardian of the Keys had run up debts.

From the moment Laertes set foot outside his own country, he was a dead man. It had only been a question of timing. Cassandra understood. This was the way of the world. It was the next part she had trouble comprehending. The fact that the murder had not only happened in *her* world, but that the killer specifically intended to discredit the Oracle.

And she did not mean the assassin.

His job was over once he'd established who could be bribed, and how much. Even the method of execution was out of his hands.

Poison ...

Extracted from the deadly nightshade, its juice induces dry mouth, impaired speech — all the things, in fact, that she had witnessed from inside her sanctum before Laertes' eyesight failed and he'd find difficulty breathing, prior to lapsing into unconsciousness and finally death. The heat from the column diffused into her backbone. It all came back to that tiny phial of liquid that had been fed to him inside the temple, she reflected, and that was the sad part. *Inside* the temple. For in this killing, timing was crucial. And, standing beneath the stars and the moon that saw everything, Cassandra knew that the hand that had delivered that fatal dose of belladonna belonged to someone not only familiar with the temple, but who knew the sanctum inside out. Who understood not only the mind of the petitioner, but also the intricacies of the disorientation process — and was in a position to play on both. Manipulating the timing of the drug, so that Laertes wouldn't notice anything out of the ordinary, whilst ensuring that the

Oracle's suspicions would not be aroused, either. Someone, in short, who knew she would set the supplicant a riddle. And be discredited when Laertes collapsed of natural causes...

It was not coincidence, she realised with a chill, that the temple physician was laid up with a broken leg. His fall from the Shining Cliffs was a nudge, not a stumble, and her stomach churned as she remembered who it was, who'd raced down the cliffs to sound the alarm –

'So that's where you're hiding!'

His voice broke the silence now, and as she turned, Cassandra's limbs were shaking.

Ah, but she was a wonderful actress, her father said of her mother. *But you. You are even better.*

This was true. Her smile was wide as she greeted him brightly.

'Jason!' She injected relief into her voice. 'I thought you'd gone back to bed! So now tell me. What symptoms did you find on Laertes' body?'

'That's what took me so long,' he said, and when he moved towards her, she backed away. 'No matter how hard I pleaded, no matter what tricks I pulled, the Guardians of the Vigil would not let me near him.'

Cassandra wished she could have sounded surprised.

In the darkness of the inner sanctum, music that was a combination of Persian and Egyptian, Phoenician and Arabic filtered down from the temple. Behind the partition painted to resemble the rockface, the doves of prophesy cooed, and in the tripod, sweet-smelling herbs emitted their scents. Lemon balm, oregano and mint.

She was a wonderful actress, but you, child, you are better.

In the past, whenever a sibyl had heard the true voice of Apollo, she had complained of smoke rising from a fissure in the floor that gave off a light, scented odour. The breath of the god. After which she fell into that fateful, delirious trance –

Wailing and thrashing in her created odour, Cassandra's actions quickly attracted the attention of the priests and acolytes above. Jason burst through the false wall in alarm.

'What is it, my love? What's the matter?'

When she didn't respond, he called for 'Water! Light! Give her air!' And when he tried to lift her off the stool, he found that he could not. A crowd gathered round, her father among them, his face a picture of agony.

I'm sorry, so sorry, she wanted to tell him. *I know this is how you found my mother so long ago, but truly I know no other way ...*

The Oracle could not – must not – be discredited.

Even at the expense of her own father's pain.

Soon the Council came running, the heavyweights who ran the administration, and the aristocrats who governed it. Through her twitching and groaning, Cassandra saw the face of her cousin, Hermione, at the edge of the crush. Familial concern tinged with more than just a little hopefulness, she noticed through her jibbering. Poor, sweet Hermione. Fated to be disappointed again.

'I see death which is not a death,' she howled, and there was no need to disguise her voice. This was Apollo speaking through Cassandra's own voice, just as he had through previous sibyls.'

'Laertes,' someone hissed in translation. 'She means it was murder.'

Her arms flailed. 'From fruit which is not a fruit.'

'Poison,' whispered somebody else.

'I see the shadow of the Ferryman inside this chamber.'

Beside her, Jason's frame had gone unaccountably still and, as her frenzy caused her to toss more herbs of prophesy into the eternal flame, she reflected again on how handsome he was. How funny. How virile. *How cunning.*

'Who?' one of the priests asked. 'Who killed Laertes?'

But the Oracle was passing into convulsions, and as she thrashed, Cassandra noticed her father slip away from the sanctum, tears streaming down his bearded cheeks. She ached to go with him, hug him tight to her breast, show him that his daughter was not dying. But the Oracle could not leave. Rooted to her stool — to her destiny — Cassandra tore at her hair in grief and despair.

You are better than your mother...

She was not, she was not, this anguish was real. Here, before the Governing Council and the enterprise that was Delphi, she was betraying the only man she'd ever loved.

'Can you see in your flames the face of the murderer?' one of the Elders asked. 'Do you see the face of the man who sought to bring disgrace on this place?'

Not in the flames, she wanted to scream. I see his face here, in my heart.

'Zeus is the foundation of the earth and the sky.' She was supposed to be rambling. She might as well ramble from the hymn that had kept her awake all through the night. And the images that had tormented her with it. 'Zeus is the breath of all things.'

'She means divine retribution will befall him,' someone interpreted.

'I see two heads in a womb and two quivers of arrows. And the bear will ride on the back of the dolphin and smite the beast that tried to kill him.'

'Twins!' an acolyte shouted. 'She means twins,' and

suddenly all the priests were chorusing at once.

'The dolphin is Apollo — '

' — his arrows are rays of light!'

It must be the shock of the Oracle's trance, she decided. Otherwise they'd have realised instantly that the dolphin was Apollo's sacred emblem, just as the bear was his sister's.

'Apollo is telling us that sacrilege has been perpetrated against him, but that Artemis, the huntress will strike down the assassin on behalf of her brother.'

Mutterings ran round the sanctum.

'The killer has already left Delphi — '

' — but we need take no action ourselves — '

' — because Apollo will have his revenge through his sister!'

'Justice is served,' someone pronounced.

But what was justice, if not a matter of perspective? From the corner of her eye, she glanced at Jason. His face might as well have been carved of stone. Tasked with ensuring Laertes' death, the assassin had been true to his mission, and in so doing he had saved a crown and a dynasty. To his king, crushing rebellion was righteous. The assassin would be a hero when he returned — but what justice for the man who fed Laertes the poison?

With a final shriek, Cassandra threw her arms into the air then collapsed onto the floor. This was the sign that the Oracle had stopped prophesying. Visions were only possible when seated upon her sacred stool. The crowd gasped.

'It's a miracle!'

'The trance hasn't claimed her life after all.'

Even Hermione appeared relieved.

'Apollo has spoken without killing his mouthpiece — '

' — he wants us to know that this sacrilege will be avenged.'

As they trickled out, the Council, the priests, even Jason, who she noticed was shaking, four words echoed inside her head. *Sacrilege will be avenged.* Yes, it would, she thought dully. Sacrilege would be avenged, but not in the way they imagined.

Only she, Cassandra, had the power to do that ...

Alone in her sanctum, the Oracle wept.

'I'm so sorry, Cassandra.' The priests bade the stretcher bearers lay down their burden. 'You have our deepest sympathy.'

The body was covered by linen, but the red stains told their own story. She stared with a heart that was broken.

'It was the will of the gods, Cassandra. Apollo needed a sacrifice, and since he spared your life, he took the life of someone you loved.'

Not Apollo, she thought heavily. He took his own life ...

'We found him lying at the foot of the pinnacle.' The priests shuffled awkwardly. 'There was ... nothing anybody could do.'

Knowing sympathy was inadequate, they retreated, leaving her alone with the body. How long, though, an hour? before they trooped back? Not long, that's for sure, since it was essential that the obsequeries commenced as quickly as possible, and since women were not allowed inside the temple mortuary, this was her only—and last — time alone with him. She wished she could make peace with him, too.

We named you Cassandra, your mother and I, because during the time of the Trojan War, Cassandra's curse was to prophesy but not be believed. Her father's words echoed in the stillness. *We thought, no we* hoped, *it would spare you the fate of the previous sibyls. But you, child* — he had smiled — *you were always so headstrong.*

'The name Jason means healing,' a voice rasped at her shoulder. 'Which I will, if you will allow me.'

She looked up at him, blond and bronzed, and thought her heart would break in two. He knew. He knew the minute he'd tried to inspect Laertes' corpse that something wasn't right ...

'I prised it out of the Keepers of the Vigil in the end,' he had told her. 'If no one was allowed near the body, then only someone in authority could have issued that command. I made them divulge who, then I knocked up the temple physician.'

That's why he was gone so long, he explained.

'The physician said that Periander had been acting oddly for a few days, and that he'd been worried.'

It was why the physician agreed to go for a walk above the Shining Cliffs with him, and why he'd accepted it had been Periander's clumsiness, not malice, that had caused him to fall and break his ankle.

Jason stared at the blooded sheet on the bier stained by one tear, then another, then another. 'Your father was not a bad man,' he whispered.

'With so many choices open to him, so many different paths he could have taken,' she sobbed, 'why did he choose to become a cold-blooded killer?'

'Because, darling, he loved you.'

Anger replaced grief. 'It was not for him to decide Laertes' fate,' Cassandra spat. 'Between us we could have used the oracle to divert Laertes from his murderous intentions, or at least warn him of the assassin at his back. After that, it would be up to him how he proceeded, not for my father to decide.'

Jason watched her tears darken the shroud.

'Laertes came to Delphi to receive sanction for the rebellion he was planning. The king's assassin followed,' he said. 'By listening and observing, he found a willing implement in, yes, this temple's seer of all people, but don't be too harsh on your father, my love. We all have something we want desperately, and we all have something to trade. Your father simply wanted to save his daughter's life.'

Old sequences replayed in her head. Periander grief-stricken when his beloved wife fell ill to the noxious vapours inside the sanctum. But not half so pained as the day his only child announced that she was following the same career path as her mother.

'To spare you the agony of dying young, your father became the assassin's instrument, feeding Laertes belladonna in the belief that, whatever happened, Laertes was a dead man, but this way he could at least save his daughter.'

If only it were that simple, Cassandra thought. He argued that, if he discredited the oracle and another prophetess took her place, what did principle matter, provided his daughter was safe? But did he not realise? That she not only understood but accepted, when she donned the bridal robes, that the deadly vapours that rose from the rock would probably kill her. But weighed against the balance of life, the opportunity to become the holy Oracle at Delphi was the most exciting, the most challenging, the most invigorating role any woman could hope to take on.

'To live a few years fully is better than to live many years badly,' she said, hugging her arms to her breast.

Once again, the decision was not her father's to make, but the tragedy was, with Jason's assistance, she had arranged that circus this morning specifically to convince Periander that his daughter had breathed the vapours of death and that there was nothing for him to live for. Sacrilege in Apollo's shrine had indeed been punished. But at what price, she wondered —

'Come,' Jason said. 'The priests are returning. Let's go back to the sanctum.' He kissed her cheek-stained tears. 'There's a fissure I want to block up.'

Healing, he said. The name Jason means healing and maybe, just maybe, Cassandra would grow to love him as much as he adored her.

Right now, though, she doubted it.

How could she love him, if she hated herself?

The climax of this Claudia mystery falls among the ruins of an Etruscan temple, many of which were already crumbling by Roman times. Which is a pity, because if you've ever seen inside an Etruscan tomb, you can't fail to be blown away by the vibrancy of the colour and the stunning action-shot figures. Their temples were equally spectacular, with fiery red columns, steep steps leading up, and lifesize terracotta statues gazing down from the roof.

GIRL TALK

Sometimes, when Destiny calls, it's best to pretend to be out.

This was, after all, the Circus Maximus — and amid pulsating excitement and a frantic rush for seats, what was one more silly rumour? Ignore it, Claudia told herself. Rumours are like fires, they fizzle out unless you poke and prod them. But instead of moving on down the steps and bagging a seat near the racetrack, Claudia Seferius found herself edging that little bit closer ...

Two minutes later, she'd cleaved a path through the surge of humanity and was elbowing her way out the turreted entrance which, despite mid-morning, lay deep in shade from the Palatine Hill.

"Alms?" A grubby hand with bitten-down nails thrust a container towards her and rattled it. "Alms for a one-legged warrior?"

"Unless you wish to wear your nose on the back of your lice-ridden head, I suggest you move out of my way."

Skewered by her glare, the beggar, whose sole brush with the army had been to doss in the lee of the barracks, forgot his sham disabilities and hopped smartly aside, and when he looked in his bowl, he could have sworn he was two asses down. Bugger! He'd planned to buy a pie off the vendor with that!

Claudia bit deep into the hot crumbly pastry as she marched beneath the steep escarpment. How dare he! How bloody dare Hector Polemo spread vicious gossip, insinuating she watered down the wine she sold! Claudia glowered at the flagstones, which sped beneath her feet. That's where he belongs, Polemo. In the sewer which runs below these wretched cobbles! And that, by all the gods, is where I'll have him crawling.

The street being narrow, she ducked into the spice-seller's to avoid a braying donkey, its panniers bursting with melons, dates and pomegranates, and took the opportunity to sneak a pinch of pepper on her pie. Holy Jupiter, wasn't she having enough trouble keeping the business afloat without some reptile spreading lies? I mean, it's all fine and dandy people calling you lucky, just because that ageing lardball you married popped his clogs years before expected, what do they know? Rich, wasn't he, the old wine merchant? Huh! It was only *after* the funeral feast had been cleared away that Claudia discovered her luscious inheritance was tied up in stock and trusts and property — and you just try spending an apartment block in Naples or half a brickworks on the Via Tiburtina!

Claudia tossed the last corner of her pie to the hopeful mongrel who'd been pattering behind and brushed her hands together. Offers to buy the business had come flooding in, including one from Polemo so tempting that Claudia had almost drawn up the contract. Until, that is, she discovered profit margins on wine were virtually double that of any other business! Goddammit, she'd be a fool to cash that in. Why not take a chance and break out on her own?

The street veered left, a bustle of shops and shoppers concerned exclusively with luxuries — perfumes, emeralds, books of vellum, tunics woven with wool spun as fine as babies' hair.

Why not? Because the Guild refused to deal with women, that's why not. Unheard of, don't y'know. A woman's place was in the bedroom, ha-ha-ha, and the proposals, which had at first been oh-so-fair became hard-nosed ultimatums, until finally they petered out — and it was at this point Polemo revealed himself to be a pirate in commercial waters.

"Take what you want by whatever means you can, that's my motto," he had laughed in that distinctive boom of his. "Sooner or later you'll have to sell and when you do, my pretty widow, I'll be the one who's mopping up the spills."

He'd had the gall to approach her during the very parade in which her husband, had he lived, would have been at the fore, Polemo and that stuck-up bitch he married — what was her name? Selina, that's right. Selina, with her predatory green eyes and flawless skin.

"My family's produced wine for generations," he said, unmoved by shining breastplates and caparisoned white horses. "When we set out to expand, we expand and nobody — I mean nobody — stands in our way." He smiled a lizard smile to emphasise his point. "So why don't you reflect on that?"

Auburn-haired Selina was standing at his shoulder.

"I don't need to," Claudia had replied, keeping her gaze fixed on the swords held aloft by purple-robed riders. "Your threats don't frighten me, Polemo and my response remains a raspberry."

Selina slipped in front of her husband, and Claudia had been able to smell her expensive perfume above the acid tang of horseflesh and leather and dung. "You'd be wise not to cross us," she purred. "Hector always gets his way in the end."

For the first time, Claudia wrenched her eyes away from the dazzling display of weaponry and armour. "Not only am I immune to bullying," she replied, "I won't be *cowed* either!"

Selina's breath came out in a hiss, but Hector's restraining hand on her shoulder had cut short retaliation. Well, that little interchange had taken place exactly one month ago today, and clearly Polemo wasn't a man to let the grass grow beneath his finely tooled sandals. Already the rumour-mongers were putting it about that Claudia Seferius watered her wine — what a cheek! The thought never entered her head! Not while she was palming it off as eight-year-old vintage …

On the corner by the basilica, a score of male prostitutes draped themselves against the columns and the walls, kohl-eyed and preening, but Claudia paid scant attention as she swept into a Forum ablaze with late summer sunshine and seething with advocates and acrobats, charlatans and hucksters, with slaves pushing handcarts and porters balancing amphorae of sweet olive oil. Pungent aromas exploded all around. Sausages sizzling on a spit, incense from the temples, fragrant roots from the herbalist.

"The sun's high in Libra," an astrologer said. "Would the lady like me to draw up her horoscope?"

His scrolls scattered across the travertine flags as the

whirlwind blazed on, half-expecting to see Polemo striding towards her any minute, mastiff at his side, lackeys at his heels, brushing his hand through the air as he waved interruptions and issues aside. By the gods, Claudia fumed, I'll choke you with your chitterlings for this! Influential he might be, but Hector Polemo wasn't above being knocked off his perch and exposed for the worm he truly was.

Handsome enough, though, she conceded. Knocking forty with a thatch of hair envied by many half his age and, to be honest, they made a handsome couple, him and his foxy-faced wife. There was a teenage daughter, too. Lotis, wasn't it? Though rumour had it, raising children was a job for nannies and for nursemaids as far as those two were concerned.

The house lay just off the Via Sacra. A respectable house, in a respectable neighbourhood, with a respectable white cat washing on the windowledge until the clatter on the knocker sent it diving under the laurels.

"Where are they?" With the flat of her hand, Claudia barged the doorman aside. "That slimeball Polemo and his poisonous wife. Where are they?"

"Who ...?" The elderly janitor strove to keep up as Claudia flounced through the vestibule and into the bright, airy atrium. "Who ...?"

"What are you?" she asked, throwing up her hands. "An owl?"

"I believe," a deep voice intercepted from the corner, "the janitor is enquiring after your own name."

I don't believe this! Holy Jupiter, Destiny must be doubled up with laughter!

Ignoring the baritone, Claudia instructed the janitor to fetch that lowlife weasel, Hector, and be bloody quick about it. Rheumy eyes darted to the corner and back again, but the doorman didn't move.

"The lowlife weasel's out." The baritone made no attempt to eliminate the amusement from its vocal chords. "Or so everyone surmises. He's not been seen since last night."

Down in the Circus Maximus, grim-faced competitors would be racing each other on thickly greased hides, much to the delight of the crowd, while here, finches in an aviary chirrupped and sang as though this was the happiest day of their lives. Shit! Claudia ground her heel into the nose of a mosaic dolphin and was damned if she'd turn around.

"In that case." Claudia's eyes bored so hard into the old man's, his began to water. "You can wheel out the frosty-faced old haddock that he married."

Wouldn't you just know the poor janitor would be pipped to the answering post!

"Selina," the baritone pronounced, "is still in bed."

The fountain in the pool juggled droplets of water in sunshine which turned bronze ancestral busts to gold.

"Orbilio," Claudia said wearily. "Why do you persist in bugging me?"

She really did not need this. Not here. Not some ferreting investigator snooping around to rattle the bones in her closet. And sod's law meant it was Marcus Cornelius Orbilio she had to bump into! The only man in Rome who knew the dark side of her past! Not, of course, that it was her past which was the problem at the moment. For reasons best known to themselves, the Security Police are attracted to offences which result in things like exile. And when it came to sniffing out crime, Orbilio had the snout of a trufflehound.

"Me?" The wool of his toga squeaked as he slid off the polished table he'd perched against and Claudia caught a faint whiff of his sandalwood unguent. "I was under the impression it was the other way around."

Claudia heard a grinding sound and, in the absence of any quernstones in the atrium, concluded it was the gnashing of her teeth.

"After all," he continued mildly. "I got here first, remember?"

Crossing her arms, Claudia stared at the sky through the opening in the roof and wished something would happen up there to break the blue monotony. Nothing did, of course. No honking geese, no passing butterfly, not even one tiny puff of cloud. Though for a busy household, it seemed odd that she could hear only the thumping of her heart against her ribcage.

"Perhaps," he suggested, and she could feel the twinkle in his eyes boring deep into her shoulderblades, "you would care to join the treasurehunt?"

He came into view, then. Casting his tall, broad shadow over the pool and for half a second Claudia allowed herself the hope that maybe, just maybe, he was here on a social visit, patrician to patrician and all that ...?

"Are we," she enquired, "talking cryptic clues on scraps of parchment?"

"N-not exactly." Bugger. "The hunt is for one Justus Capella."

"Oh, and what might the Security Police be fitting this poor sod up with?"

Dark eyes crinkled at the corners. "Strange as it may seem," he said, " we have a preference for villains." He leaned his weight against a marble podium, and Claudia watched a pulse beat in his neck. "Prosecutions tend to stick more easily, although in Capella's case we'll have no problem. His attempt to kill the Emperor was quite blatant."

Assassination! Curious, despite herself, Claudia trawled her memory. Capella. Capella. She knew that name, surely? Ah, yes. The half-baked revolutionary! Like father, like son, so they said, and whilst his father might have died fighting at Mark Anthony's side, Justus had retained his father's papers, met with his father's friends and still found time to whip up sympathisers of his own.

All very noble, Claudia supposed, all very idealistic — had it not been for the fact that the Anthony rebellion had been quashed twenty years ago!

Mind, she'd seen Justus in action on the Rostrum, and not only were his tones persuasive, he was a head-turner, too. Small wonder most of his devotees were women, but then women always did go for dimples in the chin. Makes even brutes seem somehow vulnerable.

"Let me get this straight," she said, running her fingers lightly back and forth across the aviary. "Justus Capella takes a pop at the Emperor and you come here to arrest him on your own. My hero."

"More hack than hero," Orbilio said wistfully. "Capella's disappeared and while the army gets the glory, searching every crevice and shaking down every cart, your champion is reduced to tramping round the city, questioning the man's associates."

"Or not questioning them, as the case may be," Claudia corrected cheerfully.

"Did I say it was easy being a hero?"

His fingers closed round the bars of the birdcage, she could see the short dark hairs on the back of his hand, smelled the rosemary in which his tunic had been rinsed ... She forced her mind back to business.

"Is Hector involved in the assassination plot?" Two birds with one stone and all that!

"Who knows. Capella called yesterday and there was one humdinger of a row between Hector and his wife, though the slaves couldn't hear what it was about. Unfortunately, since Selina has left explicit orders not to be disturbed —" the fingers released the wooden bars and spiked their way through his curls "— I'm forced to wait for Lotis to return, in the hope she can shd light on the whereabouts of either her father or, better still, Capella. Patience — " he released a weary grin and Claudia's heart seemed to bump that little bit harder. (Proximity of the law, of course. What else?) "— is but one of my many virtues."

"Patience," she said, marching towards the bed chambers, "is a damned good waste of drinking time."

As her footsteps echoed down the corridor, Claudia was again struck by the opulence of Hector's house — Parian marbles, painted frescoes, gilded stucco ceilings — and her resolve hardened. Polemo might be an aristocrat whose family tree has its roots intertwined with the vine, but the moral was clear. Stick at it, girl, and you too will be rolling!

"Upsy-dupsy, Selina," she trilled, flinging wide the bedroom door. "It's time we girls had a little chat."

Claudia had not taken three paces before she pulled up sharp, clamping her hand over her mouth. Selina was indeed still in bed. Her lush auburn hair streamed across the damask pillow, her emerald eyes wide and lovely, even in death.

And make no mistake, Selina was dead. Her head had been neatly detached from her body.

That, though, wasn't why Claudia reeled out of the room. She'd seen enough blood spilled in the arena not to be squeamish. No, it was more the fact that the body upon which the head had been placed did not belong to Selina.

The torso belonged to a man.

Marcus Cornelius Orbilio stared at the bed for several minutes without so much as blinking. Through his current work and during his stint as a tribune in the army, he'd seen death in all its guises and it rarely, ever, fazed him. He'd seen men writhing on the battlefield, whores stabbed in alleyways, vagrants with their throats cut and whilst he'd been saddened by it, in turns angered and debased, one thing Orbilio never underestimated was man's capacity to savage his fellow human being.

Thus, anyone watching now, as the sun dazzled the eyes of a mosaic lion, would have been surprised to see him standing motionless, his face set solid, apparently in shock at the grotesque arrangement on the couch.

Orbilio would have been flattered, since his introspection was considerably baser than concern for Selina or Polemo, or even tracking zealous revolutionaries. All that mattered, as far as he could see, was that fate had catapulted Claudia Seferius – the woman who broke laws the way a trainer breaks horses – back into his orbit ... and this time she would not slip through his grasp!

And slip she would, given half a chance, she had more tricks up her sleeve than Circe, the enchantress who had bewitched Odysseus on his return from the Trojan War. Take this morning, for example. What magic inspired such passion, such lust inside him that, even when she stumbled into the atrium, whey-faced and shaking and any fool could sense something was seriously amiss, his sole impulse had been to take her on the spot, there and then! Orbilio closed his eyes and inhaled the memory of her spicy, Judaean perfume. Mother of Tarquin, how he yearned to watch the pale blue cotton of her tunic slither to her ankles, to loosen her breast band and feel the –

"So."

Her voice in his ear sent colour rushing to his cheeks. She could read minds now? He wouldn't put it past her!

"Double suicide?"

"Undoubtedly," he grinned back, and felt something lurch in his gut when he looked at her. "What else could it be?"

Then he glanced down at the body/bodies and the storm inside him subsided. At last he understood why they called it the Security Police, because that's how his emotions were, now his brain was centred again. Secure and in control. Oh yes, a chap knows where he is with a maniac running wild ... He heard the door click as she closed it behind her.

"I gather," she said, "from the routine hum of housework, that this is still our little secret?"

Secrets, Claudia? With you? The prospect brought a tightness to his chest, but he forced himself to focus on her words. Strange how the instant he'd read the horror in her eyes, he'd dismissed the janitor. Pure instinct, but that self-same instinct had been quickly vindicated, because the last thing he needed was a houseful of panic-stricken slaves screaming their heads off and trampling any evidence the murderer may have left in his wake.

"They were killed elsewhere," he said needlessly. She knew as well as he there was barely one drop of blood on the sheets. "And positioned here later."

But why?

"Do we have a madman on the loose?" Claudia turned to examine an onyx flask as Orbilio pressed the back of his fingers against Selina's alabaster-white skin.

"Not in the sense you mean, no."

The sun reflected ripples from the washbasin in lines

against the wall, and he noticed her gaze was fixed on these as he drew down the shutters on Selina's emerald eyes.

"I don't, for instance, envisage a killer on the rampage, mismatching wives to husbands." He heaved Hector's body onto its front. No marks. He rolled the body back again — it seemed proper, somehow, to align it with the head. "On the other hand, however many enemies they made, these two —" he shot Claudia a sharp glance —"this doesn't seem the work of a sane and balanced mind."

Orbilio straightened up and wiped his hands on the counterpane.

In fact, unless he missed his guess, Selina's body and Hector's head would be lying next door in Hector's bedroom.

Life is rarely as we plan it, otherwise we'd all be millionaires with perfect figures, perfect marriages and a deep all-over tan. Clicking her fingers, Claudia marched up and down the atrium. By rights she ought to be ensonced in her seat at the Capitoline Games, cheering the competitors and making furtive bets as she nibbled honeycombs and winecakes. Ought, though, was the operative word! Supersnoop had spoken and she was grounded, stuck not with wrestlers and racers, but with a couple butchered in their beds. Destiny must have a stitch in her side!

"Sorry," Orbilio had said, looking as contrite as a puppy with a slipper. "I need you as a material witness."

Material witness be buggered, he was on to her! Claudia slapped her palm against her forehead. What an idiot she'd been! The instant she found him here, in Polemo's townhouse, she should have spun on her heel and to hell with rumours about diluting wine!

She plumped down in a chair and stuffed a cushion into the small of her back. What was that word, when you pass one thing off as another? A five letter word, was it not? Starting with F, ending with D, and didn't it have an R and an A and a U in between ...?

She bounced out of the chair and resumed her pacing. Think you're clever, do you, Marcus Trufflehound Orbilio? Think that by keeping me hanging round the murder scene I might let something slip and you can lure me into a confession? You can forget those slugslime tactics. Find yourself another mug!

Claudia pulled up short at the family shrine. Hang on. There might just be a way out of this …

Orbilio was in Hector's bedroom and the furrows in his brow could have been left by a ploughshare, they were that deep. But there was disappointment, as well as perplexity, etched on his face.

The room was a mess. A bloody mess, in fact, with the counterpane strewn across the floor, the rug crumpled in a corner, feathers bursting out the bolster. Unfortunately for Hotshot's investigative prowess, it was a room in which someone had lost their temper rather than committed double murder. Not a cadaver in sight, leaving Claudia torn between relief and reservation.

Relief, because she didn't have to confront the grisly spectacle he had predicted.

Reservation, because without the bodies she was stuck with this cocky patrician who might, if the gods sided with him, solve three cases in as many hours — and if nailing an assassin, exposing a murderer and catching a fraudster didn't hasten his path to the Senate, what would?

Claudia's objective was to persuade the gods to settle for

two out of three.

An overturned lampstand had left pools of olive oil and Orbilio trod carefully as he searched the rare wood caskets and probed the heavy clothes chests. In contrast to Selina's taste for greens and gold, Hector had chosen earthy colours for his room. Wars were fought on walls and floor, visceral and vivid. Horses reared, shields rolled, javelins rained from the sky and Claudia decided that if murder hadn't actually been committed here, it damned well should have! The room *was* Hector. Brutal, domineering, riding roughshod to achieve his own ends and it was hardly surprising he'd met with such a violent end.

"As I thought!" Orbilio waved rolls of parchment in triumph. "Confirmation that Polemo was financing Capella's operation!"

Claudia chewed her lower lip. "You think this is an execution?"

"Quite possibly," he said, leafing through the sheaths of paper. "Augustus has followers so devoted, so fanatical they would kill without conscience to protect the emerging concept of Empire, the same way Justus would kill to have it revert."

True. Thirty years might have passed since the Roman world had been wrenched in two, Augustus taking control of the West, Mark Anthony running the East, but old wounds still festered and grievances passed down. Even now, philosophers debated the case around the Rostrum.

Mark Anthony, the neutrals argued, was no less a patriot, but had he been wise to ally himself with the Egyptian whore, Cleopatra? She who'd already tried — and failed — to ensnare Julius Caesar?

Some said yes, definitely. Anthony (unlike others they could mention), would not have stopped at the Danube but pressed on to annexe Germany and the Belgica tribes, perhaps even Britannica, and by making Alexandria his capital, almost certainly Arabia and the Orient would be ours.

Bollocks, others scoffed. For ten years Anthony had ample chance to change things. Instead, he waged continued civil war, he'd never have given us half what the Emperor has. Look around! We have peace and prosperity, food in our bellies, gold in our temples — and moreover, our sons don't lie dead on the battlefield.

Oh yes, thought Claudia. To retain such stability, men would kill gladly — but did Hector pose such a threat? A few sesterces thrown to Capella's cause was probably more of an insurance policy, should the political scene change in the future.

"Wouldn't the executioners want to leave a clear message?" she asked. A warning to others sympathetic to rebellious causes?

"This isn't clear?"

Hmm. Since Supersnoop had already checked the bedrooms for bodies, it was with curiosity as opposed to trepidation that Claudia left him to his scrutiny and slipped into Lotis's chamber. Usually a 15-year-old surrounds herself with clutter bridging infancy and womanhood — the latest robes, pots of perfume, new cosmetics alongside her cracked miniature teaset and a ragged knitted doll. Because by now she'd be affianced, there should be tokens from her future husband, too — a fan, perhaps a parrot. This could pass for a guest room, it was so bare!

A stone dropped in Claudia's stomach and suddenly she felt considerably less sympathy for Hector and Selina, dedicating themselves to the pursuit of pleasure and ambition with not a thought to little Lotis. Fumbling in vain for a ragdoll tucked inside the bedclothes, her vision clouded as she pictured a small child with a light in her eyes and a laugh in her voice rushing up to show Mummy her new tambourine, her gown, her brand new whistle, only to be coldly turned away. Little Lotis would not have sat on Daddy's knee, pulling at his ears, or have him rolling on the floor as they played knucklebones together — and the tragedy was, Lotis would have known what she was missing. Growing up in a house full of slave children, chortling and happy as they bounced balls off cellar walls and played piggy-in-the-middle, her isolation would have been complete.

With a lump in her throat, Claudia left the dismal void of Lotis's bedchamber and passed into the peristyle. Orbilio was browsing through the ledgers in Hector's office and without him noticing her, she approached the bath room door.

"Sorry, ma'am, the mistress says you can't go in." A dumpy kitchen maid scurrying past with a brace of duck and a skillet tucked under her arm paused to admonish the visitor.

The visitor saw no point in mentioning the mistress was in no position to countermand the order. "Why's that?" she asked.

The girl giggled, before remembering herself. "Well, she likes her privacy, does Miss Selina."

Claudia considered the implications. Selina had been dead some hours, probably since last night …

"When did Miss Selina give this order?" she enquired.

"Ooh." The wench thought back. "Yesterday afternoon, it would have been, when —" She stopped short, her cheeks aflame, and by somehow indicating that the duck were so urgently required by the cook that to delay might cause reverberations right across the Empire, she scampered out of sight.

Claudia opened the door to the bath room and peered in.

"Hey, Trufflehound," she called out. "There's something here which might interest you."

Marcus Cornelius Orbilio heard, rather than observed, Claudia pass behind the office and he was intrigued. When he'd informed her she was required to stay as a material witness, he'd been prepared for a battle — and found instead compliance!

He bit his lip. She was up to something, he could smell it. Ask her to hang around a murder scene when the dead are virtual strangers and the Capitoline Games are in full swing, and you don't expect her to shout "yippee." At best, he'd have envisaged her sprawled across a couch, one long leg swinging with an air of nonchalance as she maybe read a spot of Virgil or nibbled chestnut bread, but never in his wildest dreams (correction, nightmare) did he imagine her assisting his investigations on a voluntary basis.

She was digging a pit for him to fall into.

All he had to do was to spot it —

Vaguely uneasy, but unable to say why, Marcus was checking Polemo's accounts when he heard Claudia call out. The grim set of her face said it all, and through the open doorway his eyes scanned the sunken floor and frescoes of winged cupids. Blast! While he'd been chasing rabbits, she'd stumbled on the bodies ...

He ran along the peristyle and skidded to a halt inside the doorway. There were no windows to the room. Illumination came from two bronze lampstands each supporting six small hanging lanterns — ample light to reveal the painted waterfall under which two painted nymphs cavorted with a painted satyr and the cleaver propped against the rocks. Except the cleaver wasn't art. Blue steel glittered in the lamplight, flickering and wicked, its handle in a pool of dark brown sludge.

Orbilio swore beneath under his breath. Bloodstains by the bucketload where the bodies had been chopped up — but no trace of the remains! Where the *hell* could they be? A prolonged and penetrating scream cut short his musings. Damn! He sprinted back along the corridor. He'd given —explicit orders to keep clear of Selina's room —

Oh, shit. Orbilio passed his hand over his eyes and experienced a wave of nauseous shame. In his efforts to link Polemo with the plot against the Emperor, he'd completely overlooked the fact that he'd originally been waiting for the daughter, Lotis.

Who'd now returned — and paid a call upon her mother!

Morning turned to afternoon to evening and the smell of scapegoat hung rank in the air.

Between them, the slaves travelled every single gamut of emotion and as the shadows lengthened and the air cooled down, they retreated into silent huddles, terrified and stiff. Unless the killer was unmasked and quickly, the entire contingent faced execution on the grounds that the murderer must, by default, be one amongst them.

Not all the gods they prayed to were Roman.

Not all the gods they prayed to were listening.

Undertakers came and went, military boots left mud on fine mosaics, metal styluses etched notes in wax tablets and the atrium became lit, not by sunshine, but by the golden glow of lamplight as the finches in the aviary tucked heads under jewel-coloured wings.

Claudia, amusing a family of kittens with a lengthy skein of wool, reflected that the Circus would be swept clean of litter and in darkness, while exhausted competitors rehydrated in taverns thronging to the rafters as spectators walked home girls they'd met at the racetrack.

She sighed as she twirled the tail of wool. By rights, she should be revelling, too, but she'd got herself into this mess and now she had to get out. Preferably without the word 'exile' bandied, even in jest! Unfurling her legs and leaving the kittens mauling a sardine apiece, she wandered into the garden. Water lilies bobbed luminous and silent on the dark, still waters of the fishpond and a tabby coiled its lazy limbs beneath a hibiscus, alert for careless moths. Someone had been collecting herbs, the air was redolent with borage, mint and thyme, and the moon was not yet up. Such was Polemo's wealth, street sounds— drovers, carters and carousers — were muffled by high walls faced off with honey-coloured travertine. Only a subdued clatter from the kitchens and ragged sobs from deep inside the building disturbed this oasis of tranquillity.

"Still here?" Orbilio's eyebrows lifted off their launchpads as he emerged from the body of the house, and Claudia thought she caught something other than surprise in his eyes "Someone has to solve the crime," she said cheerfully.

"Silly me," he murmured. "Here I was, thinking you didn't give a damn who killed Polemo and his wife, them being an unscrupulous couple who attracted enemies like flies in their ruthless quest for power — yet here you are, competing with me for a job."

Claudia smiled ingenuously and tried not to think of sixty chained slaves thrown into an arena howling for justice and for blood. "How's Lotis?"

If her change in tactics threw him, he didn't let it show. "A real chip off the Polemo block," he said, plucking petals from a purple aster. "As the undertakers wheeled the ... bodies away, she stood by, white-lipped, clench-fisted, but none of the wild hysterics you might expect."

You might expect, thought Claudia. Not me! The instant that girl sees emotion, she wrestles it to the ground and sits firmly on its chest to show who's boss. Although, in this case, Lotis could be forgiven for breaking down, poor cow. Tradition decrees that, for the nobility especially, the body lies in state for several days, feet towards the door with torches burning at each corner and cypress laid around. In Hector's case, of course, there was no head to decorate with wreathes of oak and to say it would be in poor taste to display Selina's bonce on its own was an understatement! No doubt something would be worked out before the funeral, but in the meantime, the undertakers had collected the remains and Lotis had stood stoical throughout. This before her sixteenth birthday!

Absently Claudia drummed her fingernails against a bronze Apollo. "Suppose," she said, "I'm in a position to have you feted by your peers and cited for your — Orbilio? Are you listening?"

His pupils were dilated, his expression distant. Claudia blamed the twilight, and thought she heard him mumble "Circe."

"Circe?" she frowned. "Circe was an enchantress!"

"And how." He gave a strange and distant smile. "She turned men into swine."

"That's not magic, Orbilio, that's human nature. Now are you ready for my proposition?"

"Always, Claudia," he muttered, and she wondered whether he'd been sniffing hemp seeds on the quiet. His eyes were raking hers intently, and any other time she might have thought he was ...

"Right." She settled herself on a marble bench and wondered why his sandalwood unguent seemed so fresh after such a full and busy day. "My proposition is simple. In return for delivering a killer, you overlook my little scam. Is it a deal?"

"Hmmph."

Claudia spun round. The poor chap seemed to be having a coughing fit in his handkerchief, his shoulders were shaking, his eyes watering, though for one ridiculous moment, she mistook the bout for laughter.

"I'll take that as affirmative," she snapped.

The moon, rising now, reflected whiter than the lilies in the fishpond and it was in this dark mirror she watched her tall protagonist settle his weight against a scarlet fluted pillar.

"While you were playing Centurions and Soldiers, I've been collating information. One." Crisply Claudia ticked the points off on her finger. "Capella and Polemo were in fact the best of friends. Hector, being a dyed-in-the-wool expansionist —" (she should have guessed!) "—held similar political beliefs."

Polemo, dear soul, being power mad, also believed Augustus wrong in consolidating the Empire when he could be conquering the East and subduing half of Dacia.

"So friends they were. Point two."

She swivelled round to check she had Supersleuth's attention and, finding the wicked glint in his eye offputting to say the least, swivelled back again.

"Selina and Capella were embroiled in a passionate affair. It began eight, ten weeks ago and in the beginning, when their furtive assignations took place up in the hills, only Selina's maid knew anything about it. Then the unimaginable happened. Selina — hard, ambitious, cold Selina — fell in love."

And who could blame her, really? Justus Capella was, what, six years younger than her workaholic husband, he was handsome, dashing, charismatic, he simply swept her off her feet. Lately they'd meet here, making love in the bath room, in the garden, in the bedroom, until—

"Yesterday. " Claudia ticked another finger "When — and I confess it's guesswork from now on — Selina announced she was leaving."

Across the garden, the tabbycat stretched, yawned and decided that, moths or no moths, she really ought not abandon her kittens. Tail crooked, she padded back to the house.

"Hector went ballistic," Claudia continued. "Never, he said, had he imagined such treachery, an adulteress under his own roof, cavorting with a man he trusted. He shamed her, blamed her, threatened to disown her — "

"Ah, but did he threaten to kill her in this hypothetical scenario?"

Claudia ignored the interruption. "In fact, Hector was on the very point of throwing her into the gutter, when Guess Who turns up? Well, Polemo, being as mad as a dog with its nose in a wasps' nest — "

"Threatens to shop Capella?"

Claudia's lips pursed. Fine. Cleverclogs arrived at the

same conclusion by himself, so what? A deal's a deal, and he had given his word. (All right, if you're going to be pedantic, he'd actually given his cough, but when fraud was the issue, a girl can't afford to be fussy!) Now where was she? Oh yes, Hector was on the brink of exposing Capella.

"When Justus realises his friend is serious, he brains him with a statuette — that's why Hector's head is missing. Selina, of course, is witness to the act, and the gal is horrified. Leaving Hector is one thing, but she'd been married to the man for twenty years and not without affection, and suddenly not only is she a widow, her lover is his murderer. Maybe she attacks him, perhaps she, too, threatens to call the army out, but whatever the circumstance, by now Capella is a desperate man. Drawing his dagger, he runs her through — hence Selina's body also has to be disposed of ."

"Hm." Stroking his jaw, Marcus began to pace the path which criss-crossed the peristyle. Something was clearly bothering him, presumably the issue of why Capella would need to hide the evidence of his atrocities.

"Because," Claudia explained, without waiting for him to ask, "Justus needed time to make good his escape. By laying the two — er, pieces together in bed, he could make it appear as though there was some maniac on the loose. So!" She paused for effect. "Am I brilliant, or what?"

Time passed. A chilly breeze capered round the peristyle, wafting late summer roses and heliotrope into the air. Claudia drew her wrap tighter round her shoulders. She had expected applause, though bouquets at her feet would be nice, a standing ovation even better. Instead he kept loping up and down the path like a cheetah in a cage. Oh, well. You can't rush fraud ...

Eventually the pacing stopped and Marcus scratched his

chin. "Plausible," he muttered, "apart from —"

"Plausible!" she gasped. "Is that all you can bring yourself to say? Goddammit, Orbilio, you have a dangerous, devious killer on the —" She broke off, as the impact of his words sunk in. "Apart from what?"

"Apart from the fact, you may be wrong," he said, so quietly he had to strain to catch the words.

"I may be many things, Orbilio, but I am never wrong," she sniffed. "And if I read Capella correctly, he won't run before he's had another pop at Augustus. If I were you, I'd stop haunting this place like a lovelorn ghost and start looking for him in — "

"Oh, I know where Capella is," Orbilio said, sucking in his cheeks.

"What?" He had the assassin banged up all along? Double-duplicitous-vermin-tongued skunk! He'd been winding her up ... and enjoying every single minute! Claudia managed to turn her indignant "What" into a mildly curious "Where?"

"Lotis, you see, was quite adamant," Marcus said, and clearly Claudia hadn't explained herself. He was rambling along at a tangent.

"Orbilio, you deaf clod, I'm asking what you've done with Capella."

"And I'm telling you," he grinned, and she was tempted to mash his nose with her fist. "You see, Lotis stumbled in on her mother, and shocked as she was at finding her dead, as I say she was one hundred percent certain."

A strange sensation crept over Claudia. "One hundred percent certain of what?"

"That the torso was not that of her father," Orbilio said with a sad, lopsided smile. "Which means —"

Claudia nodded in weary understanding. "The man in

the bed was Capella."

Confirmation arrived within the hour.

The marble merchant whose house backed onto the public gardens on the Esquiline Hill had despatched his steward with a doughty club to silence the mutt which had been howling for the past two hours and the man reported back, not with tales of a rabid dog terrorising the neighbourhood, but of a nobleman hanging from an oak, his mastiff baying at his feet. Despite the suffused face and black, protruding tongue, the steward believed he recognised the man as one Hector Polemo, regular guest at the marble merchant's table.

Lotis, orphaned now in earnest, responded by listening carefully to the legionary's report then calling for a scribe and parchment. To the astonishment of both Claudia and Orbilio, she then proceeded to dictate a letter to her fiancé, informing him that, now she had inherited the empire from her father, the marriage contract would be terminated.

There was no mention of regret.

As the breeze grew cooler and bright stars appeared, Claudia's eyes scanned walls dripping not with opulence, but with undiluted hatred. She shivered, and not from the cold.

The army had moved in, clodhopping over every room as they tried to decide whether Hector had committed suicide out of remorse or fear of public execution and searching for some hint of where he'd left his wife's torso and his arch rival's head. Would they, for instance, when dawn had broken on another glorious late-summer day, find the star-crossed lovers laid out in another ghoulish embrace?

In the atrium, Orbilio debriefed a tired centurion as soldiers trickled back and forth and the kitchens filled with smoke in an effort to feed the uniformed invasion. The silence from Lotis's room was electrifying. Claudia shuddered. The venom in this house was cloying. Contaminating. It gripped you by the throat and by the heart and refused to let you go, and she was sickened by the whole damned sordid business. She had to get away. To think. To maintain some balance of perspective!

Find a place well clear of scheming, plots and lies, where the air was fresh and uncontaminated by treason, spite or murder ...

Without a word, Claudia slipped through a side door, where the night quickly swallowed her up.

The little road coiled its way up the hillside like a cobra, and with every rumble of the wheels the trackway narrowed that bit further. Weeds grew waist high along the roadside, potholes frequent, and the greenery encroached lower by the cubit — hawthorn, oak and juniper.

"Are you sure this is where you want to go?" the driver enquired, and Claudia nodded, picturing the ancient temple cut into the rock high upon the hill, far (so far!) from the viper's nest which formed Polemo's house. A place of solitude and peace, where air was fresh and birds warbled from the treetops, where the wind would tug your hair and tease your skirts. Oh yes. This was the place, all right! Shunned by locals scared of ghosts who bent knees to ancient gods and who, while doing so, painted their bodies red like blood, the only worshippers today were lizards scuttling over fallen columns and swallows nesting in the crumbling eaves. Across the wooded valley, wide and distant, a buzzard mewed and circled.

"We can't go no further, ma'am." The driver indicated the weed-choked road.

"Then wait here," she instructed, jumping down. "I shan't be long."

The ascent was steep. Tendrils of ivy laid snares across the stony path and from time to time Claudia had to duck beneath an overhanging branch. Who cared, she thought, if her wrap snagged on a bramble? Anything to get away from the bitter atmosphere in that house just off the Via Sacra — but at least with Polemo dead, there'd be no more ugly rumours to contend with! Had, though, had she pulled it off? Had she done enough to make Supersnoop keep his bargain? Idly, she wondered what progress he and the military might be making.

Panting from the climb, Claudia approached the decaying temple, its stone now pitted by the elements, its grandeur and its elegance eroded by the forest closing in. Faint traces of paint remained — a figure dancing, a leopard in mid leap — but only rats made their devotions at the altar and these days rainwater poured the only libation. What was that? A scuffle from the hillside, a flash of —

"Stay where you are!" a voice commanded.

Claudia jumped, and despite the heat, her blood turned glacial cold. From the bushes to her left a bow protruded, its string pulled taut.

The arrowhead aimed directly at her heart.

Like a coney caught in torchlight, Claudia stood mesmerised by the tiny sliver of wood which could, with one brief twang, cut short the thread of life. Her tongue was dry, her legs had turned to granite. This can't be happening! It has to be a dream.

A dream. I'll wake up any second ...

But the sun beat down upon her back, the buzzard mewed and, high in the canopy, a squirrel pulled seeds from a pine cone. The bow flexed backwards in an arc, the knuckles drawing it white from the effort. Fear curdled Claudia's stomach, her head swam. Sweet Jupiter, don't let this happen. Not here. Not to me. In a spot so isolated, wolves would tear the flesh from my corpse, ants would devour my bones.

"I —" A dormouse could have squeaked louder. She cleared her throat and started again. "I know what happened at the house," she said, and this time there was no quaver in her voice. Like Lotis, Claudia was also well-versed in concealing emotion.

"Do you really?" The voice, from deep within the bushes, was heavy with sarcasm.

"Why do you think I'm here?" she said. "To gather huckleberries?"

She knew now why the bodies were mismatched. Why it was so important the missing parts should not be found.

"What did you expect to achieve?" the arrow sneered. "A confession?"

Claudia caught a movement down the path. Brown. The driver's leather jerkin?

The eyes behind the bow followed the direction of her glance. "If you're looking for the young man who brought you, you're looking in the wrong direction. Try over your shoulder!"

An eagle clawed at Claudia's heart. Oh, no! Mighty Juno, say it's not true ... With a neck made of wood, she forced herself to look down. From this dizzy vantage point, one could see clearly the dappled mare chomping on the grass which had finally impeded their progress. The horse seemed unaware of the driver slumped face forwards with an arrow in his spine ...

Claudia blinked back the tears and tried not to remember how he'd boasted all the way from Rome about his new-born son and pretty wife and the impending birthday celebrations for his daughter –

The bowstring. Surely the arm must be tiring? Somewhere in the recess of her mind, she remembered that killers are supposed to brag about their crimes, about how easy it was to fool the authorities.

"You'll never get away with it," she taunted. "If I, a mere civilian, can find you –"

"The army can? I doubt it!" The figure in the bushes laughed. "I know your sort," it scoffed. "In fact, we're not so very unalike when it boils down to it. You came here to satisfy yourself that you were right, to crow a bit, perhaps gain credit with the army, and you never once considered failure. I admire that."

The analysis was closer to the mark than Claudia cared to acknowledge. "Good." She drew a deep breath. "Because I didn't trek up to this godforsaken rathole to get killed, I thought you might care to hear a proposition."

A long silence came from the bushes and Claudia wondered whether her last view of the world would be a broad valley with leaves just turning for autumn and paint flaking from columns. Her nails bit deep into the palms of her hands, and she felt a small dribble of blood run down her thumb.

"What put you on to me?" the voice asked, and in her mind, Claudia punched the air and thought *yes!* The killer's ego had triumphed!

"It was," she said, with a studied air of nonchalance, "the body hanging from the oak."

The shrubbery rustled with undisguised curiosity. "Go on."

"It occurred to me that Hector might use many methods — violence, blackmail, extortion — to achieve his ends." Results meant more to him than methods. "But at heart he was a self-serving son-of-a-bitch. Men like him," she said pointedly, "don't kill themselves." They have an unerring belief that they can get away with it!

The arrowhead drooped as laughter boomed out of the bushes. "Brains as well as beauty, eh! And courage — coming here alone!"

Courage? We shall see. For here, at last, was the moment of truth. Claudia drew herself up to her full height and stared straight at where she imagined the eyes in the shrubbery to be. Her mouth was dry, her knees like aspic, she forced her voice to be even.

"That left two possible conclusions," she said. "Either someone was dressed up to look like Hector. Or Hector had been murdered. I asked myself, who, then, had a motive — and the answer, of course, was you. So I suggest we stop playing hide-and-seek, and if you do intend to fire," the nails bit deeper into her hands as she glanced around the temple, "you can bloody well look me in the eye."

Slowly the figure emerged from the thicket. "Ballsy little creature, aren't you?"

Even with the bow and quiver, he still looked dashing. Floppy sandy hair made him look younger than his years. As did that distinctive dimple in his chin. Justus Capella moved into a single shaft of sunlight. "Care to tell me how you worked it out?"

Funny how the memory plays tricks. Had Claudia not passed the basilica yesterday morning, with the rent boys preening on its corner, she might not have put two and two together.

Or in this case, two and one, for three murders had been committed yesterday. Clever, really. Because who, under such horrific circumstances, would notice a few superficial differences between Justus and the body in the bed? Same age, same height, same build — but, ah, the head, the tell-tale head! Capella had to stage his disappearance, and how better? Identifying Selina was straightforward — it was but a short leap to connect the torso with her lover.

The blame would fall on Hector, but Capella had already strangled him. All it required was to hang up the body under cover of darkness and let his mastiff raise the alarm.

"What did you do with the head of the boy you killed and left in 'your' place?" Claudia asked. "Where's the rest of Selina?"

"Jackal bait," he shrugged, and Claudia feared she might throw up any second. For gods' sake, Selina loved this man! Had he *no* compassion?

"How many times did you and Selina make love here, with the sun warming your naked backs?" she asked. "Did you feel nothing for her, knowing how you intended to use her, should your attempt on the Emperor's life fail?"

"Selina?" he frowned, as though the name was unfamiliar. "She was like a bitch on heat, played right into my hands. But you." He edged forward. "You are an altogether different woman."

Claudia realised she was supposed to feel flattered, and the queasiness inside her increased. "Then suppose I tell you we share the same cause?" she said. "That I, too, believe Mark Anthony to be a daring visionary who saw a dazzling future for our people in the East, not merely consolidating what we have, but pushing out?"

"You?" Capella's eyes travelled over her breasts.

"Don't flatter yourself," Claudia tossed back her curls "that you're alone in fearing Augustus has weakened Rome by reducing our soldiers to a mere peace-keeping force."

"Well, well, well." Capella nodded in grudging admiration. "Let's hear your proposition, then."

Claudia felt her breath come out in one loud blast. She hadn't realised, until then, she'd been holding it. "I'm rich," she explained. "I want to continue where Hector left off." Through her mind flashed the image of the driver and her stomach flipped. But man, alas, cannot turn back time —

"Croesus, we need people like you!" he said, passion firing his features. "People with courage, guts and spirit prepared to make whatever sacrifice is necessary to get that pretender, Augustus, out the way. And I shall, you know. Tomorrow I'll complete my task, we'll have a true democracy once more."

"Long live the Republic!" she cried.

He grinned. "Exactly. Do you have a coin?"

Excuse me?

"You do see, don't you," he said sombrely, "that the cause is greater than the man?"

Oh, no! Scarcely able to believe her eyes, Claudia stared at the weapon in his hands. Suddenly the arrow was pointing once more directly at its target, and she wondered whether Capella could hear the frantic pounding as her heart wriggled to escape its fate ..?

"So close am I to achieving my goals," he shrugged, "I can afford to leave nothing to chance. Although if there is any consolation in your death," the bastard even sounded as though he might have meant it, "it's knowing I take no pleasure in the act. The coin, now, if you please."

Claudia did not recollect fishing the bronze from her purse, but she recalled it glinting in the sunshine.

"Put it in your mouth, " Capella instructed. "You'll need to pay the ferryman to cross the River Styx."

"Sorry." Claudia tossed the coin so it landed at his feet. "I get seasick."

She watched his jaw drop open in amazement.

"But you'll need it, you callous little turd, and your crossing will be rough! Publicly and in disgrace, you'll die a lingering traitor's death in the arena, mocked and jeered by the very people you sought to save — and I tell you, Capella, I'll be in the front row, relishing every single second that you suffer!"

"Bitch," he snarled, pulling back the bowstring. "I was right not to risk my trust on you! Say 'hello' to Hades."

"You say 'hello'," a deep voice growled, as thirty men stepped out from under cover. Some brandished spears, some lances, and at least a dozen bowmen aimed at Justus.

The revolutionary's eyes bored into Claudia's. "You set a trap, you bitch! You kept me talking —" He made no effort to finish, as he released the bowstring.

There was a whoosh of air. A twang. Claudia spun through space. She heard a scream. A thud. And then came blackness.

Nothing else but blackness ...

"Next time I throw myself on top of you," said a disembodied baritone, "the least you could do is to struggle."

"Mmffff!" Claudia's protest, she thought, might have been more forceful, were it not for the greenery wedged in her mouth. She spat the thistle out and rubbed grit from her eyes. "Orbilio, if you ever, *ever*—"

She broke off, because he'd trotted off to supervise the arrest to which Capella, it would appear, had not taken lightly. Blood gushed from his temple as well as his knuckles, his clothes were in total disarray. Claudia picked herself off the ground, shook the dust from her skirts and wondered why sandalwood outweighed the smell of dank weeds.

Embedded in a silver birch behind her, an arrow quivered.

"You were saying?" Marcus grinned, taking the temple steps two at a time.

Claudia's response was a stinging slap across his face. "You took your bloody time!" she spat. "Because of your pathetic dithering, that poor sod," she jerked her thumb towards the driver, "took an arrow in the back!"

A red mark flared down the side of his cheek, but the twinkle in his eyes flared brighter. "He was one of ours," he said. "We had him padded out with leather and a man hidden from the rig to warn him when and what would happen. In fact." Orbilio sniffed miserably. "We'll probably lose him to the theatre after this."

He deftly ducked the chunk of masonry which whizzed past his ear.

"So I was not in any danger?"

"None," Orbilio said, swerving the branch of blackthorn she was brandishing. "While you were diverting Capella's attention by making your ascent, our men were circling from behind — "

"I was scared witless!"

"Which is why Capella was so completely taken in," Marcus said. "In fact, your performance was even more convincing than the driver's."

"That," Claudia said haughtily, "is because I never, ever fake it!"

His laughter echoed round the crumbling temple. "Can I give you a lift back to Rome?" he asked.

"Never in your life," she snapped. "We're quits, remember?"

Marcus bounded down the path behind her. "Yes, about that little scam you wanted me to overlook?"

"Hm?"

Her mind had already dismissed her role in coercing a confession from Capella. Life moves on, not backwards and Claudia had a call to pay on little Lotis. Fifteen years of age? Far too young to cope with Polemo's massive empire — my, my, if ever a child needed a friend, it's now! Someone she can lean on, someone she can trust, can let her feelings go with. And who better than an expert in the trade?

Orbilio paused to examine the bark of a wild pear tree and his shoulders, from the back, appeared to be shaking. "I don't suppose you'd care to tell me what that scam was, by any chance ...?"

Claudia gazed back at the ancient temple which had been gouged so painstaking out of the rock and which had now virtually been reclaimed by the land. What more perfect spot, she wondered, in which to hide a body? Especially that of a tall, dark, handsome investigator.

"Marcus," she said artlessly. "Why don't you take my arm, dear?"

Women's rights in Ancient Rome? You can sum that up in one word. None. Meaning strong, independent women looked for other ways to skin a cat...

HONEY MOON

The roar of the crowds followed Claudia as her procession wound its way down the Via Sacra, past the Temple of the Divine Julius into the Forum. Hardly the quickest route to Arlon's house — but, by Jupiter, it was the one that would attract the most attention! She'd hired the best for today. Jugglers, tumblers, musicians and dancers, with a stilt-walker to bring up the rear. But that was only half of the story.

'My dear child.'

Claudia had been buffing her fingernails in the peristyle when the priest burst in, his long white robes billowing in his wake.

'You do realise that only brides on their wedding day are entitled to wear the orange veil?'

So?' she had asked, without glancing up.

'So this is *sacrilege*!' he exploded, as much at her disdain as the religious outrage. 'I cannot allow it.'

Claudia examined her cuticles, buffed again, then, satisfied with the shine, adjusted her pendant, checked her pearl ear-studs and picked up the small, battered bowl from the marble bench beside her. Finally, she tossed the veil nonchalantly over her head.

'This dye isn't orange,' she said levelly. 'It's flame.' She watched the priest's eyes narrow in fury before adding cheerfully, 'The valance which veils the top of my litter is orange.'

Imbecile. Did he imagine she didn't know what she was doing? Did he think she'd let an occasion like this pass, without having half of Rome turn out to witness it? And what a feast the procession was for their eyes! The young widow of the wine merchant Gaius Seferius being transported shoulder-high on an open litter through the streets of Rome by eight of the most handsome and muscular bearers in the whole of the Empire, accompanied by the finest entertainers in town.

'For gods' sake, slow down,' she told the bearers. 'This isn't a bloody foot race.' Dammit, any faster and they'd be there in ten minutes, with an Olympic medal to boot. 'There's an extra denarius apiece if you take another half-hour.'

The bearers eased up so quickly, she was almost thrown off the cushions. The crowd laughed, believing it was part of the act. She laughed back. And made a mental note to reduce the bearer's tip to only half a denarius.

'Good luck, love!' cheered the throng.

'All the best!'

'May the gods smile on you, darlin'!'

They were all there. Coppersmiths, perfumers, mule doctors and rent boys, cleaving a path for her noisy cavalcade. Auctioneers, surveyors, stevedores and barbers stepped aside to watch her pass. Fishwives, sack-makers, tax collectors and chandlers whistling and clapping their hands. Claudia returned every wave with equal vigour. Dear me, so many well-wishers, it brought a mist to her eyes. Young and old, rich and poor, sick and healthy, they stopped what they were doing to cheer her on. Cradling the battered bowl to her breast, she didn't realise she'd been rubbing it until :

'In my country,' an Arab with rings in his ears called out from the crowd, 'we use lamps to conjure up jinni.'

Thank Croesus her face was hidden by the veil. She adjusted her expression, lifted the linen, a perfect smile pasted in place.

'My good luck charm,' she retorted. 'I never go anywhere important without it.'

'Looks like an old begging bowl to me,' someone else shouted.

'It is,' she laughed, waving the battered bronze cup in the air. 'I begged Apollo for sunshine and look! Not a cloud in the sky.'

As she planted an ostentatious kiss on the metalwork, she felt her stomach churn and quickly dropped the veil back over her face. *But there was no going back now—*

'Be happy, love!' the crowd chanted.

'May you and your husband be blessed!'

Ah. Husband. On her soft swansdown pillows scented with chamomile, Claudia shifted position.

Tall as a Dacian, lean as an athlete, bronzed as Adonis himself, Arlon was one of Rome's most eligible bachelors. With his glossy blond hair and marble quarries spread across Africa and the Aegean, not to mention a flush of stud farms down south, Arlon had it all. The big house in Rome. Villa in the country. Winners galore at the Circus Maximus racetrack. And today, on this twenty-first day of June, on the shortest night of the year and under a clear sky when a full moon would transmute blackness into silver, Claudia Seferius would be plighting her troth to this man.

Widow and widower, bound together until death do them part.

She considered the gifts she was bringing. Most, like the ivory-inlaid chair and the thick Persian carpet, had been despatched separately, but others, like the beads of Arabian frankincense, resin, and the heavy gold betrothal medallion, were not the kind of presents which should be delivered by an anonymous household slave. Neither — she patted the onyx perfume phial and the engraved silver hip flask in her lap — were these. Such treasures were to be handed over personally. When the occasion demanded.

Having circled the Forum, the procession now left the way it had come. Behind the Temple of the Divine Julius, back up the Via Sacra, then branching off towards Arlon's great sprawling mansion on the Esquiline Hill. There were no crowds lining these elegant, patrician streets, but Claudia didn't care. She had done what she set out to do. The orange drapes round her litter and the orange veil on her head might have contravened the odd convention or two, but since when had conventions mattered to Claudia Seferius? She had been noticed today. *That's* what mattered.

For the men in the crowds, there had been only goodwill wished upon her. In the women, though, she had seen mixed emotions. Most of them, of course, had turned out for no other reason than to enjoy the acrobats, give their toddlers their first sight of a stilt-walker and to cheer on the bride-to-be.

Others had a different agenda. They were the ones standing pinch-lipped and smug. Brought to book at last, the uppity bitch. I mean, who did she think she was, taking over her husband's wine business, indeed! These women had lined the route, arms folded over their chests in grim satisfaction that everything she owned (or at least, everything the gold-digging bitch had inherited!) would pass to Arlon after the wedding.

Arlon would see she kept her place. Arlon would make sure she'd do what she should have been doing a long time ago. Keeping house and dropping babies like everyone else. To that section of the crowd, not fooled by her misuse of the veil, Claudia waved harder than ever.

But there was a third group of women which had caught her attention. A minority, true, but they were the ones who weren't smiling either in joy or schadenfreude. Who hadn't thrown rose petals into her path.

You had a chance, said their sad, accusing eyes. *You had the chance to pave the way for other women to take on the men in their own world. Instead, you betrayed us. You sold the sisterhood out.*

The litter drew to a halt outside Arlon's villa. Trumpets sounded. A carpet of red shot with gold thread was thrown out across the pavement to welcome her. Rainbow ribbons soaked in lavender and cedar wood oil streamed down from the rooftops. In a vestibule lined with lilies in tall silver pots and elegant floral frescoes, liveried slaves carried her in on their hands to an atrium gleaming in marble and gold. Here, light streamed in through the roof, fountains danced, and bronze charioteers guided Arlon's bronze stallions in an eternal victory lap. Surrounded by priests, family, friends, business colleagues and neighbours, the man of the house stepped proudly forward.

Claudia stretched out both hands to greet her blond Adonis and smiled. I ask you. *What* sisterhood?

'I shall cherish this moment for the rest of my life.' With great tenderness, Arlon rubbed the ring he had just slipped on Claudia's finger and brought it gently to his lips.

'Ah,' sighed the congregation, and one or two of the

women surreptitiously dabbed at their eyes.

'The physicians tell us there's a nerve which runs from the ring finger direct to the heart,' Arlon murmured, smiling deep into Claudia's eyes, 'and that it is this nerve which governs our happiness. Sealed for eternity by this gold band of love, may the gods strike me dead if I ever have cause to harm you.' This time he raised both her hands to his lips. 'I love you, Claudia. I love you with all my heart and with all my soul, and nothing and no-one can change the way that I feel. You do know that, don't you?'

Claudia felt an unaccustomed rush of colour to her face. 'Yes,' she said quietly. 'I know that, Arlon.'

Now the women were sobbing quite openly, and there were a few sniffs from the men in the audience as well. Even the priest had to swallow.

'Let us make sacrifice with offerings of spelt,' he intoned solemnly, 'that the gods may bless this joyful betrothal.'

They made such a good-looking couple, he thought, so in love, that he had forgiven Claudia her transgressions over the veil. Her previous husband had been old when they'd wed. Fat as a pig, if he recalled correctly. With bad teeth and a bald spot. A marriage of convenience for both parties, and that now the husband was dead and looking at a lifetime of happiness with a dashing and virile young blade, what woman wouldn't want to advertise her wedding twice over? The priest, laying spelt cakes on the altar and pouring libations, couldn't begrudge her the orange veil for her betrothal, as well as her marriage.

All the same, he wondered why she hung on to that battered bronze bowl, even during the ceremony, when tradition decreed both hands should be free. It had made his task of exchanging rings and medallions virtually impossible, and he'd had to call one of his acolytes to assist. Most unusual woman, this beautiful young widow, and the priest resolved to have a word with Arlon before the wedding. Intractability is no asset in a wife and if this wilfulness looked like it was persisting, the priest would recommend a jolly good beating. A tactic which had certainly brought his own wife to heel.

'When did you sweethearts meet?' one old hen clucked.

'Yes, do tell us. And where?' clucked another.

'It was last Saturnalia,' Claudia told the middle-aged female crowd which had knotted around her. 'I'd laid on a sumptuous banquet and invited a select group of merchants round, in the hope of persuading them to sign up for barrel loads of Seferius wine, when—'

'When Arlon persuaded you to love him, instead!' the hens shrieked.

'Well, no, actually,' Claudia said. 'His first words were, "How much would you take for your cook?"'

Everyone laughed.

Claudia slipped away.

Outside in the garden, it was hotter, not cooler. The mosaics and marble, the honeycomb screens and gently waving ostrich feather fans conspired to keep the atrium at an ambient temperature, despite the crush of the revellers. But there were too many people talking at once. She needed the space. And the quiet.

Her gown trailing over the path, she found a secluded bench in the shade, overhung by clusters of fragrant pink damask roses. Jewel-coloured birds chirruped and preened in an aviary set in the wall, and marble nymphs danced round fountains which splashed prettily and made prisms as the drops caught the sun. She sat down on the marble bench and stretched out feet shod in the softest white leather. The air was heavy with birdsong and the buzzing of bees, and scented from swathes of bright purple lavender, with valerian, pinks, and a thousand sweet-smelling herbs.

Why, then, could she feel no peace in her heart?

'I suppose there's no point in my asking what you're up to this time?' the bay tree to her left asked in a melodious baritone.

Claudia spun round. The bay tree was grinning.

'Marcus Cornelius Orbilio, don't you ever think of approaching people in a normal fashion, instead of creeping up on them?'

'If you'd seen me coming, you'd have run off.'

'Doesn't everyone?'

He stepped out from behind the bush, his dark eyes twinkling. *All the better to see you with...* 'I'll have you know, there are some people who actually like me,' he said, settling himself beside her on the bench.

'Name one, and your mother doesn't count.'

'Not everyone sees the Security Police in a sinister light,' he laughed, tugging at his right ear lobe. *All the better to hear you with...* 'There are those who actually believe we're an asset to the Empire, rooting out assassins, rapists and thieves.'

'Oh well, then. If it's gardening you're into, the potting shed's over there.'

The grin broadened, to show white, even teeth. *All the better to eat you with...* 'Trowel by jury, you mean?'

Orbilio folded his arms behind his head, leaned back against the trunk of the sycamore tree in whose shade they were sitting and closed his eyes. Claudia did not fall into the trap of believing he was asleep. And now she knew that his sandalwood unguent was truly the scent of the hunter.

Time passed. It could have been minutes. Then again,

lifetimes might have elapsed.

'Tell me about Arlon,' he said at last. 'Tell me why you're playing this particular charade.'

Until Claudia exhaled, she hadn't realised she'd been holding her breath. She counted to five. Then—

'You're the law,' she said brightly. 'You know how the system works.'

Rome needed babies. As the Empire swelled, so did its population, but it was swelling with the offspring of slaves, not baby citizens. A victim of its own success. With peace came prosperity, and with prosperity came luxury goods, gourmet foods, safer streets, marble temples, libraries, sewers and the dole. It provided everyone with better education and better health. Which, for women, led to improved contraception. Oh, come on. When the risk of dying in childbirth was one in ten, who could blame the poor cows? So a law was passed to reverse the downward trend.

Widows of childbearing age had two years in which to find themselves a new husband. And if it wasn't a man of her choosing, then by Jupiter, she would be forced to accept the choice of the State.

Claudia shot Orbilio a radiant smile. 'My two years are nearly up,' she said cheerfully. 'Arlon is the man I have chosen.'

He grunted and closed his eyes again. Cicadas rasped, bees hummed and the heat in the garden pulsed harder. She watched his profile. The patrician nose. The decisive jaw. The vein that beat at the side of his neck. She swallowed. Watched a bumblebee scour the pink blooms of hyssop in its quest for nectar. And found her gaze locked on the flowers long after the bee had flown off.

'Tell me how you two got together,' he said.

'It was last Saturnalia,' Claudia began. 'I'd laid on a sumptuous banquet and—'

'That,' he murmured, 'is word for word what you told those old ducks indoors, and an investigator always mistrusts the account which never varies.'

'You don't trust your own shadow,' she snapped.

A muscle twitched at the side of his mouth. 'Flattery will get you nowhere,' he said. 'Tell me what happened *after* that.'

One. Two. Three. 'Very simple. I told Arlon, "I can't sell just one slave. If you want my cook, you'll have to take his wife, his three daughters, his mother-in-law and an aunt, I won't have the family broken up.'

'Claudia,' he growled warningly. One eye opened. 'Explain to me — *please* — how it was that several months passed before you and Arlon met up again.'

Something tightened beneath Claudia's rib cage. He was the Security Police. What did he know? Correction. How *much* did he know ...? Lies formed into a plausible story, but before she could open her mouth, Marcus said,

'You do know the rumours about his late wife?'

Again, Claudia breathed out. 'Rumours? Good grief, Orbilio, the woman committed suicide nine months ago. That's hardly a secret.'

No one throws themselves off the Tarpeian Rock without the whole of Rome knowing, much less a rich merchant's wife. After all, if you want privacy when you die, you don't leap from the Capitol Hill, right in the heart of the city.

'She jumped at night,' Orbilio reminded her. 'There were no witnesses to the suicide.'

'So?'

'So she wasn't a pauper,' he said dryly. 'She brought considerable capital to her marriage, and she had no heirs to claim on the estate. Arlon inherited the lot.'

Claudia reached up and plucked a rosebud from the truss. 'You have my undivided disinterest, Orbilio.'

One eyebrow rose in scepticism, but he did not presume to contradict her. Instead he said, 'Just humour me, and tell me how exactly you and Arlon got together. How soon it was, after Saturnalia, that he started to court you?'

A weight lifted from Claudia's stomach. She felt light. Free. Free as the birds in the dovecot.

'Arlon court me?' She tossed the rosebud into his lap and danced off down the path. 'My dear Marcus, for an investigator, you really do have a long way to go.'

'Excuse me?' He was alert now. Tense and poised.

'Maybe you should follow the family tradition and become a lawyer instead.'

'I don't understand.' He was on his feet now. Frowning.

'I'm the one who pursued Arlon,' she trilled over her shoulder. 'Like a terrier, if you must know.'

He caught up with her after the betrothal feast, after most of the guests had gone home. Claudia wasn't surprised to see Orbilio at the banquet. Being an aristocrat himself, his own house was a mere stone's throw from Arlon's superlative mansion and he'd probably have been on the invitation list as a matter of course. Neighbour to neighbour, and all that. But Claudia knew that he would have inveigled an invitation anyhow. It was his nature.

As the last guest stumbled out on distinctly unsteady legs and a bawdy song on his lips, she stared around the banqueting hall. Crab claws, lobster shells, cherry pips and meat bones littered the floor between the couches, and a couple of kitchen cats were probing the debris with delicate paws in search of tasty titbits. The sun was sinking fast, casting a vermilion glow over the dining hall and turning the bronze couches to the colour of molten gold. It had been a memorable feast, Claudia reflected with satisfaction. The affianced couple linking arms as they drank a loving cup between courses. Musicians. Poets. Performing apes. Plus a tightrope walker who walked backwards as well as forwards whilst entertaining the gawping diners with ballads. The food had been exquisite. Sucking pig, honeyed dormice, venison and boar, served with asparagus, milk-fed snails and white truffles which had been fetched from the Istrian peninsular. From time to time during the meal, rose petals showered the guests with their fragrance from a mechanical contraption overhead, and iced wine flowed down a river into a pool from which female slaves dressed as water sprites filled the jugs.

Now Claudia watched as, with a snarl and a hiss and with thrashing wide tails, the tabby and the tortoiseshell squared up to one another over a prawn. Too late. The porter's rangy mongrel strolled in through the open windows, scattering felines to the four winds as it proceeded to snaffle up everything in sight, shells and all.

'That dog needs worming,' Orbilio said.

'And you need a bell on your collar.'

He leaned against the side of a couch, one hand resting lightly on the carved antelope armrest. 'That,' he said looking round, 'was a very good show.'

'I thought the snake charmer rather went a bit off-key, but the fire-eater was pretty impressive.'

'I'm talking about you,' he said. 'If you ever fancy a career in the theatre ...' He let his voice trail off. Then: 'What's behind this chicanery, Claudia?'

She scooped up a handful of petals and tossed them the air, watching as they floated down like pale pink snowflakes. 'You're just worried that, once I'm married to Arlon, I'll set your career back a year.'

Know your enemy. It was a good rule to live by. And Claudia Seferius knew that this fiercely ambitious young investigator only kept such close tabs on her, because she sailed so close to the wind. She was his fast track to the Senate. The more results he clocked up, the closer his seat in the Assembly. Why else would he dog her every step?

'Or is it merely a question of dented pride?' she added. 'That your hundred percent success record will be broken, if I wriggle off your investigative hook?'

Orbilio sucked in his cheeks. 'Whatever you do, Claudia Seferius, and wherever you go, it will always involve some degree of illegality. Believe me, my career is not in jeopardy here.'

She stared at the bowl in her hand. He was probably right. She was destined to live life on the edge, pushing herself to the limits, because danger was as vital to Claudia's constitution as oxygen. Without testing yourself, how can you be truly alive?

Outside, the sun had sunk below the rooftops and the sky was the colour of blood. Cicadas buzzed like blunt saws, the heat pulsed, and bats darted round the eaves of the building. Soon, slaves would come to light the oil lamps, but for now the twilight and Claudia were one.

An age passed before he pushed himself away from the couch. She could not make out his expression in the dusk, but she knew without looking that the dancing light in his eyes had died.

'He's a sleaze ball, Claudia.'

Something changed inside her, too. 'What do you know about Arlon?' she sneered.

She saw his fists clench. 'I know that no-one gets that rich, that fast, without being a ruthless, callous, grade-A bastard — and Arlon's all that, in spades.'

'Strangely enough, Marcus, I'm inclined to agree with you.' Claudia scooped her bronze begging bowl into the wine pool. The ice had long melted, making the wine warm, but not unpleasant. 'And bloody sexy it makes him, too.'

Orbilio frowned. Spiked his hands through his fringe. 'Claudia, if this truly *is* about you needing to find a husband before the State imposes—'

'Why? Are you offering?'

He cleared his throat. Stared at his feet. Shuffled. 'You could do worse.'

Now who's talking about careers in the theatre? Him, an aristocrat with a lineage going back to Apollo, marry a girl from the slums who'd adopted the identity of a woman who died in the plague in order to hook a wealthy, if ancient, wine merchant? Hades would take day-trippers first. Welcome to my atrium, said the spider to the fly. Oh, really, Marcus Cornelius. Do I *look* like I have wings?

'You don't get it, do you?' she said over the rim her bowl. 'I love Arlon.'

'Bullshit. And don't give me that crap about him loving you, either. Arlon wants to get his hands on your assets, Claudia. Nothing more.'

Did he really think she hadn't done her homework? Her agents had dug and dug until they hit bedrock and one of the first things that Claudia discovered was that, like herself, Arlon had also married for money the first time around. His wife's fortune had enabled him to buy a marble quarry in Euboea, then another in Alexandra, then another on the island of Chios, until one way and another he'd acquired quite a collection. When the Emperor was hell bent on turning Rome into a city of marble monuments, from temples to baths, statues to fountains, Arlon's quarries worked round the clock to meet the demand. This income in turn funded a string of stud farms round Apulia and Lucania, which, wouldn't you know it, simply couldn't stop turning out winners. At the age of thirty-three, Arlon was rich beyond his wildest dreams. Good grief, by the time he hit forty, he'd have amassed so much wealth, even Midas would turn green with envy!

But that wasn't the issue here.

Claudia cleared her throat. Turned to face the ardent patrician.

'Trust me, Orbilio, there's only one thing Arlon wants to get his hands on,' she said pointedly. 'And I've promised him that as a betrothal gift.'

Even in the twilight, she could see the colour drain from Orbilio's face. 'You aren't serious?'

Her heart was drumming. Her mouth was dry. 'Never more so,' she assured him.

'For gods' sake!' He spun her round to face him. 'Claudia, you *can't* sleep with that bastard. He's a monster. A fiend. He killed his wife, for Croesussakes.'

She shook off his hands, turned away, but could still smell the sandalwood in her nostrils, taste his minty sweet breath in the back of his throat. And where he had touched her, two handprints burned a hole in her gown.

'He was dining with friends the night his wife committed suicide,' she said levelly.

But then, as an investigator, he must surely know that.

'Claudia, please, anything but that. I couldn't bear—'

Enough. 'I'm not asking you to bare anything, Orbilio. Now, the betrothal party is over. The music's ended, it's late, the wine's warm, and you're the last guest left, so I'd be obliged if you'd kindly leave me and my husband-to-be in peace.'

'Don't go to his bed, Claudia.' His voice was ragged with an emotion she couldn't place.

A bad oyster. It must be. She felt nauseous. Faint. Her legs wouldn't support her. But they had to. By all that was holy, *they had to ...*

'What I do or don't do is none of your goddamned business,' she snapped, and there was no quaver in her voice, none at all. Attagirl. 'Now get out, before I have the guards throw you out.'

She put a hand on the couch to steady herself. Please, Marcus. Please. Go. Go now—

'I'm not going anywhere,' he said, and his voice was a rasp. 'Unless you come with me.'

The room swayed. I can't, Marcus. Don't you understand? I can't walk away. I have to go through with this. *Have* to. Something wet trickled down her cheek.

'What?' she sneered. 'Sneak off with some uptight, upright, prissy law-enforcer on a penny-pinching salary, when I've got all this?'

Now will you bloody well go?

He prised the begging bowl out of her grasp and threw it onto the floor, where it clattered and bounced under a couch. 'For gods' sake, you've proved your point.' He grabbed both her wrists. 'You don't have to go through with this—'

The skin burned, she pulled away so fast. 'Oh, but I do,' she said dully.

As the moon started to rise, its light picked out the burnished metal among the crab claws and chop bones. Scooping it up, Claudia spat on the bowl, polished it on the hem of her gown. Saw the full face of the midsummer moon reflected in the bronze.

'Believe me, Marcus,' talking to herself as much as him, 'I do have to go through with this.'

'So that's where you're hiding!'

Laughing, Arlon stepped through the open double windows from the garden. In the moonlight, his fair hair shone like silk, and corded muscles bulged out the sleeves of his tunic. There was wine on his breath. Perhaps one goblet too many.

'What in Jupiter's name are you doing in the banqueting hall at this hour on your own?'

So then. He hadn't yet noticed that she wasn't alone. From the corner of her eye, Claudia watched Orbilio step backwards into the shadows, as silently as a fox.

'Sorry, darling, I lost all track of time re-living the banquet,' she said, turning her back on the shadows. 'Arlon, it was an absolutely wonderful party. Thank you.'

'Mmm.' His attention was no longer on the betrothal feast. 'You know, you've showered me with everything from rugs to rubies to Arabian resins, but—' One bronzed hand slid round her waist and pulled her close as the other brushed a strand of hair from her eyes. 'There's one gift you still haven't given me.'

'Don't sell yourself short,' she laughed, releasing a curl from its ivory hair pin. 'I'm banking on you enjoying more than one, if you don't mind!'

'Then let me unwrap it,' he said thickly. 'Right here, and right now.'

With a backward sweep of his hand, the plates and bowls went flying off the low table. At home, everything would have smashed to smithereens, but being Arlon, of course, the metal merely clanged, rolled and bounced.

'I've been celibate for two years,' Claudia said huskily, arching her back as his hand travelled slowly, expertly, down her backbone. 'I don't intend to rush this. Quite the reverse, in fact, darling. I intend to savour every delicious moment, both in the comfort of a soft bed and —' she walked her fingertips lightly down his chest '—all night.'

'That's cheating,' he laughed. 'You know damn well this is the shortest night of the year.'

'Then we mustn't waste another minute,' Claudia said, and felt something burning into her back from the shadows.

'Absolutely,' Arlon agreed, releasing the rest of her hair from their pins.

Slowly, his lips closed on hers, and the kiss was deep and unyielding. In the inescapable light of the moon, Claudia could not control the shudder that rippled over her body when his hand moved to her breast. As his passion intensified, she squeezed her eyes shut and surrendered to Arlon's embrace.

Therefore, she did not see Orbilio slip out of the shadows.

Or the mist that clouded his vision.

The windows in Arlon's bedroom had not been shuttered and, high in the heavens, the moon flooded the room with its silvery blue light. Standing in the limbo land of doorway between bedroom and peristyle, Claudia inhaled the scent of the night stocks and listened to the soft tune played by the fountain. From here, she could see clearly the bench beneath the sycamore tree where she had been run to ground by an investigator in whose veins ambition coursed as fast as his blue blood. For a second, she thought she caught a movement in the bay tree to the left. But she was mistaken. He would be long gone.

'Come to bed,' Arlon whispered.

'Soon,' she promised.

'My family think you're after my money,' he chuckled.

'Not true,' she assured him.

'I know that, but all the same, you're a complex woman, Claudia Seferius. You tell me that stupid bowl in your hand is a good luck charm, that you refuse to be parted from it, yet I've never see the bloody thing before in my life.'

'After tonight, Arlon, I promise you won't see it again.'

She might not have spoken. 'And then you woo me and pursue me until I fall helplessly in love at your feet, and promptly withhold all your treasures.'

He was right. She had used every trick in the book, every feminine wile, to win Arlon over. It hadn't been easy. It had taken weeks of relentless and painstaking effort, ensuring she was accidentally seated beside him at the theatre, at the Circus, at banquets, at parties, coincidentally bumping into him at temples, libraries, in the Forum, on the Field of Mars, by the bonnie, bonnie banks of the Tiber. But Claudia knew her man. Had researched him like a thesis. Knew exactly which strings to pull, and which to let go …

'Then it's time I gave you my final three gifts,' she whispered. From the depths of her gown, she withdrew the onyx phial. 'First,' she said, removing the delicate glass stopper. 'Balm of Gilead.'

'Claudia!' he gasped. 'That's the most precious oil in the

world.'

'If it was good enough for the Queen of Sheba to give Solomon, then it's good enough for my bridegroom,' she said. 'Lie back while I rub it over your chest.'

His muscles were hard from working out in the gymnasium, his flesh firm. He groaned in pleasure as she applied the pungent oil.

'Next comes the mead.' She held out the engraved silver hip flask. 'Brewed by a small tribe in the Peloponnese, its principal ingredient is fermented honey. What the Immortals call nectar,' she added.

'Something of an acquired taste,' he grimaced, and then grinned. 'But to paraphrase a certain young lady, if it's good enough for Ganymede to serve to the King of the Gods, then it's good enough for the bridegroom.' He upended the flask and wiped his mouth with the back of his hand. 'That, my darling, is one strong brew they mix up there in Greece.'

You don't know the half of it. My darling.

'This the old country proverb, isn't it?' he said. 'When it comes to oil, the oil scooped off the top is the best. With honey, the sweetest lies at the bottom. But wine—' he reached out to her, but his hand missed '—of wine, it is the middle which is unsurpassed.' He tried to prop himself up on his elbow, but his body seemed weighted. 'God, I can't wait to taste Seferius wine. Take your clothes off. Let me gaze at the vessel.'

'In your dreams, you bastard.'

Consternation flickered in his eyes. He couldn't decide whether he was hearing correctly. Venom? From the luscious lips of his beloved? Surely not. 'Enough teasing tonight, Claudia. Come to bed.'

There was no mistaking, however, the snort of derision.

The contempt which blazed from her eyes. 'Arlon, I would go to my grave before I went to your bed.'

Again, he tried to sit up. Again, his muscles failed him. 'I — I don't understand.'

'See this bowl?' She pushed the bronze into his face. 'It's a begging bowl, you bastard. It belongs to a crippled, broken, old woman, blind in one eye, who is unlikely to live to see another full moon.'

And the story came out.

It was April. Colder than usual, wetter than anyone could ever recall. Claudia had been hurrying along the Via Nova, the part where the road narrowed into a high, vaulted passage, when she almost tripped over the beggar. Hardly surprising. They tended to cluster there, as well as under the porticoes and aqueducts, to shelter from the rain. She was about to move on, when there seemed something familiar about the voice of the cripple. She stooped for a closer look.

'Phyllis?' It was. It was one of *her* slaves. 'Phyllis, is that you?'

The weeping sore that was the woman's one good eye narrowed to focus. 'Mistress Claudia?'

And another story came tumbling out.

A story that started on the day of Claudia's Saturnalia banquet—

As she told the old hens, she'd invited a select band of merchants, with a view to converting them to the produce of her vineyards. The idea was simple. Lay on lavish entertainment, ply them with gourmet food, unlimited vintage Seferius wine — dear me, the contracts had been drawn up long in advance, they were all ready to be witnessed and signed!

Certainly, marble merchants with quarries dotted over

Africa and the Aegean were high on Claudia's priority list. Especially when those merchants had access to hundreds of contacts in the racing world, too! But it was no joke, despite what she'd told the old hens. Arlon's first words to her were indeed,

'How much would you take for your cook?'

And her reply was exactly what she'd repeated to Orbilio on the bench. 'I can't sell just one slave. If you want my cook, you'll have to take his wife, his three daughters, his mother-in-law and an aunt. I won't have the family broken up.'

Arlon hadn't bought Seferius wine, but he did pay a good price for the slaves, and Claudia had thought no more of it. Before handing them over to their new owner, she had established that none of his slaves, not even those in the quarries, were harshly treated. The subject had passed from her mind, especially since the cook had been a stand-in for Verres, her permanent chef, who had been laid up with a broken leg at the time.

But the tale Phyllis told had made her blood run cold.

Phyllis was the cook's mother-in-law, sold as part of the family unit. Grandmother to his three young daughters, aged nine, eleven and thirteen. Arlon, she quickly discovered, had no need of a cook. The first thing he did was despatch the poor man to Africa, his wife to Chios and the aunt to Alexandria. The old woman he did not think would be a problem. He merely sent her to Apulia in the south.

The three children he took to his stud farm in Lucania. Stud being the operative word ...

'You like them young, don't you, Arlon?' Claudia said. As he struggled to bring his vision into focus, she pressed on. 'Oh, not you personally. Your tastes are far too refined. But you know plenty of men who like little girls. Officials at the Circus, for instance. Magistrates, judges. Those who decide who wins by a nose — and who doesn't.'

As she said, know your enemy. Claudia had done her homework on Arlon. Didn't take a broken old woman's word. She had checked up on the men who officiated and judged the race winners. Those who were in a position to dope Arlon's competitors. *For a sweetener of their own—*

'From a position of respectability, you procured innocent young children and passed them to men who abuse and debauch them without conscience, and have no conscience about the foul deed yourself.'

'You don't understand,' he gulped. 'You don't know what it's like to be poor. To grow up in the slums, half-starved, wearing rags, watching your siblings die in the cradle, your parents grow old before their time.'

Don't I? Claudia swallowed. Said nothing. And had the small comfort that at least her parents hadn't suffered from premature ageing. They were both dead before they'd reached thirty.

'I vowed to myself, that I'd never be poor again. Never,' he said. 'That I'd do anything, *anything*, not to go back to the gutter.'

How rich does a man have to be, she wondered? How high is the price of a man's soul?

Arlon recoiled at the contempt in her eyes. 'I love you,' he insisted.

'Purely because I fed you drugs that would make you addicted to me.'

Or the smell of her, to be precise. (Oh, she had a lot to thank those cunning Orientals for!) But Arlon, completely indifferent to his Saturnalia hostess, could not possibly become addicted unless Claudia contrived to be regularly by his side, slipping the drug day after day into his wine –

'Your mistake,' she said, 'was sending Phyllis to another stud farm. You should have sent her to Africa with the others.'

In his complacency, he had forgotten the overlap among the racing fraternity. Gossip quickly spread to Lucania about the scandal in Apulia that had to be hushed up. How the cook's middle daughter fought, and died, for her virtue. Prompting the eldest to hold a pillow over the face of the youngest, before slitting her own wrists. At thirteen ...

'Phyllis confronted one of the paedophiles, and his idea of remorse was to have her beaten and left for dead. But Phyllis is an indomitable old woman. She survived.'

For how much longer, though, was debatable. Her lungs were ulcerated, she was coughing up blood, growing weaker and weaker every day. But at least she was growing weaker under Claudia's roof, with the attentions of Claudia's physician. And, Juno willing, she would not die before the ships docked, bringing her daughter and son-in-law home.

'You can't prove it,' Arlon said, and his voice was weak now, his limbs leaden. 'You can't prove any of this.'

'I know. Just as I can't prove that you killed your wife or that fifty other small girls have been raped and defiled before conveniently disappearing.'

He must know. Orbilio must know about this. He called him a fiend. A monster. Oh, he knows –

'Then what do you gain by this betrothal?' Arlon asked.

Claudia stood up, shook out her sleeves, adjusted her girdle. 'Haven't you guessed?'

The moon was still full, but this was the shortest night of the year. Already the sun was starting to rise, prompting the birds in the aviary to sing their hearts out.

'Well, you're a clever man, Arlon. You worked out the

country proverb, and I'm sure you'll work this out, too.' She tucked the phial and the hip flask back in the folds of her gown. 'Sooner or later.'

Nine days later and the heat had not abated. The moon, shrinking fast, still cast a silvery light over Claudia's garden, accentuating the feathery foliage of the wormwood, but now the constellations could be seen bright in the heavens. The great bear, the little bear, the dragon, the lynx. And from the northern horizon to the east, the great white swathe of the Milky Way stretched into infinity.

Claudia sat on the edge of the pool with her gown hitched up to her knees, dangling her feet in the cool water. Beside her, gnawing on a fresh sardine, her blue-eyed, cross-eyed, dark Egyptian cat, Drusilla, stiffened. Half a sardine dropped from her mouth, and a low growl emitted from the back of her throat.

'I know, poppet.' Claudia stroked the hackles flat. 'I smelled him, too.'

Sandalwood among roses and pinks.

His tall frame cast a shadow over the papyrus as he untied his high, patrician boots and eased himself down on to the marble rim adjacent to Claudia, his toes making slow ripples over the surface of the pool. Moths fluttered round the night stocks and herbs, and Drusilla fused with the night.

'You didn't attend the funeral today, then?'

'Prostrate with grief,' she replied.

'It must be tough,' Orbilio said, and it might have been the moonlight, but she could have sworn she saw a flash of white teeth.

'You have no idea,' she said honestly. Stuck indoors for

nine days, she'd missed out on the Festival of Fortune, two days of bull fights and the Celebration of the bloody Muses.

'Still.' He plucked an orange marigold and twirled it slowly between his fingers. 'The period of mourning is up now. I'm sure you'll be fully recovered by tomorrow.'

'Sarcasm,' she said, snatching the bloom out of his hand, because the significance of its colour hadn't escaped her, 'doesn't suit you.'

He snatched it back. 'Any more than black suits you. Which,' he added mildly, 'I presume is the reason the grieving bride-to-be isn't wearing it ...?'

'Cut to the chase, Orbilio. What do you want?'

His eyes took a leisurely journey over the tumble of dark curls round her shoulders as he inhaled her spicy Judean perfume, watched the rhythmic heave of her breasts. 'What do you think I want?' he murmured.

'Oh, I rather imagine it entails handcuffs and chains. Things like that.'

He pinged a pebble into the pool. 'I never do bondage on a first date,' he said. 'But you should have come to me with your suspicions about Arlon, not take the law into your own hands.'

Claudia held out her hands, first palms downwards, then palms up. 'I see no law.' Several minutes passed, cicadas rasped, and the heat of the night intensified. 'Are you going to charge me?' she asked, and her voice was so quiet, and so much time elapsed, that she wondered whether he had heard her.

'With what?' he asked eventually. 'Arlon died alone in his own bed on midsummer night, choking to death on his own vomit after drinking too much.'

But he knew, she thought. He knows everything. And in

the moonlight, she waited.

'It was a dangerous ploy, Claudia.' Marcus stretched out on his elbows on the marble path, his legs still dangling in the pool, and stared up at the night sky. 'It could have backfired, and badly.'

'What could?' she asked innocently.

'The honey trap you set for Arlon.'

Classic in its own way. Girl lures man. Sets him up. The perfect entrapment. Like a fly in amber, there's no escape. Men are such fools when it comes to sex.

'Honey*moon*,' she corrected, stretching out beside him. Up there, Polaris twinkled the brightest.

'Whatever,' he laughed. 'But it was clever. Immoral, mind you. But clever.'

Pfft. How can rubbing a pungent oil on a man's chest to disguise the bitter soporific with which she'd laced his mead compare to the terror of fifty young children? Immoral, my eye! Yes, of course she knew Arlon would choke. Everyone saw how much he'd drank, it might have happened anyway, all it needed was a slight nudge. One less scumbag, fifty children avenged, hundreds more spared the same sickening fate.

The celestial zoo tramped across the heavens. A pink light began to tinge the sky to the east. The first blackbird broke into song from an apple tree already swelling with tiny green fruits.

'Let me at least reimburse you for the expense,' Orbilio said sleepily.

'No need,' she replied.

Rugs? Gold medallions? Balm of Gilead? Ivory chairs? Cheap at half the price, she reflected, as the first bees began to buzz round the lavender.

The State understood grief. Accommodated the bereaved. Made allowances.

Thanks to one bright orange veil, a noisy procession and an ostentatious plighting of her troth, Claudia Seferius had two more fabulous years of freedom stretching ahead of her.

'Breakfast?' she said.

Set in Umbria, the famous "green heart" of Italy, this story evokes the rolling hills and rich woodlands for which the region is famous. Not to mention the delicious wines, black truffles and arguably the country's finest olive oil.

STAG NIGHT

Fat and replete against the trunk of an ancient oak tree, the old boar suddenly snorted awake. What was that? Hairy ears pricked forward, straining, craning — but through the dappled shade they discerned only the liquid trill of a flycatcher, the rustle of foraging beetles. Unconvinced, he lifted his snout and sniffed the sultry air. Ripe woodland raspberries. Chanterelles. The musk of a badger who'd passed through last night. Familiar scents, which should have reassured a seasoned tusker — yet the bristles down his back, refused to be pacified. Obedient to a million years of instinct, the old boar lumbered to his feet.

Then he smelled it.

Dog! Dog and ... and — He was halfway up the bank before he placed the memory.

Man.

Dog and *man,* and as he shambled towards the brow of the hill, the glade behind him filled with alien sounds. The clash of steel. Shouts. Baying. And the sickening scratch and slither as frantic claws sought a purchase on the slippery leaf litter...

Only once did the old boar glance back. The hunt was gaining. One man was way out in front now, the sunlight off the hunter's long spear blinding the boar's button eyes. This was not his first brush with the enemy. Last time, when he'd stupidly allowed himself to be cornered, he escaped only by goring two dogs to death and leaving one human male badly gashed. Even then, someone shot an arrowhead in to his haunch, but he'd been lucky. The barb dropped out as he ran and the wound quickly healed. Nevertheless, it was a lesson learned the hard way and today the stakes were higher than ever.

The first litter of the year had been raised, this was the mating season again. The old tusker had sows and his territory to protect …

And so it was, crashing through the undergrowth, with the smell of sweat and metal closing fast, that the wily boar prepared his defence –

"Disappeared?" A little worm wriggled in Claudia's stomach, leaving behind an icy cold trail. "Cypassis, grown men don't vanish in broad daylight in front of a dozen other men."

But her tone did not match the strength of her argument – goddammit, the hunt was turning into a nightmare! First her bodyguard, Junius, was stretchered home, bloodied and unconscious, having lost his footing up on the ridge. Then two more men returned, wounded and weak. And now we hear that another member of the party's come a cropper …

"Exactly how is Soni supposed to have performed this feat of magic?" she asked. Dear me, the lengths men go to for a few yellowed tusks and some antlers to hang on the wall! "Taken wings, like Pegasus?"

"I know it sounds ridiculous," said her ashen-faced maid. "But apparently Soni was leading the hunt one minute and — pfft! gone the next. There was talk of a boar — perhaps that distracted him, maybe he took off alone, but the point is, he hasn't come home — and — and —" Cypassis spread her large hands in a gesture of helplessness. "And the worrying part is, no one really cares that he's missing."

Yes, well, Claudia thought. They wouldn't be the first rich bastards not to give a toss about their slaves. "Have you questioned the bearers?" she asked. Surely they'd care that one of their number might lie at the mercy of ferocious wild beasts?

"That lot!" Cypassis sneered. "Within ten minutes of returning, they were too drunk to string two words together!"

"And Junius?" Claudia ventured. "I suppose he can't shed light on the matter?"

"Still no change in the poor boy's coma," Cypassis said sadly, and a nail drove itself in to Claudia's heart.

It was her fault Junius was on the ferry landing, poised to cross the River Styx. A lump formed in her throat and refused to subside. The trouble was, the young Gaul had been so *eager* to join this morning's hunt! She paced her bedroom floor and put the stinging in her eyes down to the brilliance of the setting sun. Max, the hunt's organiser, had been against it from the start — Junius being a rank amateur and all that— but Claudia had prevailed, pleading her bodyguard's case that the last time he'd been hunting had been as a ten-year-old lad with his father, long before he'd become a slave through the wars.

Also, she wanted to give Junius a treat.

Max's hunts were famed the length and breadth of Italy — rich businessmen handed over small fortunes for the privilege of being one of the few — and if her bodyguard was to go hunting, dammit, he might as well go with the best! And now look. Waxy and pale, barely breathing, they'd scraped him up from the foot of a gully and carried him home on a stretcher.

"He'll be fine," she assured Cypassis. "I've seen these head wounds before, it's simply a question of time."

Liar. She'd never seen one in her life, had no idea whether Junius would pull through or not, but there was no point in both of them worrying themselves to a frazzle.

"And you can stop fretting about Soni. He was the star of today's show and, trust me, heroes don't pop like bubbles." Sweet Minerva's magic, to hear them talk, you'd think the boy was a god in the making, not simply another bearer Max had trained up!

"They said he led the hunt from the *start,*" Cypassis said breathlessly. "Ran like a hare, according to one. Even uphill. Even weighed down with his javelin and arrows!"

Remembering his bunched muscles and stomach harder than permafrost, it was easy to see why Cypassis had been so eager to fulfil her errand of seeking out the young slave. Claudia glanced at the girl's bosom, bouncing and generous like puppies in hay, and knew that no man alive had yet rejected charms given so freely and yet totally without obligation. Cypassis loved 'em and left 'em, usually with dazed grins on their faces and memories warm enough to last them a lifetime, and Soni — red-blooded hunk that he was — would be putty in those broad Thessalian hands. If Wonderboy was missing, it was certainly not because he was hiding!

With Claudia's bodyguard out of action, who better, she'd thought, than Soni for a replacement? His skill, his courage, his cunning had been praised from the rafters, and let's not forget his strength and his stamina. Thus, Cypassis had been despatched to fetch him with a view to sounding him out, but that had been over two hours ago …

Across the atrium, where cedar-scented oil lamps hung from every pillar, where water cascaded down five circular tiers of a fountain and where marble athletes wrestled, boxed or weighed up the discus, an orchestra suddenly struck up, making her jump. Every note from the horns and the cymbals, the trumpets and drums dripped testosterone.

"Oh, no! The banquet!" Cypassis clapped her hands over her mouth. "I didn't realise it was so late!" She scurried across to Claudia's jewel box and rooted out a handful of ivory pins. "There's your hair to pin up, your shoes need a buff — "

"You concentrate on finding Soni," Claudia said. Any fool can give their sandals a rub on the back of her calves, and as for her curls — well, they'd simply have to get on with it. "Unless," she grinned, "you'd rather I approached someone else?"

Deep dimples appeared in Cypassis' cheeks, and some of the colour returned. "I'll settle for Soni," she grinned back. "I hear he holds his women as tight as his liquor!"

Masculine voices boomed out in the hall, laughing, recounting, re-living, as they made their way to the banquet and Claudia clipped on earstuds shaped like a bee. Gold — naturally. A present from Max. She buffed up her armband, inlaid with carnelian and pearls, another gift, and fixed a filigree silver tiara into her hair. The tiara had been the first in this generous line, along with alabaster pots containing precious Arabian perfumes, intricate onyx figurines and rare spices all the way from the Orient.

Despite knives scraping against plate, silver platters being cleared and replaced, despite music and voices growing louder and louder, as though each had to compete with the other,

Claudia made no move to join the men in the banqueting hall. Instead she leaned her elbows on the warm windowsill. The setting sun had sponged the enveloping hills a warm heather pink and the mew of the peacocks strutting on the lawn cut through the rasp of the crickets and the low-pitched croon of the hoopoe. Far in the distance, a wagon clattered over the cobbles, bringing home the last of the harvest. Down in the fertile lowlands of the Tiber, the wheat would have been threshed and winnowed a whole month before and would already be piled in granaries guarded by tomcats. But this was Aspreta, hilly and wooded, deep in the Umbrian hills.

This was the land of the huntsman.

Of one man in particular, Max — who had tamed the wild woods around his sumptuous villa to create vast landscaped gardens awash with artificial lakes, temples and grottoes. With watercourses rippling their way down the hillsides. With fishponds and porticoes and foaming white fountains, which the dying sun had transmuted into molten copper. A skein of ducks flew overhead, and the air was rich with the smell of freshly scythed grass and the merest hint of ripe apples. It was surely impossible for anything sinister to have occurred in this Umbrian idyll. There would, Claudia felt certain, be a perfectly simple explanation for Soni's disappearance ...

She poured herself a glass of chilled Thracian wine and sipped slowly. Dear me, Max's lands were so vast, a girl had to positively squint to even *see* the hunting grounds from the villa. A smile twisted one side of her mouth. Oh, yes. This was definitely the right decision, accepting his invitation to stay ...

She pictured her host, tanned and blond, lean and muscular, and knew that the sight of him in an open-shouldered hunting tunic cut high above the knee had fluttered many a female heart in its time —

Max. She rolled the name around on her tongue. Max. Ducatius Lepidus Glabrio Maximus to be precise, but known (for obvious reasons) as Max. And this fabulous estate was his. Or more accurately, was his *and his alone.* No wife — Max divorced wives like most men shuck peas — but more importantly, no heirs either. Claudia sighed happily. That's right. No little Max's running around, waiting to inherit the pile. Idly she wondered how quickly a girl might conceive, to redress this obvious imbalance ...

The sun sank below the hilltops, swamping the valley in its garnet embrace, as swallows made their final parabolas over the lake. A perfect night for seduction, she reflected. A perfect night for —

A gentle tap on the door cut through her reverie. "Claudia?"

Many a fair-skinned man will suffer for a day outdoors in the sun, but the hunt had had the opposite effect on Claudia's host. It had deepened his tan, lightened his hair, and set off the white of his linen tunic to Greek god perfection.

"Are we too raucous for you, darling?" Aegean blue eyes ranged over the arch of her breasts, her exquisite jewels, the rich tangle of curls piled high on her head. "Is that why you haven't joined us?"

"Are you sure you want me?" she countered, as the door closed softly behind him. "I am, after all, the only female guest and... well, boys will be boys and all that."

"Janus, how could I not want you?" His eyes were smoky, his voice a rasp. "Claudia —" He opened his clenched fist to reveal a shining sapphire ring. "It's a betrothal ring."

Oh, Max. How predictable you men are!

"Oh, Max, this is so unexpected!"

For a minute he said nothing, and she watched the rise and fall of his magnificent chest. Then, as he was about to speak, the moment was broken when, emitting a cry not unlike a strangled cat, one of the peacocks on the lawn shook its tailfeathers then spread them in a brilliant display of iridescence to a pair of peahens who continued to strut with total indifference.

"Isn't it risky, allowing such precious birds to roam free?" Claudia asked, as he advanced towards her, his soft leather sandals making no sound on the dolphin mosaic. He smelled faintly — very faintly — of almonds. "Suppose your wild beasts fancied a nibble? They'd surely be the easiest of targets."

"In my business," Max whispered, his hand slipping round the curve of her waist, "a man can leave nothing to chance."

For a beat of six, Claudia watched as the drab peahens flapped in to the branch of a walnut tree, to settle down for the night. Then she gently removed his hand. The peacock's fantail fell limp.

"Over that hill —" Max swept the rejected arm towards a spot far on the horizon as though that had been its original intention "— runs a high perimeter fence with some pretty ferocious spikes on the top." He laughed. It was a melodious, gentle, masculine laugh, pitched seductively low. "The only threat to these beautiful birds is my cook. He claims their roasted flesh is delicious!"

And when searching blue eyes bored deep into her own, Claudia saw a man who was very much pleased with himself. Not smug, not self-satisfied. Just quietly confident, like a man who's achieved something special. Any other time and she'd have put that down to his counting all those lovely gold pieces that he'd fleeced off the men who were so noisily swilling his wine — had it not been for that little matter of the sapphire ring.

*"That perimeter fence," he continued, "was erected not only to keep my hunting beasts in, but also to keep other animals out. Since I breed my own stock," he whispered, and she felt his breath on her cheek, "I can't risk weakening the strain by letting them loose with the native population. My bears, for instance, are particularly belligerent and it's touches like these that give my hunts their — shall we say, *competitive* edge."

Claudia knew what he meant. Only last year, the scion of one of Rome's leading tribunes had died of wounds received whilst tangling with one of Max's famous wild wolves — an incident which, far from deterring others, had in fact doubled the hunter's trade. The greater the danger, apparently, the more men wanted a slice — especially rich men, who had never seen action in war. It was a pretty bizarre consequence for two decades of peace, but man's compulsion to tango with Death had made Max wealthy in the extreme. Who was Claudia Seferius to decry a system that worked?

"Somehow we seem to have drifted away," he said quietly, "from the subject of this little trinket ..."

The drifting was not accidental. "Max, this isn't the time." Claudia kept her gaze on the horizon. "With the banquet in full swing, you should be there for your guests."

He lifted the back of her hand to his lips and kissed it lightly. "Beauty. Intelligence. And impeccable manners, as well. Darling, you and I will forge a brilliant alliance."

Claudia said nothing, and it was only when she was alone once more in her bedroom that she realised that, somewhere along the line, Max had pressed the betrothal ring into the palm of her hand. She slipped it on to her finger and watched the light reflect off its facets.

Hot damn, this was working out well.

"To Claudia!"

"Hurrah for the lady!"

"A toast to Claudia Seferius!"

One cheer after another ran round the banqueting hall, drowning the flutes in the background. All this, she thought, because I was the one who put Max on to Soni at the slave auction — what *would* they have been like, had she suggested he purchase a whole string! Goblets chinked, roasts were carved, and plates of salmon and oysters and hazel hens were passed round as slaves continuously topped up the wine. *Except.* Claudia coaxed a scallop out of its shell. Except Max had only bought the one slave, and what a magnificent specimen he was, this Soni from Gaul.

As a Greek balladeer recounted Jason's triumphant lifting of the Golden Fleece, Claudia leaned against the arm of her couch and thought back to her first meeting with Max. Was it really only three weeks ago? So much had changed in that short space of time. She popped the scallop into her mouth and reflected that, without that chance meeting at the slave auction, she would not be here tonight as … well, as "guest of honour," shall we say, of the man on whom Rome's wealthiest citizens descended with greater regularity than a double dose of prunes and where small fortunes changed hands for the gamble of turning wives into widows …

"See this?" A portly marble merchant on the couch opposite lifted the hem of his tunic to show his fellow diners a livid red scar. "The puncture wound was so bloody deep, I'm left with a permanent limp, but he was a plucky bugger, I tell you. Game to the end."

"Call that a scar?" The magistrate beside him yanked at his neckline to expose a long and jagged line, barely healed. "Compared to mine, yours is a scratch."

Much to the balladeer's confusion, all eight then began dismantling expensive clothing in a bid to compare injuries, each insisting theirs was the worst while swearing at the same time that their quarry was the bravest, the toughest, possessing by far the most guile — *ever*. The singer's words became drowned in the melee and Max shot a slow, but happy wink at Claudia. He had noticed, then, the ring which she wore on her finger …

Perhaps not as rich as Midas, hunts which were famed the length and breadth of Italy had enabled Max to not only purchase this fabulous villa stuffed with antiques and fine art, but lands that stretched to every horizon. No, sir. Claudia impaled a prawn on her knife. Without that chance meeting in Rome, Claudia Seferius would not be sitting here tonight with the man around whom Great Plans revolved …

Sometimes, she reflected, the gods on Olympus *do* smile down on mortals. Her mind drifted back. She'd been crossing the Forum from the east and another man had been crossing the Forum from the west. Marcus Cornelius Orbilio, to be precise, but — But dammit the man's name was not important! What mattered was that the sweetest of all goddesses, Fortune (may her name live for ever), Fortune arranged for the slave auction to be held smack in the middle of their crossing paths. And Marcus Cornelius, god bless him, knew Max …

Marcus.

Marcus Cornelius.

Marcus Cornelius Orbilio.

Something skittered inside her when she pictured his face

and she gulped at her wine to settle the jitters. Pfft! So what if he was tall and dark and — all right — not exactly bad looking? Who cared that his hair was wavy, except where it sometimes fell over his forehead, and that he wore the long tunic of a patrician? Marcus Whatsisname Thingy meant nothing to her. Nothing whatsoever. Less than zilch. In fact, the only reason her pulse raced now was owing to the lack of legality of certain scrapes she'd been in, seeing as how Supersnoop was attached to the Security Police.

In fact, that's what she'd been doing in the Forum, returning from some rather dodgy dealings, but hell, what other option is there, when merchants conspire to freeze a young widow out of the wine trade that she'd been thrust into after inheriting her late husband's business? Goddammit she'd married the old goat for his money, the least others could do is allow her to spend it, but no. Supersnoop's always there, sticking his investigative snout in her business, hoping to catch her red-handed. One day he'd cotton on that she was too damned smart for him, but in the meantime Marcus God-but-I'm-handsome Orbilio had, for once in his miserable life, come up trumps.

Until then, Claudia was stuck with relying on money-lenders, con-tricks and bluff to keep the creditors at bay, but Fortune was favouring more than the brave that day. She was favouring Claudia Seferius. It was obvious, from their frosty introductions, that the two men weren't exactly bosom buddies and chances are the meeting would have come to nothing — had Max not then excused himself, saying he needed to purchase a slave from the block.

"Just the one?" Claudia had asked. Normally people picked up quite a number. "One is hardly worth coming to Rome for."

Suddenly the opening was there for the blond hunter to score points over his aristocratic rival. "My lovely Claudia," Max had rasped, his eyes stroking her curves. "For me, one person is *always* enough." Arched eyebrows indicated the auction block. "Which of those slaves would you recommend?"

"It depends on what qualities you're looking for," she'd purred back, with barely a glance in Marcus' direction.

"In men," Max replied huskily, "it has *got* to be staying power. Don't you agree?"

"I wouldn't settle for anything less." From the corner of her eye, she saw the flush rise on Marcus' face and, noticing Junius jabbering away in his native tongue to a fellow Gaul beside the auction block, she found it delectably easy to add, "Personally, I've always found Gauls to have extremely strong backs ..."

Marcus by that time was glaring daggers and Max, capitalising on this sexual undercurrent, instantly bid for the Gaul, whose name, it transpired, was Soni. The same Soni who had done the hunt so proud today.

All in all, Claudia thought, things were going exceedingly well ...

Especially that exquisite moment when, swallowing his pride, Orbilio enquired whether he might attend Max's forthcoming hunt. Knowing these were extravaganzas to die for, Claudia watched his face turn to thunder when Max oh-so-politely informed him that, alas, he only ever took ten men on a hunt and, he was so very sorry, but the next was fully booked ...

As it happened, Claudia had been in the courtyard this morning when the hunt had set off. And there were eight men present, not ten. Dear me, she really must remember to mention that numbers thing to Marcus next time she saw him –

If she saw him again. The chances were, now he knew she

was ensconced here with Max, he'd stop pestering her and stick his nose into someone else's illegal wranglings.

"... I parried to the left, made a feint, dodged back to the right, but he was too smart for me..."

"... I was impaled once, right here." More linen was bunched up to expose violated flesh. "Tossed me right on to my shoulder, he did ..."

He! A wave of disgust washed over Claudia. They talk about boars, bears and wolves as though they were the hunter's equals, yet how often do you see stags armed with a slingshot, or running with their own pack of dogs? She looked round the banqueting hall, at watery red eyes, fists thumping on tables, where words were already slurring, and wondered how these cloistered, overweight city-types would fare in one-to-one combat. With no bearers carrying their spears or their arrows. With no dogs at their side to hound wild creatures into panic. Just them out there, with only their wits to keep them alive ...

"Having fun, darling?"

"Absolutely."

And what it would be like, living with a constant succession of drunken braggarts, day in and day out? Max coped admirably, but then the post-hunt entertainment — this orgy of showing off afterwards — was part and parcel of the package he sold. He was, she decided, a magician. An illusionist. A man who — *abracadabra!* — turns fat slobs into young bucks, and should they look in the mirror back in Rome and see who they really are, then hey presto! All they need do is hand over more coins and suddenly they're heroes again. The "war" wounds were not only worth the pain and aggravation. They were fundamental to the whole process.

She recalled their return this afternoon, whooping and

hollering in the courtyard amid carcasses of slaughtered beasts and a welter of blood-caked spears, concerned only with the glory of their own achievements and not a single thought for the wounded. Or a lowly slave, who hadn't come home …

"Is our hero not invited to join the celebrations?"

For perhaps a count of ten you could have heard the proverbial pin drop following Claudia's question, then everyone clamoured at once, most of them bursting in to raucous, drunken, astonished laughter.

"You mean *Soni*?"

"Not in here, love!"

"Soni? Join *us?* Now that's rich!"

Claudia felt a tug on her elbow as Max gently steered her away from the couch. "That," he said, speaking through his forced smile, "was extremely embarrassing, darling. My guests comprise merchants, politicians — the cream of Roman society." He paused. "They do not take their dinners with slaves."

"They take their dinners with dogs."

"Cyclone and Thunderbolt are exceptions," he said, and his blue eyes were steel. "The other dogs remain in the kennels, and never, ever do *any* of the bearers join in the banquet."

"No matter how competent?"

"No matter how competent." She felt his whole body unstiffen. "I admire your liberated ideas about slaves and equality," Max said, winding one of her curls around his little finger. "But it's my job to give these men what they want, and believe me, they don't pay several thousand sesterces to dine with common slaves. Ah! The desserts."

Platters of melons and cherries, quinces in honey, almond cakes and dates stuffed with apple passed by in mouth-watering succession.

"Come sit by me while we eat, it gives me an excuse to slip my arm round your lovely smooth shoulder."

"Shortly," Claudia promised. "There's something I must attend to first."

"Of course." Max gently released the ringlet. "Hurry back, darling," he whispered, rubbing the sapphire ring on her finger. "Your beauty is all that makes the evening tolerable. Oh, and Claudia —"

"Yes?" She turned in the doorway.

"Betrothal rings go on the left hand, my love."

The room in which Junius lay was lit only by a single lamp of cheap oil, whose stuttering flame cast staccato shadows against the far wall. No mosaics covered his floor, no painted scenes brought bare plaster to life. Even the welter of bandages which swaddled his head seemed uncared for.

"You blockhead," Claudia whispered, wiping a bead of sweat from his cheek. "What did you have to go and get yourself beaned for?"

Dust motes danced in the wavering flame, and the scent of her spicy Judaean perfume blocked out the smell of caked blood. He was lucky, according to Max's physician, that no bones were broken, he'd taken one helluva tumble, but watching the shallow breathing and the waxy texture of his skin, lucky was not the first word which came to Claudia's mind. Her hands bunched into fists. Dammit, Max knew the terrain up on the ridge like the back of his hand, he should have warned Junius that shale was dangerous. The stretcher-bearers told her what happened — how he'd lost his footing under the weight of the weaponry he was carrying — but the fact that the accident happened at all was the problem. She should not have allowed Junius to go. Max knew he was inexperienced, dammit he should have insisted the boy stayed behind — but since he hadn't, then he should bloody well have taken better care of his charge!

She opened the shutter, allowing a small breeze to sport with the flame. From here, there was only a view of the cowshed, plus a hint of the moon through the oaks. Far away, a fox barked and she felt, rather than heard, the door open behind her.

"How is he?"

Claudia's heart flipped a somersault. It can't be. Sweet Janus, this isn't possible — She waited until her pulse settled down. "Lazy as ever," she said, not turning round. "But that's servants for you these days. Not a thought for anyone but themselves."

The baritone chucked softly, and her heart began to spin like a top.

"I've just come from the banqueting hall," Marcus said. "And I think it's a reasonable prediction to say there'll be some jolly sore heads in the morning."

Claudia did not smile. "Orbilio, what the hell are you doing here?"

"Oh." He rubbed a hand over his chin. "Just passing."

"On your way where, exactly?"

"Home."

She took in the long patrician tunic, the high patrician boots, the firm patrician jaw. And wondered why it was that little pulse always beat at the side of his neck when they were alone. "Isn't this something of a detour for you? Say, of some one hundred miles?"

His teeth showed white in the darkness and she could smell his sandalwood unguent, even through the pongs from the cowshed. Then the grin disengaged and his voice, when he spoke, was a rasp. "Claudia, you must leave, it's dangerous here."

She closed the shutter, and the flame straightened up. "It's the Emperor's fault," she told the comatose bodyguard. "He will keep subsidising theatrical productions, some of the drama's bound to rub off. Or could it be, Junius, that this aristocrat's simply jealous of Max?"

"This has nothing to do with — *Is that a betrothal ring on your finger?"*

"See what I mean?" she asked the welter of bloodstained bandages.

"It is! It's a betrothal ring! Claudia, you can't marry that man, he's worn out five wives already."

"Six has always been my lucky number."

"Fine!" He threw his hands in the air. "Fine. Do what you like, only for gods' sake, let's discuss this back in Rome. I have horses outside, we —"

Claudia spun round to face him. "Who the bloody hell do you think you are? My guardian? My husband? I'm not one of your flunkies."

"You've got me wrong —"

"I haven't got you at all, and that's the root of it. You're jealous as hell that I'm here with Max, and moreover, I intend to stay here, Orbilio. I have Great Plans for my future —"

"As Soni had Great Plans for his!"

Claudia felt the ground shift underfoot. "Soni?"

"Dammit, he was one of our best undercover agents." Orbilio slammed a fist in to the palm of his hand. "When he failed to report back, I came looking — only I can't find him anywhere."

The floorboards became marsh, and Claudia slumped

down on Junius' narrow pallet bed. "Soni's a *policeman?"*

"Of sorts," Marcus said. "Why?" She saw him stiffen. "Do you know anything about his disappearance?"

Claudia rubbed at her forehead. "Yes ... No ..." The room was spinning around her. Umbrian idylls crumbled to dust as she explained how Soni hadn't come home from the hunt.

"Shit." Orbilio sank on to the bed beside her, and buried his head in his hands. "That means someone rumbled his cover and took the opportunity of this morning's excitement to kill him."

But how? When? Obviously suspicious, Soni's idea of life insurance was to keep himself in full view of the hunt. How could he possibly have been eliminated without witnesses? What was it the head bearer had said? *Now you see him, now you don't —*

"What —" Claudia could not bring herself to say 'who'. "What are you investigating?"

Orbilio spiked his hands through his hair, and when he spoke, his voice was weary. "Max," he said slowly, "makes too much money for my liking. I mean, look at this place, Claudia. A man doesn't make legitimate millions from stag hunts and bears! So I started making some enquiries and ..."

"And what?"

For a long time, the only sound in the room was the shallow breath of the unconscious bodyguard. Then: "I couldn't be certain — after all, the top echelon of Rome are visitors here. I had to tread softly. So I set up that business at the slave auction —"

Soni was a plant?

"Goddammit, Orbilio, you set me up, too!"

That was no accidental meeting, that day in the Forum — Supersnoop had been waiting for her! He knew where she'd been, she knew where she was going, and on top of it all, he damn well knew Max would be there. Both of them, plums for the picking!

"I needed you to add authenticity," Marcus said. "That way, Max would suspect nothing and I'd have an undercover agent to sound out my theory." He scrubbed his eyeballs with his thumbs. "What the hell am I supposed to say to his mother?"

Several more minutes ticked past, and the candle guttered and spat.

"I think it's fair to say that, having rumbled Soni," Marcus said quietly, "they feared Junius was also a spy."

Nausea clogged Claudia's throat as she studied the comatose form on the bed. "His injuries aren't accidental?"

"Don't you think it's strange he has only head wounds? For a chap who supposedly tumbled down a ravine, it seems odd no bones were broken." He paused, before adding, "I'm sure they believed they were bringing his corpse home to you."

Tears scalded Claudia's eyes. Sweet Jupiter, that might yet be the case ...

"What hunch were you working on?" Claudia asked, but her words were cut short as the door to the sickroom burst open, spilling bright orange light on to the floor.

"Seize him!"

Half a dozen men rushed into the room, grabbing a kicking, struggling, protesting Marcus and hauling him in to the corridor. Claudia shot after them, but there were too many and Orbilio was quickly bundled down the slave wing, watched by a blond huntsman with Aegean blue eyes.

"Where are you taking him?" Claudia demanded, but a strong arm shot out to restrain her.

"Stay out of this," Max growled. He needed both hands to

contain his struggling fireball. "This is between Orbilio and me." To his men, he said, "Get a horse, tie him to it, then escort this *gentleman* to Rome."

"This is outrageous," Claudia hissed.

"I know," Max admitted. By the gods, she could squirm! "But I can't allow people to go around slandering me, particularly well-connected patrician policemen."

"He says —"

"I know what he says, and perhaps he genuinely believes I'm up to my ears in extortion or blackmail, but Jupiter's balls, I'm no gangster. I won't have the slur bandied about. Now, Orbilio's pride might be hurt, riding home hog-tied, but it *will* only be pride."

He released her at last, leaving them both panting and red from exertion.

"What of his claim that Junius' injuries aren't consistent with a fall?" she spat, and to her astonishment, Max burst out laughing.

"Have you seen the bruises on that poor bugger's body? Junius hit his head on a rock, Claudia. Knocked himself out - and you know yourself what happens when drunks roll about. The body goes limp."

Actually, that was true ...

"Orbilio's problem," Max chuckled, "is not that I might be a gangster, not even that I make more money than Midas by ripping off rich bastards hand over fist. His problem is, I have *you!*"

Claudia slipped off the armband, the one set with carnelians and pearls, and ran it round and round in her hand. "Like you have Soni, you mean?"

Aegean blue eyes flickered briefly. "Soni," he said, "is a slave. Yes, I own slaves. Yes, unlike you, I don't treat them as equals. And yes, I've been married five times, if that's what you're driving at, but I never think of women as chattels." He drew a deep breath. "Whether you believe me or not is another matter," he added.

"Whether I believe you," she said slowly, "rests on my seeing Soni, face to face, right this minute."

An astonished expression crossed Max's face. "Are you serious?"

"Is there a problem?"

"No. No, of course not," he stuttered. "It's just that … It's just that I'm jealous, my love. I know I can't compete with a stripling half my age and whose pecs are solid steel, but … well, I'm not in bad shape and, unlike a slave, I can give you wealth unimaginable —"

Not unimaginable, Max. I've imagined it many times.

"I want to buy Soni," she snapped, "not sleep with the boy." If everything was above board, then there would be no obstacle. Max had denied her nothing so far.

"Ah." For a moment, he faltered, then the old seductive laugh was back as he led her back through the lofty atrium, rich with its cedarwood oils. "In that case, darling, you must accept him as a gift, with my compliments. May he serve you as well as he's served me."

Claudia felt a tidal wave of relief wash over her. For once, Supersnoop was wide of the mark. Junius *had* simply cracked his head on a rock before falling down that ravine! But what of Soni?

Suppose, she thought, trailing her hand in the fountain as she passed, Max had decided to satisfy himself that Soni was all that he'd seemed? Soni's refusal to comply with a criminal act would have blown his cover right out of the water, and suddenly Claudia was extremely keen to meet the man who had staged his own disappearance in broad daylight without arousing suspicion and yet had returned with a convincing explanation!

Glancing at Max, suave and easy, Claudia found no problem in picturing him up to his ears in racketeering, using the hunts as a front, both to make deals at the highest of levels and also to enforce any threats. He led her in to his office and clapped his hands. Immediately, a negro slave answered the call.

"Fetch Soni here, will you?"

"Master?" the old man's face creased in a frown.

"Stop dithering, man. Just fetch him. Shoo!" Strong hands poured two goblets of rich honey mead, hesitating a fraction before handing her hers. "You — You aren't going to marry me, are you?" Max asked quietly.

"No," she admitted. "I'm not."

His gifts were welcome, of course — the tiaras, the earstuds. But the Great Plan had been to ingratiate herself with his wealthy clientele and sign them up for hefty consignments of Seferius wine. Well-oiled (thanks to Max) they'd be pushovers for good, vintage wine and would be in no mood to worry about loaded prices. Especially when the alternative was this sickly concoction. Yuk. Two parts thunderbolts, one part bile, it was watered down with three ladlefuls of the River Styx. No wonder they had to add honey!

"Claudia —"

His voice came from down a dark tunnel, and the tunnel was closing in all around.

"Claudia?"

The voice echoed like stones in a barrel and her vision grew cloudy. Bloody mead! Filthy stuff.

"Is everything all right, darling?"

"Perfectly."

But everything was not all right.

Jellified knees gave way. Lights went dim. And Claudia collapsed in a heap on the floor.

Was she dead? Was this blackness Stygian gloom? There were no three-headed dogs about, but there was barking. Claudia tried to lift her head, and found it had been glued to the floor. When she finally raised it, she needed to hold it with both hands to prevent it rolling into the corner.

Except... Except her hands had been glued down, as well. She couldn't lift them. Ignoring the hammering inside her head, she tried harder. *And found not hangover lethargy, but ropes binding her tight.*

"I'm sorry it ended like this," said a familiar voice from the corner. The chair creaked when he stood up. "But you would keep pressing the subject of Soni. Oh, Claudia. If only you'd let it go."

Primeval creatures slithered down Claudia's spine. And how strange. High summer, yet her teeth were chattering ... She struggled, but the knots were professional and her skin chafed itself raw.

"You know." When he knelt down, she could smell the leather of his boots. "You really are very lovely." He ran a hand gently down the length of her cheek. "Had your brain been full of feathers, we could have had a wonderful marriage and raised some damned good looking kids." He sighed at what was not to be. "Unfortunately, though, dawn is breaking. Time to leave."

Cold. So very cold. "People will come looking for me," she gabbled. "Marcus, for one, won't let it drop -"

"Ah, but this is terrible country for bandits. So many tragic accidents can befall a beautiful woman." Either Max had thought it out carefully during the night, or else he'd done this before. "Oh, don't look like that." He dragged her to her feet and propelled her to the door. "I'm not so hard-hearted that I won't pay for a lavish funeral tribute and endow the most magnificent of marble tombs you could imagine in a prominent position along the Appian Way."

"You spoil me."

The door cranked open and two hefty bearers pushed her into the pale pink dawn light. The barking escalated, and some of the dogs started baying. The sound, she realised with a chill, was caused by impatience. Their desire to get underway. "Max?" Surely he wouldn't kill her? Not Max.

But Max clicked his fingers, and the bearers manhandled her into the courtyard, where eight fat city men in short tunics milled around. None looked in Claudia's direction. Terror gripped at her throat.

"Please —" She could hardly breathe. "Help me. For gods' sake, one of you, help me!"

Last night, these men were her friends. Business colleagues. They'd laughed at her jokes, given her contracts for rich, vintage wine.

A vice tightened round her ribcage. Oh, sweet Juno in heaven. It's not that they can't hear me. It's not that they imagine I'm drunk. They're not helping, for the simple reason they're busy. Checking spears and arrows and slings ... And when they do glance around, it's not a terrified girl that they're seeing. *They're simply assessing the strength of their prey.*

The true horror of Max's hunting parties slammed into her, filleting every bone from her body. Finally she understood what had happened to Soni.

Why he was way out in front of the others.

The slave, goddammit, was the quarry.

That's why Max only wanted the one. Only ever the one ...

"You'll never get away with it," she cried, as the cart bumped over the lawns. Past the peacocks. Past the watercourses. Past the shimmering man-made lakes rimmed with reeds.

"Wrong," Max replied, as they approached the wooded hunting grounds. Behind, the bearers loped along at a steady rhythm, their dogs straining at the leash. "All over the Empire, you'll find men bored with a quarter of century's peace. Sons of warriors who've only ever heard about the clash of weapons, the bittersweet fear of hand-to-hand combat. And since they've never ridden into battle themselves, they hunt boar, they hunt stag, they hunt bear for their thrills and to affirm their manhood. Unfortunately, with some, that's not enough." Slowly, he reined in the horses. "Some seek a further dimension."

Aegean blue eyes scanned her face.

"Can you imagine how much these men are prepared to pay to hunt humans? Thousands, Claudia. Thousands upon thousands, and you know the best part? There's an unlimited market out there. Oh, I know you're going to tell me your clever friend, Marcus is on to me. He's suspected me for some time, but what can he prove? Nothing! Not one bloody thing."

Drawing a broad hunting knife, he cut through her bonds in a businesslike fashion. For how many others, she wondered, had he done this?

"You have intelligence, cunning and resilience, Claudia Seferius, you will be a worthy adversary." Max took her trembling chin between his thumb and forefinger. "Your tomb will do you credit, I promise."

Claudia spat in his face. "Go to hell."

"I probably shall," he agreed. "Now then. We always give the quarry a chance. Here's a slingshot, a javelin and a short stabbing dagger. Try," he whispered, glancing at the businessmen, "to take at least one of them with you."

Breath was too precious to waste on this son-of-a-bitch, her mind whirled like a cap in the wind. The estate was fenced in; the gates closed behind them; guards were posted; and ferocious spikes topped the perimeter fence. What the hell chance did she have?

"We normally give a count of a hundred," he said, "but seeing as how you're a woman, I think two hundred is fair —"

Claudia made no effort to kill him. He'd be prepared, would only injure her, consigning her to a lingering death. She had no choice. She set off — a victim of the very men on whom, only last night, she had wished this particular fate.

Behind her, she could hear Max counting aloud. "Sixteen. Seventeen."

Father Mars. Mighty Jupiter. Can you hear me up on Olympus? Can you help?

"Twenty-two. Twenty-three."

"Nobody move, you're surrounded."

For a second, Claudia's heart stopped beating.

"Drop your weapons, put your hands in the air."

Then the breath shot out of her lungs. That was no Olympian deity. That baritone was quite unmistakable, even through the shell he used as his loudspeaker —

As one, fifty archers stepped out from the bushes, their arrowtips aimed at the group. Almost before the daggers and javelins had crashed to the ground, eight men began babbling. Explaining. Exonerating. Bribing.

"You all right?"

Claudia hadn't realised she had collapsed, until a strong hand pulled her up. Even then, her knees were so weak, the only way to stay upright was with his arm tight round her waist.

"Nothing better than a run in the country," she said, and it was odd, but her teeth were still chattering.

Orbilio grinned, and brushed the hair from her eyes with his thumb.

"I thought they'd run you out of town," she said.

"I was expecting some form of trouble," he replied. "Which is why I brought back-up." He paused. "It took a little persuading, but eventually one of Max's heavies told us of Max's plans for you. Hence the trap we were able to lay overnight."

Behind him, pleading, protesting, terrified merchants were rounded up — men of substance, yet men of no substance at all — while the bearers tried to explain how they were under duress to obey, that they got drunk to blot out the horror, that if they didn't participate, they would become the next quarry. For many years afterwards Claudia was able to recall, with blood-curdling clarity, everyone's clamouring at once. *While not one word of remorse fell from their lips.*

"You know this won't come to trial?" Orbilio said, steadying her with his grip. "Senior politicians and influential businessmen on slave hunts? The scandal would de-stabilise the Empire in no time, Augustus wouldn't risk it."

"They'll get off?" The prospect of these scum swaggering free was almost too much to bear.

"No, no!" Orbilio was certain of that. "It's suicide for these boys," he said, leaving unspoken the fact that, in at least two cases, the exit would require a certain assistance.

The soldiers, meanwhile, were being none too gentle with their cargo, yet throughout the whole ignominious defeat, one man had said nothing. Outmanned and outnumbered, Max surrendered at once, quietly and without fuss, and stood, hands bound in front of him, as his rich clientele and his poor bullied bearers were kicked in to the cart.

His passive acceptance alone should have alerted them.

"Shit!" shouted the captain of the archers. "After him!"

Sprinting through territory as familiar as his own back terrace, Max hurdled tree roots and obstacles with the grace and ease of a gazelle, heading deeper and deeper into the woods.

"Wait." Orbilio's voice was calm. His authority stopped the men in his tracks. "This is his ground, we can't hope to either catch or outwit him. Soldier!"

A burly archer stepped up. "Sir."

Orbilio relieved him of his dark yew bow and weighted it in his hands. Carefully, he plucked an arrow from the quiver. Sweet Janus, the white tunic was now barely a dot!

"Marcus," breathed Claudia. "Leave this to the archer." So many trees in between, it needed an expert!

"This," said Orbilio, notching the arrow into his bow, "is for Soni."

Claudia felt her heart thump. "I'm just as much to blame as you are," she said. "I know you put him up as a plant, but it was my urging that bought him his grave."

The bow lifted.

"This," he repeated, "is personal."

With a hiss, the arrow departed. Silence descended on the clearing — the men in the cart, the soldiers, Claudia, Marcus — watching as one as the arrow took flight. No-one breathed.

In front of them, the white dot grew smaller. Then, with a

cry, Max fell forward. No one spoke. Not even when Max hauled himself to his knees, then his feet, and then began running again …

The colour drained from Orbilio's face. "I winged him," he gasped. "Only winged him."

The arrow, they could see now, was lodged in his shoulder. Painful. But hardly life-threatening.

Orbilio wiped his hand over his face, as though the gesture might turn back time. Give him one more chance to make good.

Then – "Look!" Claudia pointed. Marcus followed her finger.

In the distance, a huge bristly boar came charging out of the undergrowth, tusks lowered. His furious snorting could be heard in the clearing. As though in slow motion, they watched as he lunged at the figure in white. They watched, too, as Max tried to duck, turn away, but the wily old boar had been there before.

This was the mating season, remember.

He had sows and a territory to protect …

Under the old Roman calendar, March, named for Mars the God of War, was the first month of the year. On the 1st, the sacred fire of Rome was renewed by the Vestal Virgins, keepers of the flame, ritual dances and processions filled the streets, and parties held to celebrate the god's birthday.

SWAN SONG

'Claudia!' Amid the harpists and lyre players, dancers and jugglers, Dexter welcomed his guest with an embrace that was perhaps a fraction too tight and lingered perhaps a fraction too long. 'I'm so glad you could make it.'

Make it? Dexter was an international merchant whose bank balance made King Midas look like a pauper. He imported white marble from Paros, green marble from Euboea and a creamy red variety from beyond the Sea of Marmora. Rumour had it that the waiting list for his yellow marble was a mile long, while in Rome his imports adorned the porticoes of the rich, formed the steps of several temples and lined the walls of practically every bath house and basilica. The profits from these enterprises had added three silver mines to his portfolio, as well as seventeen apartment blocks, sixteen high-ranking civil servants and half the countryside between Naples and Brindisi. Claudia would have clawed her way back from Hades not to miss this invitation.

On the pretext of not being able to make himself heard over

the musicians, Dexter leaned forward to whisper. His eyes were dark and intense, she noticed, and his breath tasted of mint.

'I very much hope you will be joining my domestic arrangements on, shall we say, a rather more intimate footing.'

That was the other thing. His colossal wealth aside, the marble merchant had also sired four successful sons. Claudia glanced across to where they were welcoming visitors with the same broad smile as their father and felt a flutter of immense satisfaction. Four Greek gods aged between twenty and thirty, whose circumstances, whether divorce, bereavement, career or university, had conspired to throw them into the marriage market at the same time. And while each son was very different in looks from his brother, they were united by their mother's strong teeth and round ears on the one side, and by their father's straight back and square hands on the other.

'I doubt my arm will need much twisting,' she purred.

An advocate, a banker, an orator and a poet. Plenty of choice there for a girl with youth by the bucketload, but a bank balance in serious decline.

'Claudia, you look ravishing.' Dexter's wife swept out of nowhere and linked a frosty arm with her visitor's. 'Absolutely divine, my dear.'

Didn't she know it. She'd spent weeks building up to this party, perfecting the right shade of dye for her robe, formulating the exact designs for the jewellery to accompany it, boning up on family, guest list and politics — and why not? When beauty and wits are a girl's only assets, she can't afford to squander either one. There are only so many bites to a cherry.

'Oh, you know how it is, Calpurnia.' She flicked the pleats of her gown in a dismissive gesture. 'The whole city's turned green from the decking of laurels, so I thought if you can't beat 'em, might as well join 'em!'

Dexter's wife laughed with a smile that did not extend to her eyes. Claudia wondered whether calling her "Mother" might crack some of the ice.

'I just love the Festival of Mars, don't you?' she breezed. 'Everyone's so happy.'

Present company excepted, but who knows? Maybe Calpurnia had swallowed a wasp with her breakfast sausage, or eaten a sea urchin and forgotten to pull the quills off? Then again, she mused, still feeling the hot imprint of Dexter's hand on her backbone, maybe adulterous husbands stick in every woman's craw?

'I suppose people see this as the turning point after a long winter,' Calpurnia said, casting round to see who she could palm her guest off to. 'A celebration of renewal and growth.'

Yes, it was funny how foreigners tended to think of Mars as god of war, when common sense should tell them that no general wages war lightly. Mars, like any other decent soldier, was more guardian and defender, a safekeeper of brothers and sons, and what better way to protect his people than keeping the crops in the fields free of blight and their livestock healthy and whole?

'Change is always welcome,' Claudia replied sweetly, and was rewarded with a glare of pure venom and a swift introduction to the dullest woman in Rome.

'... no idea *where* she sends her linens for washing,' the old trout was saying, 'if indeed she sends them at all...'

By the time she'd moved on to a different neighbour's shortcomings, Claudia was busy dangling four Greek gods on the twin prongs of beauty and wit.

Paulus, the oldest, was the banker, who'd been widowed

last year when his wife and baby both died in childbirth. Serious and reserved, but with an admirably square jaw, he made a bid to impress the glamorous newcomer with learning.

'Here's one thing they won't have taught you at your fancy university in Athens,' he informed his youngest brother. 'The first of March used to be the start of the new year.'

'Really?' Leon murmured, almost drawing his eyes away from Claudia's cleavage. 'When was that?'

'Back in the days when Venus was a virgin,' she quipped, and all four brothers laughed.

'Old habits die hard.' That was the second son, Arval, a respected advocate newly divorced, who'd decided pleasure was the path to a girl's heart. 'Five generations may have passed, but the feasting and revelry hasn't changed.'

'Father's excelled himself this year,' Sergius added in his rich mellow tones. 'He's brought in dancers from Spain, Arabian jugglers, fire-eaters from Kush and commissioned acrobats from the island of Crete.'

It was no coincidence that Sergius was the most muscular, working out in the gymnasium to hone his physique in the same way he trained his deep orator's voice.

'The old man's laid on a feast featuring all manner of exotic dishes.' (Bankers don't have the same way with words). 'Perhaps Claudia would allow me to escort her to the banquet later ...?'

'Why, Paulus, I would be honoured.'

'But before that,' young Leon cut in, 'maybe she'd be kind enough to partner me during the official State celebrations?'

'My pleasure,' she gushed, only this time her smile was a tad strained.

Odd how flies turn up in every pot of ointment, and she wasn't talking about Calpurnia staring daggers across the atrium, either. This year the Salian Dance was being performed outside Dexter's house, though in theory that was an honour. Twenty-four patrician men selected by none other than the Vestal Virgins performing this ancient ritual on one's doorstep? A rare privilege indeed, one of the few honours that couldn't be bought, and to even stand in such a golden shadow should have bathed Claudia with its light.

It was just that she could have sworn she recognised one of the patricians under the elaborate costume, but surely she was mistaken. True, the blood that ran in Marcus Cornelius Orbilio's blood was as blue as the Aegean in August, but of all the young aristocrats the Vestals could choose from, would they really pick the only patrician attached to the Security Police? She tapped her finger against her lip. When ambitious young investigators set their sights on the Senate, chance went out of the window, but there was no time for misgivings. Having raised the subject of feasting and revelry, Arval wasn't too happy that two of his brothers had stolen his thunder.

'Father's not only hired entertainers from all round the world,' he cut in swiftly, 'but thanks to my baby brother here,' he landed a mock punch on Leon's shoulder, 'he's managed to persuade Barrekub to recite some of his work for us this evening.'

'Barrekub?' Claudia goggled. Surely he couldn't mean *the* Barrekub? 'Not the famous Persian poet?'

'The very same,' Arval said. 'It's a measure of the esteem in which the bard holds his star pupil — ' this time he ruffled Leon's hair ' — that Barrekub has deigned to travel all this way to Rome. The old boy rarely leaves Athens these days.'

A Persian living in Athens? Just as well the old wars were a long way behind them.

'It's a tremendous honour for the family to welcome him

into our house,' Sergius intoned. 'Perhaps Claudia would consent to being my consort at the recital?'

Arval glowered, and the word *Objection!* all but hung in the air. Outmanoeuvred, a lesser man would have acknowledged defeat and retreated. But, of course they were brothers; competitive wasn't the word.

'Leon,' he said, 'has a real gift.' The others nodded. 'The rest of us are professional animals. My discipline's law, Paulus is a financial genius and Sergius is going to be a real thorn in the political side before too many more years are out, isn't that right?'

The orator tried to look modest and failed. Strangely, it only added to his masculine appeal.

'I won't say we're not good at what we do,' Arval added, 'because we are. Bloody good. But none of us has a shred of creative talent the way Leon here has — '

Leon's chest swelled out his tunic.

' — and for that reason, it would be a privilege,' Arval concluded, 'if we could stage a private recital of his work for you.'

Boom. In an instant, the outwitted had outfoxed them all and she laughed. The other three brothers might be escorting this entrancing young beauty throughout the festivities, but these were passive gestures on their part. Arval, on the other hand, had initiated an event purely for Claudia's gratification. The competition was hotting up nicely!

And so it was that, as the patricians performed their intricate symbolic movements to the haunting tune of a flute, her own senses danced in tandem. The piece Leon had chosen concerned the conception of Helen of Troy and, as the Salian Dancers gyrated in their sacred armour, Claudia shivered — and not from the wind that whistled down from the Capitol.

... many times all-knowing Jupiter watched the daughter of the Spartan king stroke the swans that drew sea-born Venus's gleaming chariot. Thus did he wait, biding his time, until black-winged Night cradled the horns of the moon in her arms ...

Leon's cadences were so subtle, his wording so fine, that she experienced the same pulsating passion that Helen's mother felt when Jupiter came to her disguised as a swan. She sensed the gentle brush of a lover's wing against her cheek. Imagined herself being drawn into his soft, downy embrace ...

Still reliving the heady mix of awe and excitement that rippled through Helen's mother when, instead of a giving birth to a daughter, a hyacinth blue egg appeared from her womb, it took Claudia a moment to realise that the dancers were out of time with the flautist. Or at least that one of the dancers was out of rhythm, and that his leaps were in completely the wrong direction as he elbowed his way through the crowd.

Then the music stopped, and Claudia also heard the screams.

Her first thought, upon seeing the body sprawled across the flagstones in the kitchen, was just how much blood the human form normally manages to keep contained. Her second, that the assailant was nothing short of a monster.

'Thank you for coming,' the dancer said.

His voice was a rich baritone and, even beneath the smells of abandoned cooking, burnished armour and the stench of clotted blood, she detected a faint whiff of sandalwood as he knelt over the body.

'You know me.' She dusted off one of her most dazzling smiles and flashed it at him. 'Anything to help the Security Police.'

Two hours had passed since a dark-skinned pastry slave, bored with a ritual she didn't understand and too short to see over the crowds anyway, slipped back to the warmth of the kitchens and tripped over Barrekub's body. Two hours. Claudia twisted the ring on her finger. How long did it take the Ferryman to row to Hades? Would he have shipped his dark oars by now? Or was the journey colder, and longer?

'I thought you were off duty,' she said, shuddering.

'Surely you, of all people, know the Security Police are never off duty?' he tossed back with a grin.

The more urbane, the more dangerous, and if there had ever been a hope that Marcus Cornelius Orbilio had forgotten about her various frauds, tax dodges and what was that other thing? oh, yes, forgery, this was a timely reminder that she was out of luck.

'Is it true you're related to the Fourth Vestal?' she asked.

It was a shot in the dark, but he hadn't been picked to perform this dance at random, and for heaven's sake, what were young women *supposed* to do when their aged husbands pop off across the River Styx leaving all their worldly goods behind? Of course, she could have sold the wine business — many times she'd wondered why she hadn't — but dammit, the old buzzard had slogged his entire life to build that up, and she was buggered if she'd sit back while his so-called friends carved it up like some common spit-roast! She just wished someone had warned her that expenditure greater than income equals one hell of a slide. The sort, it would seem, that attracted investigators like wasps to ripe fruit.

'Senior Vestal, actually.' His eyes crinkled wickedly at the corners. 'She's my second cousin twice removed.'

'And does she hang upside down in the cave at night with you?'

'Only in the summer months. We hibernate in winter.'

He was lying, of course. Bears hibernate. Wolves prowl all year round. 'You realise you're the only person in Rome who doesn't believe the cook was responsible for the Maestro's death?'

After all, the cook *was* Barrekub's nephew — a post that Leon had wangled as a favour for his illustrious tutor — and the pair of them *had* been at each other's throats ever since the old man arrived.

'Uh-uh,' Marcus said, and when he twisted his neck for a better view, sunlight from the little window bounced off his breastplate. 'There are at least two of us who share that opinion.'

'You've never heard guilty men protest their innocence?'

'You've never heard rich men proclaim that murder's bad for business?'

So Dexter was pushing to get this high-profile case closed with the loudest of snaps? What was wrong with that, when faced with a cook in blood-stained clothing and the not unreasonable assumption that the younger, stronger of the protagonists had decided to settle the dispute once and for all? 'Dexter wants the issue resolved,' she said, 'not hushed up, and in any case, not every crime has to be complicated.'

The squabbling had been in Persian, of course, but the general gist seemed to be that the cook wasn't as grateful for landing the job as the famous bard had expected, claiming that accusations of cronyism had resulted in a distinct lack of respect among the kitchen staff, to which Barrekub replied that if the boy was no good at his job, don't go blaming him — from which point matters tended to escalate.

'Very loudly, I understand,' Marcus said.

Claudia suppressed the sigh that was threatening to

surface. It was the nature of his work, she supposed. Accustomed to intricate conspiracies and complex assassination plots, he'd lost the capacity to differentiate between something really fishy in the air and a simple plate of tuna marinating in wine for tonight's banquet.

'Have you ever known Persians argue in a whisper? Their tempers are even louder than their clothes.'

Renowned for eye-wateringly bright colours, baggy pantaloons and shoulder-length tong-curled hair, they sported skull caps in summer, fur collars in winter, and even the poorest tied bows on their shoes.

'The expression "standing out in a crowd" was expressly invented for these people,' she added.

'With scarlet stripes on a cloak already bordered in purple, I am in no position to criticise another man's dress code,' Orbilio murmured, examining the wounds to the head. 'Excessive force, wouldn't you say?'

Claudia had no intention of looking in that particular direction ever again. She concentrated on the ornate decoration of his shield, currently propped up between the wood stove and a wine jar.

'I've dropped eggs on a tiled floor and seen fewer breaks on their shells,' she said quietly. 'But if Barrekub was killed in a passionate outburst, it fits.'

The shields were ancient; shaped in a figure-of-eight. In the past, soldier priests would beat them with swords to drive out the old year, then repeat the dance to usher in the new campaign season. Things had moved on a lot since those days.

'Passion, but not compassion.' His mouth twisted. 'Isn't it strange how two words so similar can mean something so opposite?'

'Not as strange as seeing his body still lying here.'

It was usually the first thing people did. Have the corpse taken away on a bier purified with laurel, in order to sanctify the blood that had been spilled in violence.

'The undertakers forgot it was the first of March, when the city decks itself with bay to honour Mars.' Orbilio's smile was pure innocence. 'I told them they'd need to use yew. It is the death tree, after all.'

Claudia pursed her lips. 'How far away is the nearest yew?'

'Another hour, with luck.'

'And Dexter swallowed your story?'

'Not my story.'

He was quick to point out that it was the undertaker who convinced the head of the household that the rules concerning purification must be followed to the letter. Not him. And until the body was shown the respect it deserved, arrests were out of the question.

'How many favours did the undertaker owe you?'

'Enough.'

Fine. As a trained investigator, Orbilio didn't believe the cook had killed Barrekub over a petty squabble and was buying time while he worked out whether it was the butcher, the baker or the candlestick maker who'd clubbed the bard's skull to a pulp. Claudia didn't see why he should have sent for her, though. Unless — Unless —

'Sweet Janus, you suspect one of the family!'

He straightened up and examined the heavy iron frying pan lying beside the body. 'I'm ruling out suicide.'

Around the walls, strings of onions, garlic and herbs were coloured with the poet's blood, contaminating the air with its stench. Arcs of red spattered gridirons and ladles, pastry moulds and egg-beaters, and, across the trestle tables, Dexter's gourmet dishes were fast becoming a feast for the blowflies. Claudia would never look at honeyed quail again without her stomach heaving.

'One word keeps going round in my head,' Marcus said.

'Only because there isn't room for any more.'

A muscle slanted one side of his mouth. 'The word "why",' he continued. 'Why was Barrekub killed in the kitchens? Why did he make such a long journey from Athens, and why in the winter as well?'

'He has family here.'

'One nephew?'

'Just because they argued, it doesn't mean they weren't fond of each other.'

She thought she heard him mutter *I'll drink to that*, though it made no kind of sense. 'What's wrong with Barrekub making the trip simply to stage this performance? Audiences are oxygen to a poet, and no audience is bigger than Rome.'

'People made pilgrimages from all corners of the Empire to hear him, not the other way round.' Orbilio leaned back on his heels and quoted from "The Song of the Sirens". *'Mothers held up their hands to the immortal gods and prayed that the Spirits of Death would not fall upon their sons — '*

' — while Grief wrung her hands at the edge of the battlefield as the dust from the fighting ran muddy with tears.'

He had a point. Goosepimples were already rising up on her skin.

'Even so,' she insisted, 'rather than arrest the one person who has been arguing night and day with the dead man, in his own domain no less, and whose clothes also happen to be soaked in the victim's blood, our trusty sleuth prefers to point the finger of suspicion at one of the wealthiest, one of the most influential, not to mention one of the most respected families in Rome?'

'Why, Mistress Seferius, I do believe you have it in one.'

'Did I mention that there isn't a single spot of blood on any of the family's clothes?'

'Did you mention that it's customary for the family hosting the Salian Dance to change into laurel green for the ceremony? Incidentally, that's a very becoming shade you are wearing yourself.'

If Claudia couldn't convince Calpurnia that dressing in this particular colour was coincidence, there was little point in trying to get it past the Security Police. (And damn that kitchen girl for sneaking back early and screaming her bloody head off! Couldn't she have shivered for another ten minutes, until everyone who was anyone in this city had seen the young widow Seferius alongside Dexter and his family wearing exactly the same shade of green?)

'Seventy-five men sit on a jury, Orbilio, and not one of them is going to accept the prosecution's argument that this killing was deliberately engineered round a change of clothes.'

'Well, that rather depends on how strong the argument is presented,' he said cheerfully, 'and what other evidence is submitted to the court to back it up.'

'You have other evidence?'

'Um…' He scratched the lobe of his ear.

'Motive?'

Slugs sprinkled with salt squirm less energetically. 'Let's say I have a hunch.'

'Nothing a decent tailor can't hide.'

'Seriously,' he said, straightening up, 'are you going to help me convict them or not?'

'No.'

'Very well. I'll have to prove it without the benefit of your razor-sharp insight.'

'*What* insight?'

'I saw you playing eeny-meeny-miney-mo with Dexter's sons. Which one did you choose, anyway?'

'None of your damned business.'

'It is, if one of them turns out to be a killer.'

'Marcus Cornelius, you are the most arrogant, the most stubborn and positively the most perverse man I've ever met.'

'You missed out pig-headed, but otherwise it's a fairly accurate assessment.'

Claudia heard a grinding sound, and realised it was her teeth. 'Has it ever occurred to you that you might be wrong?'

Much less the consequences, once the marble merchant found himself humiliated in public and without reason! No matter that Orbilio could trace his ancestors back to the sun god, Apollo. His career would be over before it had started.

'If I'm wrong, then I'm wrong,' Marcus said, and his face was unusually solemn. 'But seriously, Claudia.' He swirled his cloak over his shoulder and winked. 'When have you ever known that?'

Afternoon rolled into evening and, as the tempo of the celebrations increased, harps gave way to trumpets and drums, fire jumpers leapt through flaming hoops in the courtyard, and an Arabian snake charmer coaxed a cobra out of its basket. With the wine flowing ever more freely, the laughter grew louder, the conversation more raucous, and as people retreated from the chill winter air, so the temperature in the villa rose too. Wall-mounted braziers crackled and spat as the resins wafted scents of the Orient over the atrium, and fountains danced by the light of a thousand oil lamps, bringing the mythical beasts on the frescoes to life. Claudia recognised drunken satyrs, the Minotaur, Medusa who turned men to stone, while down the length of the portico ran the epic that had inspired young Leon. The Siege of Troy, beginning with the woman who'd started it all. Helen, hatching out of a swan's egg. Death did this, of course. Everything seemed to lead back to the poet. Association was everywhere Claudia turned, but she had learned this before. Violent death could not be outrun …

'Are you all right?' She didn't hear Dexter approach. Only smelled the mint on his whispered breath. 'That must have been ghastly for you, seeing Barrekub in the kitchens like that.'

'I've had better experiences.'

A comforting hand supported her shoulder blade. 'And you will have better in the future, I promise.' Dexter smiled. 'Much better.'

He snapped his fingers and unseen hands filled their goblets with a dark, smoky red that had been ageing in casks of oak.

'Candied cherries, my lady?' a slave girl murmured. 'Dates stuffed with almond paste?'

Claudia waved the plate of sweetmeats aside. Wine lees rubbed into her lips and cheeks had taken the paleness away, but the nausea remained locked inside. *Such ferocity …*

'I'm proud of my sons, they're fine boys,' Dexter was saying, 'and when I see you young people getting on so well, you've no idea how it makes my heart sing.'

'What tune does it play when Calpurnia sees me?'

When he laughed, the silver strands in his hair reflected the lamplight. 'You have a sharp wit, my dear. Precisely the reason I am so impatient to hear your decision — I presume you have *made* a decision?'

'Oh, yes.'

'Excellent.' Something dark glinted in Dexter's eyes. 'What —?' He cleared his throat as he slipped his hand under her elbow and led her to a quiet corner. 'What did he want?'

'Who?'

'That investigator chappie. The second he saw poor Barrekub lying dead, he shooed everyone out of the kitchens, even before he started asking his questions, then an hour or so later he sent for you. Since it was hardly an act of chivalry, confronting a young widow with that grisly sight, I was curious.'

As the host of today's riotous festivities, he had every right to wonder, but Dexter wouldn't have been the only one — murder traditionally generates interest — and Claudia had been prepared for the question all evening. Making quite certain the wine in her glass didn't stain her green gown, she fainted prettily into his arms.

'There, there, my dear,' a solicitous voice crooned. 'Try to lie still.'

Coals in a bronze tripod wafted their gentle heat round a chamber in which music from the festivities was reduced to an indistinct muffle and the laughter no more than a murmur. The lifting of half an eyelid confirmed that Claudia had been stretchered to a distant corner of the villa to allow the invalid to recuperate untroubled by the clashing of cymbals, guffaws or shrieks, and where teams playing *Hide and Seek* wouldn't burst in. The eyelid closed again, and she allowed compresses drenched with lily-of-the-valley to be laid over her forehead as the physician pronounced a combination of exhaustion and over-excitement as the cause of her collapse.

'Nothing vervain tea can't put right,' he added jovially, 'but right now my patient needs rest.'

Please Jupiter, let another medical emergency demand his attention before that infernal mixture arrived, and fortunately for her, the King of Olympus had tasted the stuff, because within five minutes the door closed with a clickety-click and now just one set of lighter, female footsteps were echoing over the mosaic.

'You can drop the act,' Calpurnia said crisply. 'I've sent the physician away.'

Men might be taken in by an elegant swoon, but Dexter's wife was nobody's fool. Claudia tossed the compress aside and swung her legs off the bed.

'Keep away from my sons,' Calpurnia hissed. 'All of them, do you understand? I will not have my husband's mistress flaunting herself around my family as though she was part of it.' Her eyes raked Claudia's laurel green robe. 'You are not, and you never will be.'

'Has it crossed your mind that I might not be Dexter's mistress?'

'Oh, please.' Calpurnia's eyes rolled in derision. 'You stage that pathetic little show then end up in this lovenest? Don't insult my intelligence.'

Lovenest? The fresco over the bed depicting Jupiter's seduction of Danaë as he came to her in a shower of gold might be a tad suggestive, and, sure, Dexter's womanising was legendary, but that was no reason for Calpurnia to jump to — Wait. Scented sheets? A quiet, empty room kept warm by charcoals? A jug of wine and two goblets on the table? Claudia's mind travelled back to her arrival and an embrace that was perhaps a fraction too tight and which lingered perhaps a fraction too long.

I very much hope you will be joining my domestic arrangements on, shall we say, a rather more intimate footing.

She'd been thinking in terms of marrying off that lump of a stepdaughter to one of his sons (Arval seeming the best bet), while Dexter had been thinking …

Your wit is precisely the reason I am so impatient to hear your decision — I presume you have made a decision?

So much for hoodwinking the family physician! Dexter, like his perspicacious wife, would have construed her faint as an invitation to make her his mistress, something this chamber suggested he'd taken for granted, with the doctor privy to the conspiracy. But for heaven's sake! What gave Dexter the idea that thinning hair and a paunch made him attractive? Didn't the man own the mirror? Not that there was any point explaining this to Calpurnia; the woman would never believe her. Far better to let her think she had won. Especially since her life was about to be turned upside down ...

'You're quite right,' she said, fumbling for her sandals. 'It's late and I should be getting along.'

'Just a moment.'

Something metallic flickered in the lamplight and Claudia saw that Calpurnia was holding a key in her hand. Belatedly, the clickety-click of the physician's departure replayed in her head and she recognised not the sound of a door closing. Rather the sound of a door being locked —

'You have something I want.'

'I … do?'

Green eyes narrowed, the way a leopard's does when it's picked out its kill. 'I am tired of playing games with you, Claudia. Hand me the scroll.'

High in the sky, the moon shone white through the bare branches of the oaks and the fruit trees. The city would be white with frost by the morning,

'This won't solve anything, Calpurnia.'

'I'll take it anyway, if you don't mind.'

'As you wish.'

From the folds of her gown, Claudia withdrew the charred remains she'd salvaged from the bread oven beside Barrekub's body. Large chunks of parchment had snapped off as she'd unrolled it, but sufficient text remained for one of the excerpts to leap out.

...many times all-knowing Jupiter watched the daughter of the Spartan king stroke the swans that drew sea-born Venus's gleaming chariot. Thus did he wait, biding his time, until black-winged Night cradled the horns of the moon in her arms ...

'Subtle, emotive, but above all — ' She stared long and hard at the singed scroll. 'Above all, familiar.'

It was word for word from the scene Leon recited earlier. 'Now I could be wrong,' she said steadily, 'but I'll bet the reason you want this scroll is to stuff it back in the fire, because these Persian curlicues strike me as somewhat distinctive.'

Unmistakably, this verse was written in Barrekub's hand.

'I've worked hard to see my sons rise to where they are now,' Calpurnia rasped. 'Not their father. Me. I engaged the appropriate tutors, sounded out the best universities to fit their abilities, hustled contacts to help my sons climb. Not Dexter. *Me.*'

Claudia swallowed. Something was happening here that she did not understand. 'You have every right to be proud.'

'Every right,' Calpurnia echoed. 'It's me they owe everything to — '

Why was Claudia getting the impression the boys didn't see it that way?

' — and nothing will prevent them from rising to the very

pinnacle of their chosen professions. I will make certain of that.'

Even to covering up murder, it seemed.

Claudia pictured Leon creeping in to his mentor's room, gradually committing the bard's work to memory. What had gone through his mind when Barrekub turned up in Rome, and as a guest of his father no less? What thoughts churned in his head when he realised the only reason the old man had made this long journey was to expose him with the handwritten proof? All the same …

'You wouldn't honestly send an innocent man to execution?'

'The cook killed Barrekub,' Calpurnia replied flatly. 'They'd been quarrelling incessantly and his clothes were drenched in the old man's blood.'

Only because he cradled his uncle's corpse! 'Does that man's life really mean so little to you?'

A soft snort escaped from Calpurnia's nose. 'You count working from dawn till dusk in a room full of smoke, steam and sweat a *life*? My son is a poet.'

Claudia felt something cold congeal in her stomach.

'Your son is a plagiarist and you cannot protect him for ever. Sooner or later he'll be found out, and before he runs out of bards to kill, isn't it better that he owns up now? Explain how Barrekub caught him in the act of burning the evidence, Leon lashed out, and it was just unfortunate the old man's skull was so thin?'

Not half as thin as that defence. Croesus, a man can strike out once in panic, but several times?

'No one is explaining anything.' Calpurnia's eyes were harder than the ice on the pond. 'This is not going to court.'

'What about Arval?' That's what lawyers got so much

money for, wasn't it? Getting guilty men off the hook? 'He can argue a good case for self-defence — '

'Self-defence! When the old fool was bent over the bread oven trying to fish out his precious — '

She stopped, and two pairs of eyes locked.

Calpurnia's, because she'd realised she'd just admitted battering Barrekub's skull to a pulp.

And Claudia's, because she knew there was no way Calpurnia would let her leave this room alive ...

Time stood still. Claudia could only watch as Calpurnia snatched up the candlestick, blew out the flame and tossed aside the still-dripping candle. She cast around for a weapon to defend herself with. There were none, and the key to the door was in Calpurnia's hand. Could she reach the window, unlatch the mechanism and shin over the ledge before the candlestick made contact? Could she hell.

'Wife and mistress fight over lover. Wife wins,' Calpurnia said.

'You will keep making the mistake that I'm your husband's whore.'

Claudia made a feint to the left. It was blocked.

'Your naked body will tell its own story.' Calpurnia advanced carefully. 'I suggest you start saying your prayers.'

Jupiter had already answered one plea tonight and Claudia wasn't sure he'd fork out for another. She dodged to the right, but Calpurnia blocked that move, as well. To start a fire from the charcoals would take too long, while to upend the oil lamps would roast them both alive. Grabbing the wine jug, she hurled it at the window. The glass shattered. Claudia waited. Nobody came.

'Scream if you want.' Dammit, the bitch was enjoying herself. 'No one will hear you down here.'

Even if they did, they'd think it was one more rowdy party game. Calpurnia had chosen her moment well.

'Orbilio will come looking for me.'

Shards of glass make sharp knives, but Calpurnia saw this and barred the route to the window. Claudia shuffled a few paces backwards.

'Oh?' Calpurnia sneered. 'Since when have the Security Police taken an interest in their host's bedtime athletics?'

No wonder she was so bitter. For thirty-five years she'd had to put up with her husband bedding his floozies under her nose, and for thirty-five years she'd never got used to it. Could Claudia turn this to her advantage?

'Dexter, then.'

A few paces more.

'My husband wasn't expecting you to capitulate quite so quickly, my dear. Until the Consul and his wife leave, you're on your own, and as you know, the Consul has always been a night-owl.'

'You stay with a man who puts business before pleasure and takes no interest in his own family?' Claudia's back hit the wall with a sickening jerk. 'Doesn't that make you the same as his whores?'

Calpurnia was too cool for for provocation. Exactly how she must have been when she planned Barrekub's murder, Claudia realised. Selecting a time when everyone was gathered outside to watch the Salian Dance, even the slaves, to seize the poet's scrolls, knowing he would follow her down to the kitchens. What reason had she given Barrekub for holding back from joining the others? Had she asked him to accompany her for the ritual? Who cared. The point was, the bard was where she knew he would be; the household was where she knew they would be; she could kill Barrekub, destroy the evidence and frame the cook in one swoop. Brilliant, in its own way.

'That poor sod was dead from the moment he confronted you.' Claudia's voice was surprisingly steady as she focussed on the candlestick that was advancing closer with every second.

'He was dead from the moment I overheard him reciting his verse in the atrium,' Calpurnia corrected, and her smile was as cold as the Styx. 'I saw no reason to let matters escalate.'

She was almost within striking distance and, with a chill, Claudia realised the bitch had no intention of bringing the weapon down on her head. She was looking to break an arm and incapacitate her first, then no doubt she would inflict a few scratches on herself once Claudia was dead, to make the scene look convincing. Calpurnia swung. Claudia ducked, but it was only a matter of time before instinct made her put out an arm to defend herself, and once the first swing connected, it was all the chance Calpurnia needed —

'Did you think you could best me?'

The candlestick swung again, and this time Claudia felt a whoosh of air on her cheek.

'Did you really think you could take me on and win?'

'You know the trouble with a posh upbringing?' Claudia grabbed the damask bedspread by its corner. 'You girls never get to play *Gladiators*.'

Swirling the counterpane, she encompassed her opponent with a flourish many an arena master would be proud of. Of course, *Nets and Tridents* was never her favourite. She'd much preferred fighting with shields made of old leather with and boar tusks found on the middens; that way you got to stick feathers in your headband and pretend it was a crested visor. But the flick of the wrist was still second nature and memories of the hidings she'd received for reducing family blankets to ribbons flooded back.

'Bitch!' the bedspread screamed. 'I'll kill you for this! I'll see you ruined and rotting in hell!'

But even as Claudia brought it crashing to the floor, she knew she could not hold Calpurnia for long. The woman was strong, she was angry, fury ensured she felt no pain. Whereas Claudia had no weapons except her fists, and already she was starting to tire. The candlestick was still under the bedspread, so was the key, she couldn't reach a pillow to smother the woman and the window was too far away. As Calpurnia kicked and raged beneath her, tears began to well. Was this full March moon was the last she'd ever see?

Then the door burst open in a blizzard of splinters. Light from the corridor flooded the bedroom and Claudia caught a faint whiff of sandalwood unguent.

'Vervain tea, anyone?' Marcus said.

'Now there's a sight I never expected to see,' he said, clamping a pair of reassuringly solid-looking handcuffs round Calpurnia's wrists. 'Claudia Seferius riding bareback on a bucking bedspread.'

Behind him, four legionaries hauled a hissing harpy to its feet. Its language was enough to make two of them blush.

'These coverlets are more dangerous than they look,' Claudia said, and someone had filleted her legs, because there was nothing left now but jelly.

'They're perfectly tame providing you feed them live mice twice a day.'

As he lifted her onto the bed, she decided that his arms were reassuringly solid-looking, too. Not to mention his chest, which seemed perfectly positioned for resting wet cheeks against.

'You realise I nearly got myself killed because of you?'

'So this is my fault?'

His tone was jokey, but his eyes, she noticed, were dark and full of pain. Jupiter, Juno and Mars, if she lived to be a hundred she'd never understand men.

'Don't try to weasel out of your responsibilities, Orbilio! And next time you embroil me in one of your devious schemes, kindly have the courtesy to come up with a cover story beforehand, because how on earth I was expected to explain — what are you doing?'

'Looking for a quill and parchment,' he said. 'This needs to be recorded urgently.'

'That Calpurnia killed Barrekub because Leon plagiarised his epic?'

'Leon didn't plagiarise Barrekub, it was the other way around.' He leaned his shoulder against the door jamb and played with the splinters. 'The bastard had been at it for years, stealing his pupils' work, but such was his reputation, who'd take a callow student's word over a legend?'

That was why Barrekub made this trip, he explained. As she so rightly said, audiences were what made a poet's life worthwhile and no audience was greater than Rome. With Leon's prodigious talent, Barrekub sought renewed fame and when he asked his star pupil to give his nephew a job, Leon could hardly have suspected that his good deed had been designed to reduce his status to that of mere toadie.

'Barrekub asks his pupils to jump, they say how high,' Orbilio continued. 'Would they do this for a man they didn't respect? A man whose words came from someone else's head? Of course not. Like countless students before him, Barrekub had Leon pinned like a winkle and if anyone complained, he could shoot down his detractors with the written proof and come out smelling of Persian roses.'

'I thought poets were supposed to commit these things to memory?'

'Memories can't be used in court.'

Orbilio knew all along, Claudia realised. It was why he didn't arrest the cook, in spite of the overwhelming evidence. *Why was Barrekub killed in the kitchens?* he'd asked. *Why make this long journey from Athens, and in the wintertime, too?* He already knew the answers, of course, and since he'd been in the kitchen for a couple of hours, he also knew about the scroll in the bread oven and, having planted seeds of doubt in Claudia's mind, knew she'd go back and poke around for herself.

'How did you know the bard was a fraud?'

'Accusations surfaced from time to time, although they were quickly suppressed.' His expression was grave. 'As a child, I remember hearing rumours of a youth who'd hanged himself, claiming he'd written "The Song of the Sirens", not Barrekub.'

Grief wrung her hands at the edge of the battlefield, as the dust from the fighting ran muddy with tears.

Didn't it just, Claudia thought bitterly. Didn't it bloody just...

'We said passion was the key to this murder,' she said, 'and we were right.'

Barrekub's passion for glory, Calpurnia's passion to protect her sons, and the tragedy was, if only Calpurnia had funnelled that passion in the right direction, she'd have had Barrekub whipped in a week. Bullies rely on their victims being cowed and intimidated. Dammit, with one son an orator, another a lawyer and the youngest one a brilliant poet, Calpurnia could have eaten the old man for breakfast and still found room for a steak.

'Ironic, isn't it?' Orbilio pushed away the thick wave of hair that had fallen over his forehead. 'Poetry killed the poet.'

What was ironic was that Claudia suddenly had no sympathy for either the dead man or his killer, and her growling stomach reminded her that she hadn't eaten since yesterday evening.

'If it isn't Calpurnia, what needs to be recorded so urgently?' she asked, linking her arm with his. (Purely for support, you understand).

'Isn't it obvious? That on the first day of March in the eighteenth year of the Emperor Augustus, Claudia Seferius was rendered speechless.'

'Very funny.'

'I thought so.' He paused by the banqueting hall and looked down at her. 'So there's going to be a next time?'

'Excuse me?'

'You said the next time I embroiled you in one of my devious schemes, I should come up with a cover story. Well, I've just thought of one. There's this case I'm working on at the moment — '

Which *reminded* her. 'Surely solving a murder counts for something?'

'I'm not with you.'

Why did he always play the damn innocent! 'I'm thinking immunity from that tax thing, perhaps?'

'You've still lost me.'

Very well. If he wanted to play games — 'Orbilio, exactly why did you come here today?'

'Ah.' He rubbed his hand over his jaw. 'You mean what makes a grown man dress up like a performing dog in the freezing cold then make an ass of himself in front of the whole city outside the very house where a certain young widow is playing eeny-meeny-miney-mo with the four most eligible bachelors in town?'

He leaned forward and his eyes were the darkest she had ever seen.

'Don't you understand?' he rasped. 'Don't you realise it's passion that brought me here, as well?'

She blinked. All that, simply because he was a patrician and proud of his heritage ...?

'Correction. If I live to be a *thousand*, I'll never understand men. Now do stop dithering, Orbilio. I am famished.'

'And I will never understand women,' Marcus laughed. 'What do you fancy? Oysters? Sucking pig? Partridge stuffed with white truffles?'

Credit where it was due. His wife might have been carted off in chains, albeit it discreetly out the back, but for Dexter, arch-businessman and entrepreneur, the show must go on. None of the high-level guests knocking back his wine or clapping his rope-walkers suspected a thing, least of all the Consul, and Claudia suddenly understood what it was that made Dexter so powerful. Already, thirty-five years of marriage were being washed down the drain as he began to distance himself from Calpurnia.

'Don't care,' she said. 'I'm that hungry, I could eat anything.'

Well. Her thoughts flashed back to the kitchens. Anything apart from eggs.

While meeting with Julius Caesar, the Egyptian Queen Cleopatra finds herself witness to murder. And discovers that the worst part about betrayal is that it doesn't come from your enemies.

THE WINGS OF ISIS

'So then.'

With two clicks of the imperial fingers, the handmaidens fell back in a wave, but it took an imperial glare before Kames, Head of The Queen's Bodyguard, retreated his men out of earshot as well. Cleopatra had to lift her head to look into the eyes of her Captain of Archers.

'What are they saying about me this time, Benet? That the Queen speaks nine languages fluently and can't say no in any one of them?'

Spies, deep undercover, kept her abreast of the scheming and plotting among her so-called trusted Council. Feedback from the common people was no less important.

Benet swallowed his smile. 'Nothing of the sort, your Royal Highness. Your people are behind you all the way in—' He paused, ostensibly to adjust his swordbelt. '—In Egypt's alliance with Rome.'

'Your tact will make you a general some day.'

And a good general at that, Cleopatra decided. Benet was a born tactician, intelligent, brave and not too dishonest.

Above all, he was that rarest of breeds, he was loyal.

The eagle of Rome was casting a shadow across virtually the whole of the civilised world. Iberia to Asia Minor, Libya to the Black Sea. Now that Julius Caesar had his sights set on the great prize of Egypt, the pickings were rich for, say, an ambitious young Captain of Archers for whom the matter of allegiance rated low on his list of priorities.

So far, Benet had shown no desire to serve himself above his country. But it would be foolish to take such loyalty for granted ...

Boom, boom, boom-a-doom-a-dum-dum. The pounding of the drums, soft and insistent, cut short the briefing.

'We'll talk later,' she told him.

Information could wait.

Mighty Isis could not.

Boom, boom, boom-a-doom-a-dum-dum.

The memory of those lazy drumbeats would stay with Cleopatra for the rest of her life. They encapsulated the point when she walked into the temple a queen — *and walked out a goddess.*

From this moment on, Cleopatra was to be worshipped as Isis incarnate. It was official. She was now the Great Mother, protectress of the Pharoah, goddess of healing, fertility and magic. Ah, yes. Never underestimate the power of magic, she thought. Rising from the throne of solid gold as the ceremony drew to its close, Cleopatra felt the brush of the goddess's wings on her face. And the wings were beating in triumph.

As she made her way across the cool marble floor of the temple, she passed Yntef the shaven-headed high priest, sweating under his leopard skin, his eyes still unfocussed from his recent trance. Renenutet, the priestess of Bast dressed as the cat-headed goddess, made obeisance. As did Tamar,

Hathor's priestess, wearing the ceremonial mask of the cow. Temple musicians lined the aisle, their harps and reed flutes playing the Queen out. The choir sang softly — young women, whose voices had been trained from early childhood to sing as sweetly as the larks which soared above the broad wheatfields of the Nile and lifted the spirits of those who laboured to bring home the harvest.

Glancing back over her shoulder, Cleopatra committed the moment to memory. The temple regalia, the black bowl of divination, the fat sacred cats, the dark ceiling studded with bright silver stars. Flaming torches high on the walls brought brightly painted frescoes to life, made them dance. Acrobats on the north wall, fishermen hauling home their nets on the south, Anubis weighing the heart of Osiris against the ostrich feather of truth on the east. Best of all was the fresh painting on the west wall: Cleopatra as Pharoah. Let the Council take the bones out of that!

Boom, boom, boom-a-doom-a-dum-dum.

As the mighty cedarwood doors of the temple swung inwards, the Queen suddenly faltered. Priests and priestesses, acolytes, the crowd outside — all would naturally assume she had been blinded by shafts of brilliant white sunshine. They could not possibly know that, for an instant, Cleopatra had forgotten where she was. That, when she stepped into the light, she had been shocked by the alien world into which she had been propelled.

A world which babbled not only too fast, but in Latin.

A world where, in place of the calm, green waters of the life-giving Nile, the Tiber ran, brown and rancid, its lush banks long since vanished under warehouses and wharves. Despite the heat of the sunshine, she shivered. This was a world inhabited by fair-skinned people whose women were chattels, handed over from father to husband without rights, and whose men swaddled themselves in thick woollen togas, even in this merciless heat. There were other differences, too. These barbarians burned their dead. Bent their knee to feeble human gods in devotions which were no better than common horse-trading.

Yet these people ruled the world...

It had been easy, while Yntef conducted his ritual divination, the cloudy water swirling in the bowl beneath a film of warm and scented oil, to forget she was no longer in her beloved Alexandria, gazing out from her palace across the Great Sea, feeling its cool breeze brush her lips. Instead Cleopatra was in Rome. A city that, to many, represented the very heart of the enemy ...

All eyes were upon the Egyptian Queen as she descended the temple steps. Precious stones had been woven into her heavy plaited wig. Amethysts, emeralds, sapphires and pearls, every facet reflecting back sunlight. Bangles and bracelets encircled ankles and arms. Each finger was adorned by a ring, as was each toe, and round her neck hung a shining pectoral of gold. There were times, and this was one of them, when Cleopatra could barely hold herself upright with the weight of the metal but, far from home, her people needed the reassurance of the pomp and the ceremony.

In short, they needed someone to look up to.

Someone to believe in, in these turbulent times.

At the foot of the steps, she held up a hand to stall her bodyguard and beckoned over her Captain of Archers. 'You were about to tell me, Benet, what the people of Alexandria really feel about Cleopatra's liaison with the Roman dictator. Do they fear I am selling them out?'

Benet had still not grown accustomed to his Queen's forthright manner. It sat strangely at odds with the long-winded words of her political advisers, and he often wondered how she juggled court etiquette with her compulsion to drive straight to the core.

'Far from it,' he replied quietly.

Across the flagged courtyard, shaded with acacias and sacred sycamore trees, Kames scowled his resentment at a mere captain's confidence with the young Queen.

'When Julius Caesar stormed the palace in Alexandria three years ago,' Benet said, 'your Majesty's people saw hope die in the dust of his four thousand troops.'

'Go on,' Cleopatra urged.

She was not blind to Kames' scowls. Benet indeed walked a tightrope, but not in the way Kames imagined. Noble from birth, as with everyone else in authority — Kames, included — the Captain of Archers was blessed with the common touch. An ability to tap into the Alexandrians' innermost feelings, secure their trust, assure them their confidences would not be betrayed. Perhaps, she reflected idly, this was because precious little of her own, highly interbred Macedonian blood ran through Benet's veins. Benet was a true-born Egyptian.

'By the time Rome trampled the city,' he said, 'our own Regency had betrayed its people twice over. First, with the coup which exiled your Majesty in Syria. Then by taking a stand against Rome, a force they could not hope to beat, instead of entering into negotiations. As a result, Egypt believed itself yoked to Rome's plough with no chance of salvation — until, oh munificent Ra! — the Queen smuggles herself to Caesar wrapped in a rug, and overnight the balance of power swings again!'

It hung unsaid that Julius Caesar imagined that, in Cleopatra, he would be manipulating a soft, sweet puppet queen …

'From the moment your son was born, your Majesty, the

people have embraced Caesarion as Egypt's heir. Nothing, I promise, has changed in the ten months you have been absent.'

Cleopatra darted a glance across to the boy who lay cradled in his nurse's arms, his rosebud lips slightly parted in sleep. Caesarion. Little Caesar. She smiled fondly. Who would suspect the child's exquisite public behaviour owed more to a splash of poppy juice on a sweetmeat than a well-trained royal disposition? Caesarion was a lusty two-year-old, with a lusty two-year-old's energy and a lusty two-year-old's lungs. His mother had no intention of curbing either. That boy was the future Pharoah and his spirit would never be tamed. Indomitable through inheritance, that spirit would soar. *Higher than his father's eagle it would rise. And the breadth of its shadow would be unsurpassed …*

'You wouldn't lie to me, Benet?'

Why should the common masses back her, when half her Council rejected Caesarion's claim to royal blood and believed the Queen wielded far too much power as it was. Power, which should rightly be theirs —

The Captain of Archers looked deep into her eyes. 'I would never lie to you, your Royal Highness.'

He knew full well that the eighteen-year-old chit who had mounted the throne on Ptolemy's death had not proved the pliable young thing these shadowy figures had hoped. A truth the Roman Dictator had yet to discover …

'Good.' She flashed Benet a wicked grin. 'Because the last man who betrayed me died the Death of One Thousand Cuts, the first slicing off his treacherous tongue.'

His eyes smiled. 'A point I shall bear in mind in the future— *Holy Ra!'*

Cleopatra's head turned in the direction his, and fifty others, were turned. For once, she was unable to control her gasp of surprise. Renenutet, still wearing the silver mask of the cat, was standing, arms outstretched, on the roof of the

House of Scribes. Her pleated linen gown billowed softly round her ankles in the sticky breeze.

'Renenutet!' The high priest's voice carried its full weight of authority. 'Renenutet, in the name of Isis, I command you —'

The screams cut him off.

For a few ghastly seconds, Renenutet seemed to hang in the air. A white pleated cloud frozen against a backdrop of azure.

Then the billowing gown disappeared —

Kames was the first to react. In an instant, his soldiers had surrounded their Queen, tried to hustle her through the nearest doorway for safety.

'Don't be ridiculous,' she snapped. 'It's not me that needs helping, it's Renenutet. Kames, take some men and see if you can do anything for her. Benet. Go with him, if you will.'

The Captain of Archers met her eye and nodded in mute understanding. If Renenutet's fall had proved fatal, it was from him that she wanted to hear it.

As the soldiers trotted off, their bronze helmets and greaves jangling, Cleopatra's instinct was for her child.

'Take Caesarion home,' she instructed his nurse.

She must remove him at once from this tainted scene.

'No, wait.'

It would not do to have Pharoah run from a crisis. Even if he *was* only a babe and fast asleep!

'Tuck this into his clothing instead.'

She handed his nurse the amulet Renenutet had given her earlier.

'The sacred amulet of Isis,' the priestess had hissed, her voice barely recognisable under the silver cat mask.

Flushed with the priesthood's recognition of the Queen as Isis incarnate, the public attestation of their powerful support, Cleopatra had barely glanced at the tiny object when

Renenutet pressed it into her palm.

'Set with carnelian,' she'd whispered, 'washed in a tincture of ankhamu flowers, fashioned from the trunk of a sacred sycamore tree.'

This had been at the very start of today's ceremony, at the moment the priestess was supposed to pay homage to her Queen and nothing else. To cover the delay, Renenutet pretended to disengage the panther tail which hung at her waist from Cleopatra's gold belt, as though the two had become somehow entangled.

'Isis is the goddess from whom all being arose,' she murmured, her eyes glittering behind the metal mask. 'From her feathers came light. From the brush of her wings came the air. She is the Enchantress, the Speaker of Spells, who protecteth the living and extendeth her protection even beyond, unto eternity.'

Oh, Renenutet. You should have kept the amulet, Cleopatra thought, picturing the nightmare vision of Renenutet frozen in space. You should have kept the amulet to protect your own soul from self-destruction.

'Let the wings of Isis cover you instead, little Caesar,' she whispered, stroking her son's soft, dark hair. She bent to kiss his cool, dry forehead and wondered how long the effects of the poppy juice would last. As she straightened, Kames and Benet came striding across the shaded courtyard, their white kilts swinging in unison. Their expressions said it all.

'I deeply regret, the priestess Renenutet has already begun her long journey to the West,' Benet said softly.

The two men knelt beside the Pool of Purification and allowed the priests to splash their eyes with sacred water to wash away the contamination of having gazed upon a corpse. Cleopatra felt no disrespect. To have deferred the task would have been to taint the Queen with their polluted sight.

Poor Renenutet, she thought. A suicide. Whose imperfect

soul was destined to wander the dark paths of the Underworld for ever. 'I suppose we shall never know what drove her to take such drastic action,' she added sadly.

'On the contrary,' Benet said. 'I know exactly what drove the poor woman across the Far Horizon.'

He hesitated. Pursed his lips.

'Someone else's hands,' he said quietly. 'Renenutet, I regret to inform you, was murdered.'

Whether for business or pleasure, the Field of Mars on which the temple complex stood was arguably one of the busiest places in Rome outside the Forum. Sited on a bend in the Tiber, it was home to seven other temples, as well as a whole host of public baths, theatres, race courses and libraries, offering works of art to admire, tombs to revere, groves to picnic in, trees for the children to climb, steps on which bearded philosophers could debate the meaning of life and open spaces for athletics. The air was never silent. Until now. Snake charmers stopped playing their flutes. Beggars bowls ceased to rattle. Peddlars stopped hawking. Only the jackdaws continued to chatter.

As the Dictator's concubine esconced in the very villa from which his lawful wife had been evicted, Cleopatra was accustomed to being gawped at by the populace. Suddenly, like wasps to honey, they swarmed to the scene of the drama, but their interest, thank Horus, lay not in the dead priestess, rather in the bejewelled Egyptian whore. Cleopatra could handle that standing on her head. No person, living or dead, had ever witnessed a crack in her armour. They certainly would not do so today.

However! As the consort of the most powerful man in the

Roman Republic, she was also expecting a different kind of attention. Any minute, Caesar's legionaries would arrive.

She turned to Kames. 'I assume from your contemptuous tutting that you disagree with Benet's conclusion?'

'Your Majesty, we *all* saw what happened,' Kames replied. 'There was no one else or we'd have seen them. With respect, that roof's flatter than the sole of my boot.'

The Queen turned to her young Captain of Archers and raised one finely plucked eyebrow in query.

Benet inhaled. Released his breath slowly. 'Because of the angle at which the body was lying, because of *where* it was lying, close to the wall, because the blood which had dried round the head wound doesn't correspond with the copious amount of fresh blood inside her mask — all that adds up to only one thing. Renenutet was murdered.'

Kames' bluster was shot out of the water. At last, he understood what the Queen saw in Benet. Drawing himself up to his full height, he cleared his throat and squared his shoulders.

'Benet's deductions are correct,' he admitted. 'Renenutet leapt off with arms outstretched, yet the body was found with one arm pinned beneath it. Likewise, when a person jumps they make a trajectory.'

'A trajectory?' she queried.

'Imagine throwing a javelin or spear from that roof, your Highness. This is the same principle. The body lands at the end of that arc. Renenutet, as Benet said, lies close in.'

Kames dropped to his knees, his forehead touching the ground.

'Your Majesty, as a soldier I should have recognised the signs —'

How fortunate, Cleopatra thought, to have two such pillars to lean on. Benet, alert to nuances, unafraid to put forward an unpalatable theory. Kames, man enough to admit his mistakes. *Or clever enough to know he could no longer get away with the suicide theory ...?*

'Don't whip yourself, Kames,' she said, bidding him rise. 'You fell into the same trap we all did. You took Renenutet's death at face value.'

Hobnail boots echoed on the Via Triumphalis, the rhythmic clink-clink-clink of scale armour, the jangle of bronze medallions as the legionaries drew closer. Grief and shock would no doubt set in later, but Pharoah was raised to consider emotions an indulgence — never more so in a crisis. As the centurion halted his troops, Cleopatra summarised the points in her mind.

The priestess Renenutet had been murdered.

Renenutet ... priestess of Bast.

Bast ... the gentle daughter of Isis.

Isis ... Protectress of the Pharoah.

Cleopatra steepled her fingers. More crimes than murder had been committed today. Sacrilege for one. The sanctuary of the Great Goddess had been defiled by the spilling of blood. Furthermore, the outrage of Bast had been invoked by the assault on her priestess.

But worse than that, by embroiling the Queen in this apparent suicide, someone had tried to pull the wool over Cleopatra's almond eyes.

And that was their biggest mistake.

In retrospect, she should have realised Caesar would not let it go at a lowly centurion.

Cleopatra studied the corded muscles of the man dismounting from his pure white stallion, noted the purple stripe on his tunic which pronounced him patrician. He had a strong face, a handsome face, and in spite of herself a shiver of desire rippled the length of her backbone. Contrary to rumours put about by certain viziers, the Queen had only ever taken one lover, and that had been a matter of expediency. The gods do not bestow virginity for it to be taken lightly. The night she had had herself smuggled through enemy lines in a rug, knowing that if she was discovered her own kinsmen would cut her throat like a dog, was the night she had given herself to the Roman Dictator.

Fast track negotiations, some might say.

The Regency had usurped the throne. Cleopatra was in exile, Alexandria was in the hands of the rioters, the palace in the hands of the Romans. To survive, she had had to act fast. Her first move was to throw her army of Syrian mercenaries behind Caesar. Afterwards —? Well, what greater assurance of Egypt's allegiance than the Queen's precious virginity?

Men. Such fools, she thought. In seducing the young Cleopatra, Caesar believed he was annexing the rich lands of the Nile through the back door, a mission he could not hope to accomplish by force. But with his entrenched Roman attitudes towards women, he had not stopped to contemplate the alternative. That she might be using him ...

Within days, Cleopatra achieved her first goal. She conceived. In the simple act of giving him an heir, something Caesar was sorely lacking, the tables turned. By the time Caesarion was of an age to rule, his father would be dead. *And Rome would be annexed to Egypt, not the other way around!*

In a journey which had taken her from royal princess to queen to pharoah to goddess, Cleopatra quite literally held the power of the world in her hands.

The power felt good.

Nothing — and no-one — would be allowed to change that.

Which wasn't to say her blood could not be stirred by a lopsided smile here or a bunched muscle there! Benet, although he did not know it, was one such contender. The patrician dismounting from his stallion, another.

'Your Highness,' he murmured, making obeisance Egyptian fashion.

'It is good to see you again, Mark Anthony.'

Nothing would come of these flirtations, of course. Cleopatra was neither stupid nor reckless — she had Caesar in the palm of her hand, and with it the eagle of Rome. But Caesar was old, he was bald and, let's be frank, when it came to the art of love, his was more a quick sketch than an intricate fresco. Other décor could still be admired.

'Caesar salutes you,' he said, rising, 'and offers his escort to the Queen, that she may return to the villa without incurring unwarranted scrutiny or gossip.'

The weight of so much gold jewellery was exhausting her, the heat from the wig almost unbearable. But when Cleopatra smiled at Mark Anthony, you would think she had just risen from her bath, calm and refreshed.

'The Queen sends her grateful thanks to the mighty Caesar,' she replied.

Heavenly Horus, she would need all her diplomatic skills here! Strictly speaking, she was a foreigner on Roman soil, subject to Roman law. If the most powerful man on earth decreed she must leave the Field of Mars, then leave she must and in the three years they'd been lovers Cleopatra had never gone head-to-head against the Dictator's wishes. Let him think he was in control. Illusion was everything.

'But the Queen has no desire to impinge upon Caesar's generosity,' she told Mark Anthony. 'The Queen shall be remaining at the temple.'

The tall patrician blinked. 'Is that wise, your Majesty?' Likewise, only a fool would go against *Cleopatra's* wishes.

Julius Caesar would not wish to lose his hold on the Nile's treasures just because some clot upset his mistress!

'Wise is a contentious word, Mark Anthony.'

She linked her arm through his and led him to the shade of the Pool of Peace, where papyrus plants swayed in the hot, sultry breeze. The silvery sound of sistrums filled the air and fragrant incense filtered out from the temple.

'Was it wise of the Queen,' she asked, as handmaidens fluttered up with plates of fresh fruit, 'to devalue Egypt's currency by one third in order to keep export sales strong? Or a gamble which happened to pay off? Was it wise of her to have her portrait stamped on our coinage, to prove to the world that Egypt's economy was stable in the hands of a woman? Or was it nothing more than female vanity?'

Cleopatra dabbled her hands in the cool, clear water.

'For that matter, was it wise of the Queen to muster an army of mercenaries to fight her own brother? Or simply the banner waving of a power-mad female with no hope of success?'

'Life, I agree, is entirely a matter of perspective,' he said, a twinkle lighting his eyes. 'Which is precisely why I am now offering my services to escort you personally to the safety of Caesar's villa.'

Cleopatra bit into a peach. 'Your concern is touching, Mark Anthony. Unfortunately, it would be disrespectful for me to leave until the rites are over.'

When the Roman General smiled, the lines round his eyes fell into deep crinkles. 'The ceremony finished an hour ago,' he pointed out, selecting a cherry.

'To honour Isis, yes, but we have yet to venerate the cobra goddess and sing the hymn to Nut,' she replied, and watched as he bought himself time by slicing an apple.

Mark Anthony had not bought the lie. True, he was ignorant of the rites conducted here, but he was keenly aware that a surprisingly large number of Roman women made devotions at this shrine. Isis had become popular in Rome, more so since the Queen's arrival last September, when additional aspects had been added. Bast, for instance. Hathor the cow. Plus numerous other female deities who, together, presided over motherhood and love, beauty and healing, all the issues important to women, Roman or otherwise.

Mark Anthony might not know the details. But he knew, dammit, when a ceremony was over and done with. Selecting a date, the Roman General changed tack.

'Listen to the baying crowd,' he said. 'Perhaps the Queen does not appreciate how much resentment her royal presence causes in the city ...?'

'The Queen knows *exactly* how Republicans view the concubine and her bastard son,' she said tartly. 'Keep the mistress — flaunt her, even — is the general consensus. After all, the Queen of Egypt is a prize for Caesar to parade, is she not? Just don't play house with the whore.'

Another lie. Marital scandal was a minor issue, the cause of gossip rather than resentment. The real fear among the Senate — Mark Anthony included — was for the future of their hard-won Republic. They suspected Cleopatra of dripping poison in the Dictator's ear every night to serve her own ends.

They were not wrong.

Come next March — no later than April — she would have Julius Caesar declare himself King of Rome, with herself crowned as Queen. Upon his death (and who knows how quickly that might come to pass) Caesarion would inherit the title.

Then all of Rome's dominions would belong to Egypt—

The scent of the oil of marjoram drenching her wig wafted in the sultry air. The gems glistened like raindrops.

'As to the mood of the crowd, my answer is this,' she said carefully. 'Rome likes its spectacles. I say, let the people enjoy this one.'

Renenutet was murdered on the sacred soil of Isis wearing the insignia of Bast. Now that Cleopatra was to be venerated as Isis, this comprised a triple sacrilege and the perpetrator must be punished. Pharoah could not simply walk away this afternoon. It was her duty to stay and see justice served. In any case, she thought sadly, she owed it to Renenutet to find her killer. Renenutet should not journey into the West without the feather of truth on her shoulder. The journey was long enough as it was.

She held out a small, sandalled foot.

The sparring light in the General's eyes died. She inched her foot out further. His expression darkened. There was no mistaking the Queen's message.

Or defying it ...

As Mark Anthony knelt to kiss the royal toe, anger and outrage pulsated from every Roman pore. He! an aristocrat! a general! one of the world's greatest power brokers! had been ... *dismissed!* There was a very different glint in his eye as he rose.

She watched him stride away, barking orders to the centurion to keep the crowd back. One day, she reflected, this man would return for more of the same. His type always did. And Cleopatra would be waiting.

Inside the sanctuary, prayers were being said for Renenutet's journey into the Afterlife. Yntef, Tamar and the rest of the attendants had lost no time in shaving their eyebrows. They would have done this, had just a temple cat died, much less one of Bast's holy disciples.

The atmosphere inside the sanctuary pulsed with emotion.

Cleopatra glanced at the sky. The sticky, midsummer heat could not last and the first rumble of thunder could be heard in the distance. Excellent. She would be able to interpret the storm as Bast's anger made manifest. Thunder would be the cat goddess's growling, lightning her ferocious spitting. Magic and superstition played a pivotal role in Egyptian life. Only a fool would fail to capitalise.

'Benet. Kames.' She beckoned them over. 'No one is to suspect this was not a straightforward suicide.' If the Romans sniffed murder, this would become a civil investigation. Much better to keep these things in-house. 'We will deal with this quietly, between the three of us. Do either of you have any clues as to who killed her?'

'None,' Benet admitted. 'But we know Renenutet was killed inside the temple.'

Cleopatra's eyes flashed. Was there no end to the insult? 'How can you be sure?'

'There is only one place on this site where people must bare their feet, even your Majesty. Inside the sanctuary. Renenutet was barefoot.'

Cleopatra picked up a sloe-eyed kitten mewing at her feet. The kitten began to rattle like a chariot over cobblestones, snuggling its head into her collarbone.

'Anything else?' she asked.

'Dried blood around the head wound suggests Renenutet died an hour before the simulated suicide —'

'How do you know?'

'Dead bodies don't bleed,' Kames explained. 'The blood was probably that of a chicken's, poured into the mask at the last moment to make it look fresh. Also, her skin was cool.'

Slowly, Cleopatra laid down the kitten. If Renenutet had spoken to her at the beginning of the ceremony, when she passed across the amulet, but had been dead for some time after Benet examined the body, there was only one conclusion. She died *during* the ritual. Meaning the killer had contrived to use the Queen of Egypt as his alibi.

Another mistake.

Beside the Pool of Peace, with butterflies and bees swarming round the fragrant flowers in the urns and thunderclaps booming ever closer, Cleopatra's memory travelled backwards in time.

It returned her to the soaring temple. Closing her eyes, she saw its star-studded ceiling, just as she had seen it earlier, the dynamic wall paintings flickering beneath the flaming torches. In her mind she once more inhaled the sacred incense, a rich blend of frankincense and myrrh, cedar and gum arabic, juniper, cinnamon and sweet flag. Her ears re-played the lazy beat of the drums — *boom, boom, boom-a-doom-a-dum-dum.* She was mounting the dais again, only everything now moved in slow motion.

'Homage to thee, Isis,' the choir sang, *'whose names are manifold and whose forms are holy. Gracious is thy face.'*

At the time, Cleopatra had hardly listened, concerned only that she had won over so powerful a body as the priesthood. With their support, the vipers in her Council could scheme until the sun set in the North and still not get their hands on the throne.

'You are the north wind that bloweth in our nostrils. Your word is truth.'

Beside the pool, Cleopatra's head pounded. From the heat, from the weight of the gold, from the hot heavy wig. From wondering how on earth Renenutet could have been killed beneath her very nose. She concentrated on re-living the ceremony...

'O, Isis of a thousand names, who watcheth over us.'

The nightingales had finished their chant. Silence had descended over the sanctuary. The flames on the torches had been dimmed. From a side door, a score of acolytes entered, each carrying a small gilded cage in reverent, outstretched hands. Gliding in long pleated skirts, they mounted the steps of the platform. The cages were lined up, side by side on the floor, the eyes of the occupants flashing like fire in the gloom. With a synchronised click, the catches were sprung and twenty temple cats tumbled on to the dais in honour of Bast. Renenutet, Cleopatra remembered, had gone forward to feed them.

She recalled, too, how Renenutet and Tamar assisted the High Priest in his divination. Supporting him when he fell into his trance. At his side when he pronounced how beneficent Anubis had shown him how the heart of the Pharoah was happy, how the heart of Osiris was glad, and how the two halves of Egypt would always be one.

'May Isis embrace you in her peace, Yntef,' Cleopatra had replied solemnly, using the *ankh* to make the ritual gesture over his head. 'For the ka of her High Priest is holy and Anubis has shown him the truth. The heart of Isis is full of joy at her servant's devotion.'

Translation : Yntef would be richly rewarded for throwing his support behind the throne.

She pursed her lips in concentration. Remembering how Yntef, unsteady still from his trance, had been helped away by Tamar as Renenutet bestowed upon the imperial wig the sacred crown of Isis, the solar disc cradled between the twin horns of the moon. The priestess's breathing beneath the replica mask had been laboured, Cleopatra recalled. But she was certainly very much alive –

'Your Majesty?' Benet's shadow fell over the pool.

'Ah, Benet, just the man!' The royal headache had vanished. The gold weighed as a pectoral of feathers round her neck, the plaited wig a gossamer veil.

'Have you worked out how the trick was done?'

The Captain of Archers returned the smile. 'I have indeed, your Royal Highness.'

'Good,' she said. 'Because if you can tell me how, I can tell you where and when.'

Between them, it should tell her who.

The how had been ingenious. The trick as audacious as Cleopatra had ever known.

'The key,' Benet explained, 'is a metal spike hammered into the brickwork at the junction of the wall of the House of Scribes and its flat roof. Wrapped round the spike were these.' He held out a few coarse fibres of hemp from a rope.

An elaborate pantomime had been staged, he explained, which hinged upon no lesser person than the Queen of Egypt witnessing what was supposed to have been a dramatic suicide. Renenutet on the roof, her arms outstretched. Renenutet jumping to her death.

The killer, though, had reckoned without Benet.

Benet was the Queen's spy and spies never take one damn thing at face value.

'The murder was carefully planned,' he told her. 'During the ceremony, that spike was hammered into the brickwork and a short piece of rope attached to it, with a noose at one end.'

Cleopatra's heart twisted. When that first lazy drumbeat began, Renenutet had no idea her thread of life had less than an hour to unravel. Except ... the priestess of Bast had sensed danger! It had been with force and urgency that the sacred amulet of Isis had been pressed into the Queen's hand. At the time, Cleopatra dismissed it as a token of Renenutet's acceptance of herself as Queen of Earth and Heaven. She should have realised. No priestess, especially one of Renenutet's standing, would need to pretend her sacred panther's tail had become entangled, had the gift been open and above board! Renenutet had passed the amulet in secret.

'Now I shall tell you when and where Renenutet was killed,' she said.

After she passed Cleopatra the amulet, the ceremony had continued as scheduled. The choir extolled the virtues of Isis (in other words a public proclamation of the priesthood's support), then the lights dimmed.

That was the moment Renenutet's thread was severed.

As she slipped out of the sanctuary to fetch the procession from the Sacred Cattery, two people were waiting. As one snatched off the silver mask, the other threw a sheet over her head.

'What odds her skull was crushed by her own metal mask?' Cleopatra said. 'The sheet would contain any splatters of blood.'

The killers had no time to waste cleaning floors. One was already clad in ritual robes. All she had to do was don Renenutet's mask and run swiftly to the Sacred Cattery. Only a few seconds would have been lost and while she was fetching the feline procession, her accomplice carried the body away, arranging it beneath the House of Scribes.

'She?' Benet queried.

'Definitely,' Cleopatra confirmed. 'The killer had to impersonate Renenutet for the remainder of the ceremony. Only a servant of Bast could possibly have known the routine.'

In due course, when the temple cats had been released from

their cages on the dias and the lights went up again, who would suspect that Bast's representative was not Renenutet? It was only, thinking back, that Cleopatra remembered how laboured the priestess's breathing had been when she lowered the horned headdress on the royal wig. The killer's hands had shaken slightly as well, she recalled. Not from the heat or exertion. But from nervousness!

'Afterwards,' Benet said, 'the impersonator climbed up on the roof. She slipped the noose from the rope round her ankle. Waited until her Majesty was looking. And jumped.'

No wonder Renenutet seemed to hang in the sky, Cleopatra thought. That was precisely what had happened. The rope suspended the killer in mid air. Dangling like a fish on a line.

'The accomplice at the upstairs window in the House of Scribes threw another noose around her wrist,' Benet said, 'cut the rope around her ankle and hauled her inside. Then they filled the cat mask with animal blood and stuffed it on Renenutet's head. Plenty of time before anyone else arrived at the scene.'

For several moments, Cleopatra listened to the thunder, watched jagged spears of lightning cut through the charcoal sky. Lost in contemplation, she did not even notice as the first heavy drops of rain fell. Finally, she summoned the Head of her Bodyguard and together all three withdrew into the shelter of the painted portico.

'Kames, I want you to observe the priestesses of Bast and, discreetly mark you, isolate the one with rope burns on her wrist and ankle. I suspect they are covered by bandages.'

Cleopatra almost regretted doubting the head of her bodyguard's loyalty. Then again, to make assumptions about even her most trustworthy cohorts was to open herself up to danger.

'Her accomplice will be a priest or a scribe,' she added. 'Someone with regular access to both buildings, strong enough to heave corpses around and he'll probably have a bloodstained sheet beneath his bed.'

The killers would not have expected events to move so swiftly. They would not have needed to take extra precautions at this stage.

In less than an hour, Kames returned. 'A novice priestess called Berenice and her lover, Ity, have been quietly removed from their duties,' he said. 'Shall I send them to the Royal Torturer for confession?'

Cleopatra shook her head. 'Have your men smuggle them out of the temple, take them into the hills. Oh, and Kames.'

'Your Majesty.'

'Be sure they bury the bodies deep.' As he left, she turned to her Captain of Archers. 'Benet, I want you to remove a few handfuls of silver from the Temple Treasury, also a small but precious statuette. Have it put about that Berenice and Ity stole them and ran off.'

Caesar might not agree, but this temple was every bit a part of Egypt as Alexandria itself. Pharoah's justice would be served — only today it would be served in secret. Only a few hand-picked soldiers would ever know Berenice and Ity had killed Renenutet, and she imagined the ill-fated lovers would be regretting the deed long before Kames' men had finished with them.

'Why?' Benet asked. 'Why did they kill Renenutet?'

Cleopatra glanced across at her son, struggling out of his drugged sleep, and pictured the amulet tucked inside his clothing. An amulet set with carnelians, washed in the tincture of ankhamu flowers and fashioned from the trunk of a sacred sycamore tree ...

'I doubt we shall ever know, Benet,' she said, tapping him cheerfully on the arm. 'Now, off you go and rob the Treasury, there's a good boy.'

She snapped her fingers and two handmaidens scampered forward. 'Fetch my litter,' she ordered. 'We shall return to Caesar's villa.'

I do believe Mark Anthony has stood in the pouring rain for long enough.

Five days afterwards, Cleopatra was seated next to Caesar as guest of honour at the games inaugurated to commemorate Rome's victories in Gaul. As befitting the Queen of the Upper and Lower Nile, she wore a gown shot with silver threads, a headdress set with amethysts and enough gold jewellery to turn Midas green with envy. The one hundred thousand Romans crammed into the surrounding tiers ought not be disappointed, she thought happily.

Syrian lions roared from the pits. Baited bulls bellowed, bears snarled, wolves howled, elephants trumpeted their rage. First in the arena, a half-starved tiger, to be pitted against a trident and net. The human did not stand a chance. After that, beast fight followed beast fight in rapid succession, and Cleopatra's gorge rose at the senseless shedding of blood, the death of so many splendid specimens.

Then it was the turn of the gladiators, their swords and lances gleaming in the sun. She watched, impassive, as steel clashed against steel. Blood spurted, bodies writhed, heels kicked up clouds of sand as Roman fought Roman to the death. From the corner of her almond eye, Cleopatra watched Caesar size up the crowd. How much did they back him? he was wondering. How far they would follow him? Would they accept a monarchy in place of their hard earned Republic?

As always, Cleopatra pretended not to care. She slipped her small hand into Caesar's. Showed the people — and the Senate — that it was Caesar she loved. Only Caesar ...

To the backdrop of trumpets, attendants dressed as gods of the Underworld hauled the mangled corpses away in chains, threw fresh sand over the blood. The crowd was insatiable. Stamping their feet they bayed for the next treat, the despatching of murderers and rapists by wild animals.

There seemed to be some activity at one of the gates. Guards conferred hastily. Glanced at the Queen. Conferred again. Then one of them made a decision. Marching over to Cleopatra, he pressed his clenched fist to his breast in salute.

'One of the prisoners insists there has been a mistake, my lady. We don't believe this is the case, but – well, he is Egyptian and swears your Majesty will vouch for him.'

'Bring him over,' she said, in her perfect Latin.

Two guards frogmarched the prisoner across. One eye was closed, his body bruised where he'd put up a fight.

'Your Highness,' he gabbled, 'tell them they've got the wrong man. Last night some thugs set upon me and the next thing I know, I'm here. In a cage full of murderers awaiting execution.'

Whatever did you expect, she wondered silently. You plant seeds of dissention in the minds of two idealistic young lovers and incite them to murder Renenutet under the Queen's nose. She leaned closer, pretending to examine his features. Features that fully expected to kill, get away with it – and then be shown the Queen's mercy.

'I have never seen this man before in my life,' she told the guard.

'But your Majesty–! It's me, Yntef! Your High Priest.'

Cleopatra smiled pityingly at Caesar. 'My High Priest is on a boat bound for Alexandria,' she murmured. 'To take up his new promotion.'

Let's face it, one shaven-headed Egyptian looks the same as

another to a disinterested Roman. Only the temple servants would know that Yntef had been replaced. And even they would not know the reason …

She watched impassively as Yntef was dragged away, protesting at the top of his voice. The crowd loved it. They would love it more, she thought, if they knew the full story.

Her mind travelled back to the beginning.

Coincidence that it was here, in Rome, that the priesthood chose to throw their support behind Cleopatra? Hardly. Had this happened in Egypt, that would have been different. But it all took place in the back of beyond, and why?

Because the priesthood did not back Cleopatra at all.

That most powerful of organisations had thrown its weight behind the traitors within her own Council. Oh, yes. The bastards planned to have her assassinated in Rome, knowing damn well the finger of blame would point to the Senate, who hated Cleopatra with a vengeance.

Just before the ceremony, Renenutet must have discovered Yntef's treachery. That was the reason she pressed the amulet into her hands. Set with Isis's sacred carnelians, washed in a tincture of the goddess's consecrated ankhamu flowers and fashioned out of the trunk of her sacred sycamore tree, no object was more holy, more sanctified, more precious in Renenutet's eyes than that which invoked the Great Mother's protection.

The amulet had been the warning. That was why she'd passed it in secret. But that loyalty cost Renenutet her life.

Yntef knew she was on to him. Enlisting the help of two sympathisers to the cause (heaven knows how many more vipers there were in the nest, but Benet's skills would root them out and Kames's men would do the rest), the High Priest was forced to eliminate Renenutet in a way that would not arouse suspicion. Set some distance from the temple, the House of Scribes allowed ample time for his accomplices to stage their pantomime then pretend to come rushing up with the others.

Once Cleopatra realised who had killed the priestess of Bast, the motive behind the murder was obvious. Yntef would have known if anyone other than Renenutet had been holding him as he came out of his trance. That meant Yntef was in on it.

Oh, dear Yntef. All those hymns and blessings and public acceptance of the Queen as Isis incarnate, How they backfired. You see, it's all very well to pretend the priesthood backs Cleopatra — provided Cleopatra is dead. Now they've made their support public, the priesthood has no choice but to stand by their decision. The die has been cast. The Queen wins. Best of all, Yntef's failure will have created division among the priesthood and the Council in a way that Cleopatra could only ever have dreamed off. Each would now suspect the others of selling them out. Trust among the conspirators would crumble like sand.

Instinctively, her hand reached for the amulet round her neck. In bestowing Isis's protection, Renenutet had saved the Queen's life at the expense of her own, but she would not go unrewarded. Plans for a sumptuous tomb were already being drawn by the Queen's Architect.

The rewards also extended to the spiritual plane.

Two of Renenutet's killers lay in unmarked graves, where, without proper burial rites, their souls were doomed to wander the Halls of the Lost for eternity. Now the third member of the trio was poised to look retribution square in the face. Kames's men had done well in delivering him to the Roman arena.

With a snarl, a panther bounded into the arena.

Bribes had ensured the beast had been tormented with

prods, whips and firebrands, and it had also been starved and denied water. Yntef screamed. Behind her, the crowd cheered and stomped on the wooden boards of the amphitheatre, unaware of what Yntef was seeing.

The figure of Bast incarnate. Leaping to avenge her devoted disciple.

As the panther sat back and licked its bloody lips, Cleopatra felt a brush of soft, white feathers against her cheek. Once again, the wings of Isis were beating in victory.

Paul Simon reckons there are 50 ways to leave your lover. I reckon it's easier to poison them.

TRUNK CALL

When a man lies on his deathbed, it is, of course, customary to send for his wife. But with Rufus Vatia, purveyor of Imperial elephants, wouldn't you just know that *three* women would turn up, each laying claim to the title? For two days now they'd been pacing his tiny apartment up on the Palatine, stiff with suspicion and hating each other's guts— yet these three women stuck like glue. Fearful lest one gained an edge on her rivals.

The sun rose. The sun set. And now it had risen again, its fiery ball casting long autumn shadows across the seven hills of Rome, its heat swirling white mists over the Tiber, enshrouding the brown sludgy waters which churned beneath the arches of the bridges. Another month and there would be frosts twinkling across the city's red tiled roofs. Would Rufus Vatia, the ultimate practical joker, live to see them? Or would Death have the final laugh?

On the table, in the corner, between a carved ivory jackal and a terracotta lamp, an old-fashioned cylindrical water clock relentlessly dripped away his allotted mortal span ...

From time to time, the women took turns visiting the sick room, returning though, only moments later, thin-lipped and shaking their heads, but today the physician had taken the unprecedented step of banning all visitors. The only exception he'd made was for Milo, Rufus's almond-eyed steward, who continued to waft in and out with his trays on silent, padded feet.

For the very first time, everything on those trays was coming back untouched.

So the three contenders sat.

And waited.

And watched.

The clock dripped on. Occasionally, one of the women would half-rise, think better of it, then sink back into position, and Claudia, observing them from the corner of her eye as she leant against the marble flank of a rearing Spanish stallion, was reminded of a pack of hyenas waiting for the stumbling beast to finally drop. The analogy was more than apt.

Africa had been the dashing trapper's life, and across his walls antelope and lion, wildebeest and zebra thundered across the open plain, while flamingos dabbled in the margins of a pair of double doors painted to resemble a lake.

Except that the young wine merchant with the flashing eyes and tumbling curls had not come to admire the artistry in the hunter's crowded apartment ...

'I could be wrong,' whispered a baritone in her ear, 'but I have the distinct impression you've been avoiding me.'

'They do say that's the first stage of paranoia,' Claudia replied, although when he followed her behind the statue, Marcus Cornelius Orbilio found himself completely alone.

'Claudia. Please.' He managed to catch up with her beside a painted hippopotamus. 'You've got to help me out here,' he hissed under his breath.

'My pleasure.' The young wine merchant smiled, keeping

her gaze on a rampaging rhino. 'The exit's just past the flamingos.'

Orbilio contrived to have his head turned by the time his grin slipped out and forced himself to ignore the gentle curve of her collarbone and the waves of her spicy Judaean perfume. This was a professional visit, he reminded himself sternly. The Emperor, being as fond of the charismatic trapper as he was of the showpieces themselves, had despatched a representative from the Security Police with a single, clear-cut objective. To thwart any scandal, stamp it out. Orbilio rubbed his jaw with the back of his hand and tried not to reflect that failure would unquestionably result in some far-flung posting abroad.

'Rufus Vatia is dying,' he pressed, weighing up the prospect of scorching Nubian deserts versus cold, damp Pannonian plains. 'My job is to establish which of those three has a genuine claim on his estate.'

Claudia tilted her head at a painted giraffe. Was it her imagination, or did the poor beast have a squint? 'Knowing Rufus's sense of mischief,' she said, 'he would have married them all.'

'Bigamy?' Marcus felt his shoulders sag. That was all his career prospects needed! And suddenly, as he glanced across to Rufus's hard-eyed harem, his original notion of fraudulent claims seemed achingly appealing —

The hunter would be what - forty? Forty-two? With half his year spent under hot African skies, trailing, trapping and transporting elephants for the Emperor's extravaganzas, it was obvious that that easy smile and lean tanned body was never going to settle for a good book on a long winter's evening and a ballad or two on the lyre!

Not when our friend Rufus could coax a sweeter tune from that sultry Arabian beauty buffing her nails in that high-backed satinwood chair.

... Or test the voluptuous charms of the girl who now sprawled lengthways on his couch, one smoky sage-green eye keeping a permanent vigil on the water clock.

... And certainly not when he could melt into the soft, milky blondeness of the creature who stood twisting her rings by the window!

'You really think these could be bigamous wives?'

'Actually.' Claudia flashed him a wicked sideways grin. 'I know it for a fact.'

A fishhook clawed in Orbilio's gut, and he battled the urge to ask the question which was uppermost in his mind. Instead, he said levelly, 'Then I suppose I should turn my investigations towards which of the three Rufus married first?' He put strong emphasis on the *three,* but Claudia did not seem to notice.

'I wouldn't waste my time, if I were you,' she said. 'The whole thing's academic.' She began to edge away from her tall, dark, human shadow. (Dammit, the last thing she wanted was the Security Police sniffing around!) 'You'll find our man Rufus is as fit as a flea.'

'Fit?'

Orbilio followed so fast, she had to check that his belt buckle hadn't snagged in her gown.

'Claudia, his steward is laying cypress round the front door and weaving funeral garlands of oak!'

'Milo can run naked round the Forum for all I care,' she tossed back, 'but trust me on this, Rufus is *not* at death's door.'

Marcus smiled indulgently. 'I think you'll find you're mistaken,' he said. 'I've spoken to the physician and he's adamant —'

'I may have my faults, Orbilio, but being wrong isn't one of them.'

The young investigator might have been able to suck in his cheeks, but he could not disguise the twinkle in his eyes. 'Remind me again when and where you studied medicine, will you?' he said.

'One doesn't need to have taken the Hippocratic Oath to work this one out,' Claudia retorted. How many men do you know who, when they're supposed to be standing at the ferry landing about to cross the River Styx, suddenly lurch out of bed to pinch a girl's bottom? She resisted the urge to massage the bruises and said instead, 'Our handsome trapper is up to something.'

I just don't know what it is yet!

'Wait, wait.' Marcus pinched the bridge of his nose. 'Let me get this straight. You think this deathbed stuff is some kind of *prank?'*

'Oh, you can bet your fine patrician boots on that.'

Except you're not the only one who can play games, Rufus, my old mucker ...

Outside, a horse whinnied as it stumbled in a pothole and a flock of goats not sold at market bleated their way back up the Palatine Hill, but Claudia was oblivious to both. Nor did she hear the squeals of children playing hopscotch in the street, or the foghorn voice of a pie-seller over the road. No, no. Whatever sport the wily trapper was engaged in, she could match him move for move, no doubt of that. What *really* bugged her was why he had —

The collective gasp of female breath made her spring round.

Three sets of kohl-rimmed eyes were fastened on the ruffled head of the physician, which had now appeared round the bedchamber door. His young face was the colour of porridge.

'I'm sorry.' He shrugged his thin shoulders to the assembly in general, though his gaze remained fixed on his sandals. 'I-I did everything I could ...' His blue eyes were tortured. 'But — I'm really sorry — Rufus is dead.'

'Impossible!' Claudia barely noticed two of the women jump out of their seats, or the other slump to the floor. She was too busy pushing past the ashen-faced medic. 'No-one drops dead from a simple cough and a sneeze!'

At first she'd thought it a joke. That Rufus would burst through the door, laughing. But there was no doubt the doctor was telling the truth. His face, his voice said it all.

'It was the quinsy,' he murmured.

'Listen.' Claudia spun round to confront him. 'When I want a medical opinion, I'll go straight to the undertaker and cut out the cost of the middle man.' This clot typified the reason why she never called a doctor. Mistakes they bury, and judging from this one's nervy, twitching manner, he had — incredibly — chalked up one more medical disaster. *What the hell had gone wrong?*

'A fever set in,' he began, but that was as far as he got, because the bedchamber door was firmly slammed in his face. Damn! Somehow Orbilio had preceded her into the bedroom, no doubt slipping in while she'd been trouncing that idiot physician!

However, what caught Claudia's breath was not the sight of the aristocratic investigator lifting to peer under Rufus's eyelids. Rather, the overwhelming number of scents which were slugging it out in this simple room of woven drapes and wooden floor, of bearskin rug and the writing desk strewn with scrolls and dice and shaving implements.

Slowly, Claudia identified the conflicting odours, one by one. Dark purple heliotrope in glazed pots out on the balcony.

The heady aromas of the physician's ointments, his tinctures, rubs and infusions. There was evidence of some over-zealous beeswax polish. Burnt bread. Lavender oil in the lamps. And from the street far below, over-ripe peaches and pitch.

Alone, each scent could have laid out a horse, but the winner, on points, was surely the smell of death which clung to that motionless figure? The setting sun reflected off the only hint of luxury in the room, his great silver bedframe, and the sunlight dazzled her eyes.

A perfect excuse, she thought, to turn away from the empty shell that had once been Rufus Vatia ...

Around the walls, his adored elephants trumpeted and reared, their characters captured as clearly as the faces of their trainers. Some bore wooden castles on their backs, from which mock battles were fought in the arena. Others danced, performed tricks, while the little ones endeared themselves merely by being babies. Moving round, she saw that the scene behind the desk recorded Rufus's skill in capturing the beasts. The pits that he dug. The way he hobbled the brutes. The ships he carried them home in. Even the odd, tragic casualty, like when two elephants drowned after one boat capsized in the harbour, or when an Oriental assistant had been trampled beneath giant grey feet.

Claudia swallowed. So much death. So much unnecessary, excessive, *premature* death ...

She stood for a moment, swaying, trying to make order from chaos. And then, while Orbilio was engrossed with his grisly inspections, slender fingers silently riffled the papers and scrolls on Rufus's desk.

Dammit, what she wanted wasn't there! Come on, come on, it's got to be here somewhere. Where have you hidden it, Rufus? Her stomach lurched. Oh, no! *Please* don't say it's under the mattress —

Claudia swivelled her eyes towards the lean, bronzed figure stretched out on what was now his funeral bier — only her gaze never reached as far as the trapper. The instant she saw the expression on Orbilio's face, ice exploded throughout every vein.

'You were right,' he rasped. 'Rufus didn't die from a simple cough and a sneeze. He's been poisoned.' He straightened up and spiked his fingers through his thick, dark curls. 'So I think now's as good a time as any for you to tell me exactly what brings a young wine merchant to this flat.'

Night had fallen. Claudia was in her own garden, where silvery trails of slug slime shone in the light of a full hunter's moon and there was not yet a chill in the air. The fountain gurgled like a contented baby, and a bullfrog croaked to the bats.

The gate hinge had been oiled far too often to creak, but she knew it had opened behind her and she felt, rather than saw him, approach. There was a faint shadow of stubble on his chin and he poured himself a goblet of wine before settling himself beside her on the white marble bench, his back tight to the trunk of the sour apple tree. He smelled of sandalwood and ambition, leather and hope. An owl hooted from the garden next door.

'See that statue?' Orbilio's voice was thick as he pointed to the nymph and her amorous satyr. 'One kiss like that from you, Claudia Seferius, and I would be faithful to you for ever.'

'Well, thank you, Marcus. I appreciate the warning.'

In the darkness, she saw him grin and the tension drained from her limbs. Slowly — very slowly — the stars tramped their way across the heavens and Claudia pulled a wrap round her shoulders.

'You were right,' he said eventually. 'About who killed Rufus.'

Claudia watched a moth flutter round the vervain, a plant reputed to have sprung from the tears of Isis, before moving on to drink from the sweet blue blooms of borage.

'What happened when you broke the news to our winsome trio that Rufus was not the rich catch they believed they'd netted, but was actually up to his eyeballs in debt?'

The trapper was a man who worked hard and played harder, and his personal slogan of 'Live now, pay later' was fine ... providing one remembered that there *was* a second part to that motto! Unfortunately, in Rufus's case, this wasn't as often as his creditors might have wished and indeed, had it not been for his dire financial circumstances, he and Claudia would not have been thrown together in the first place.

'Let's just say two of the women are already on their way back to Ardea,' Marcus said dryly. Ardea was the town south of Rome where Rufus stabled and trained his thumping great pachyderms, the place where he spent most of his time.

It would be a different town without him, she thought. No craggy smile, no easy laugh, no acted-out tales of his exotic adventures. Idly, she wondered whether the elephants would miss him, and had a mental picture of them shuffling in patient anticipation.

'And the third one?' she queried. 'The blonde?'

He shot her a sharp, sideways glance. 'I won't ask how you fathomed it out,' he said, refilling both glasses with wine. 'But you were right on all scores.'

Claudia twirled her goblet between her hands without drinking. It was obvious, from the start that Rufus Vatia had been out to make mischief. This was autumn and, fresh home from the safari he loved and facing six months in a climate he hated, he'd very quickly grown restless. So much so, that when he went down with that chill in his lonely apartment, he resolved to cheer himself up. Just a joke; nothing malicious; something to make the stablehands chuckle throughout the long winter.

Rufus would pretend he was dying!

And if three bigamous wives pitched against one another wasn't enough, he'd summonsed the little blonde's lover, as well — that young buck of a physician — in addition to Claudia Seferius, his … his …

Well, never mind what! The point was, so absorbed had Rufus been in his own machinations, that he'd failed to notice the shadow stealing over him. The shadow of someone who was aware of his charade — *and who decided to cash in on the opportunity to settle a score …*

'I must admit, I was way off target,' Orbilio said, stretching. 'My money was on the blonde — especially when she fainted at the announcement that Rufus was dead. After all, her father *is* an actor at the Theatre of Marcellus. I simply assumed she was putting it on. It's a classic ruse to divert suspicion.'

'No, her distress was real, all right. Like me, she knew there was nothing wrong with Rufus apart from a few sniffs and snuffles, so when the poor sod was suddenly pronounced dead, it came as quite a shock to think her lover had shortened the odds.'

'She thought he'd killed Rufus for the money?'

'Typical Rufus, feeding each of his wives the same line, that he was sitting on a fortune.' Greedy bitches. That was the only reason they married him! 'But you're in good company, Orbilio. Blondie was way off target in her suspicions, too!'

Claudia crossed one long leg over the other and leaned back.

'Blondie's boyfriend wasn't, as she imagined, looking sick and nervous out of guilt. The poor chap suspected *her* of bumping off her husband. He was genuinely mortified!'

She recalled the pitiful slump of his shoulders, the look of utter despair. *'I did everything I could,'* he'd said, and although his words had been addressed to everybody in the room, in reality it was a coded message to Blondie. Obviously, as a doctor, he'd realised at once that someone had slipped Rufus poison during his absence overnight and (this was the hard bit!) he also knew that he was powerless to do anything other than make the unfortunate trapper's end as comfortable as possible.

That's why he'd banned visitors. That's why he'd disguised the foetid smell of baneberries with burnt bread and lavender, heliotrope and polish.

Believing the little blonde had killed her husband for him, the physician had gone to great pains to cover up murder.

As someone predicted he would ...

'When did you realise the truth?' Orbilio asked, resisting the urge to massage her neck and rubbing his own instead.

'The minute I saw the exquisite detail on Rufus's bedroom walls.' Claudia sank half her wine in one go.

Every expression had been captured, every likeness reproduced with breathtaking authenticity. Especially the fresco recalling the accident where, boarding ship, an Oriental helper slips and is trampled by elephants. His injuries are truly horrific. His face twists. The scene is so vivid, you wince with him. Crowds gather round, men confer. The victim continues to thrash. Rufus steps forward. He slits the dying man's throat. When he's laid on his funeral bier, the dead man's mouth rests in a smile ...

'The resemblance to Milo was unmistakable.'

And who, but the steward, would be privy to Rufus's hoax? *Who better placed to avenge his young brother's death?*

'Milo claimed there had been bad blood between the two men for several months,' Orbilio explained. 'In his view, what Rufus did was nothing short of cold-blooded murder and anything less accurate than the gentle euthanasia scene depicted on that fresco Milo could not imagine. His version is that his brother simply lost his footing on the gangplank and that Rufus took the opportunity to kill his enemy, making up that story afterwards about him being trampled.'

'And as a slave, of course, bound to a master who, rightly or wrongly, he believed had killed his brother without conscience, Milo would be in a difficult position. The sense of injustice and grievance would grow, but to kill Rufus openly would only draw attention to himself. He had to either make it look like an accident or —'

'— Or throw suspicion on to somebody else.' Orbilio chinked his goblet against Claudia's. 'Exactly!'

'I expect you'll find Milo's perception has been twisted by grief,' Claudia said. There were many accusations one might level against Rufus Vatia, but cold-blooded could never be one of them. 'I daresay once you start interviewing witnesses to his brother's death —'

'Ah.' Marcus wriggled uncomfortably. 'Unfortunately, the case file is now closed. We'll only ever be able to guess at what happened. You see, Milo fell on his dagger just as the soldiers arrived to arrest him, and the Emperor wants it left at that. Just — you know — in case there *is* any truth in the rumour.'

In the darkness, Claudia smiled. 'You mean, he doesn't want any taint of scandal attached to his Imperial pachyderms?'

'Like Caesar's wife,' he grinned back, 'those elephants must be above suspicion.' A few moments passed, then Orbilio rubbed his jaw thoughtfully. 'Incidentally,' he said. You, er … never did tell me what you were doing at Rufus's flat.'

Claudia thought of the reason that had brought her and Rufus together. Two people, both in financial dilemmas. One with a product to sell. The other with a means of transporting it. She then thought of the formal, written contract which the wily trapper had insisted on securing before he would agree to ship any of her precious vintage wines to Africa unfettered, shall we say, by the burden of Imperial taxation.

The self-same contract, in fact, that she'd whisked from underneath his mattress. And which now lay as a delectable pile of white ash in the kitchen …

'Oh, it was purely a social visit,' she purred, flicking a strand of hair from her face.

After all.

What's the point of having double standards, if you don't live up to both?

A MARILYN TODD CHECKLIST

1. Books

A. In the "Claudia" series

I, Claudia. Macmillan hardback, November 1995; Pan paperback, November 1996; Untreed Reads ebook, May 2013.

Virgin Territory. Macmillan hardback, November 1996; Pan paperback, November 1997;Untreed Reads ebook, August 2013.

Man Eater. Macmillan hardback, November 1997; Pan paperback, November 1998; Untreed Reads ebook, October 2013.

Wolf Whistle. Macmillan hardback, November 1998; Pan paperback, October 1999; Untreed Reads ebook, December 2013.

Jail Bait. Macmillan hardback, October 1999; Pan paperback, July 2000; Untreed Reads ebook, January 2014

Black Salamander. Macmillan hardback, July 2000; Pan paperback, March 2001; Untreed Reads ebook, March 2014.

Dream Boat. Severn House UK hardback, December 2001; Severn House USA hardback, March 2002; Untreed Reads ebook, May 2014.

Dark Horse. Severn House UK hardback, August 2002; Severn House USA hardback, November 2002; Untreed Reads ebook, July 2014.

Second Act. Severn House UK hardback, July 2003; Severn House USA hardback, October 2003; Untreed Reads ebook, November 2014.

Widow's Pique. Severn House UK hardback, July 2014; Severn House USA hardback, September 2004; Untreed Reads ebook, January 2015.

Stone Cold. Severn House UK hardback, March 2005; Severn House USA hardback, May 2005; Severn House UK trade paperback, July 2005; Severn House USA trade paperback, January 2016; Untreed Reads ebook, March 2015.

Sour Grapes. Severn House UK hardback, September 2005; Severn House USA , May 2006; Severn House USA trade paperback, November 2006; Untreed Reads ebook. May 2015.

Scorpion Rising. Severn House UK hardback, May 2006; Severn House USA hardback, August 2006; Severn House UK trade paperback, December 2006; Severn House USA trade paperback, June 2007; Untreed Reads ebook, July 2015.

B. In the "Iliona" series

Blind Eye. Severn House UK hardback, September 2007; Severn House USA hardback, December 2007; Severn House UK trade paperback, May 2007; Severn House USA trade paperback, August 2007; Untreed Reads ebook, date of publication t.b.a.

Blood Moon. Severn House UK hardback, December 2008; Severn House USA hardback, April 1009; Severn House UK trade paperback, September 2009; Severn House USA trade paperback, December 2009; Untreed Reads ebook, date of publication t.b.a.

Still Waters. Severn House UK hardback. July 2010; Severn House USA hardback, September 2010; Severn House UK trade paperback, June 2011;Severn House USA trade paperback, September 2011; Untreed Reads ebook, date of publication t.b.a.

C. Short story collection

Swords, Sandals, and Sirens. Crippen & Landru Publishers, August 2015. Published both in signed, numbered clothbound and in trade paperback.

2. Short Stories:

[Stories in *Swords, Sandals, and Sirens* are marked with an asterisk.]

* "Girl Talk." *Past Poisons*, Headline 1998. (Reprinted in *Ellery Queen's Mystery Magazine* [hereafter, *EQMM*], May 2000.
"Fan Male." *Daily Mail "YOU" Magazine*, October 1999.
* "Stag Night." *The Mammoth Book of Locked-Room Mysteries and Impossible Crimes*. Robinson Books UK; Carroll & Graf USA, 2000. (Reprinted in *EQMM*, July 2002.)
* "Trunk Call." *Murder Through the Ages*. Headline, 2000.
"A Taste for Burning." *The Mammoth Book of Historical Whodunnits*. Robinson Books UK; Carroll & Graf USA, July 2001.
* "Bad Day on Mount Olympus." *The Mammoth Book of Comic Fantasy*. Robinson Books UK; Carroll & Graf USA, July 2001.

"The Great Rivorsky." *EQMM,* August 2001.

* "The Wings of Isis." *The Mammoth Book of Egyptian Whodunnits*. Robinson Books UK; Carroll & Graf USA, 2002. (Reprinted in *EQMM,* March 2003.)

"Michelle." *EQMM*, March 2003.

* "Honey Moon." *The Mammoth Book of Roman Whodunnits,.* Constable UK; Carroll & Graf, USA, September 2003.

* "Cupid's Arrow." *EQMM,* September/October 2003. (Recorded for podcast by *EQMM.*)

"Thoroughly Modern Millinery." *Mammoth Book of Roaring 20s Whodunnits.* Robinson Books UK; Carroll & Graf USA, July 2004. (Selected for inclusion in *Best British Mysteries of the Year*. Headline, November 2005.)

"Stakes & Adders." *Mammoth Book of Comic Fantasy.*- Robinson Books UK; Carroll & Graf USA, July 2005.

"Stage Struck." *EQMM* , September 2005.

* "Swan Song." *EQMM,* February 2006.

"A Taste for Ducking."*Mammoth Book of Jacobean Whodunnits.* Robinson Books UK; Carroll & Graf USA, June 2006.

"Distilling the Truth." *EQMM,* June 2006. (Selected for inclusion in Mammoth Book of Best British Mysteries. Robinson Books UK; Running Press USA, 2008.)

* "Death at Delphi." *EQMM,* March/April 2007.

"Awaiting the Dawn." *Mammoth Book of Dickensian Whodunnits.* Robinson Books UK ; Carroll & Graf USA, October 2007.

"Room for Improvement." *EQMM,* December 2007. (Selected for inclusion in *Best British Crime No. 6.* Allison & Busby, April 2009; recorded for podcast by Crime City Central; nominated for a Shamus Award 2008.)

"Dead & Breakfast." *EQMM,* March 2009. (Selected for inclusion in *Best British Crime No. 7*. Allison & Busby, February, 2011.)

"667 —Evil and Then Some." *EQMM,* May 2009.

"Open and Shut Case." *EQMM,* September 2010. (Selected for inclusion in *Best British Crime No. 9.* Allison & Busby, January 2012.)

"Something Rather Fishy." *EQMM,* August 2011 (Recorded for podcast by Crime City Central; selected for inclusion in *The Crooked Road Vol. 3, EQMM,* December 2013.)

"Show Time." *EQMM,* September 2011.

"Alternative Medicine." *EQMM,* March 2012.

"The Wickedest Town in the West." *EQMM,* June 2012 (Recorded for podcast by *EQMM; Ellery Queen Mystery Magazine* Readers Award winner 2013.)

* "Cover Them with Flowers." *EQMM.* November 2012.

"The Way It Is." *EQMM,* September 2013.

"Heaven Knows." *EQMM,* January 2014.

"Fruit of All Evil." *EQMM,* March 2014.

* "Bad Taste." *EQMM,* June 2014.

"Blood Red Roses." *EQMM* , September/October 1914. (*Ellery Queen Mystery Magazine* Readers Award winner, 2014; included as a separate chapbook with *Swords, Sandals, and Sirens*.)

"Who Pays the Piper." *EQMM,* March-April 2015.

"Looks to Die For." *EQMM,* March-April 2015. (Poem)

"The Longboat Cove Murders." *EQMM,* August 2015.

"Petrified." *EQMM,* September/October 2015.

"The Old Man and the Seashore." *EQMM,* January 2016.

"Saw Point." *EQMM,* forthcoming

"Beach Men." *EQMM,* forthcoming.

Swords, Sandals and Sirens by Marilyn Todd, is set in Palatino for the text and Bernhard for the running titles. It is printed on sixty-pound Natures acid-free recycled paper. The cover design is by Gail Cross. The first edition was printed in two forms: trade softcover and one hundred seventy-five numbered copies sewn in cloth, signed and numbered by the author. The clothbound copies contain an additional story,"Blood Red Rose," in a separate chapbook.

Swords, Sandals and Sirens was printed and bound by Thomson-Shore, Inc., Dexter, Michigan and published in August 2015 by Crippen & Landru Publishers, Inc., Norfolk, Virginia.